SUPER POWER LESS

ALSO BY CHRIS PRIESTLEY
(SELECTED)

Anything That Isn't This
The Wickford Doom
The Last of the Spirits
The Dead Men Stood Together
Through Dead Eyes
Mister Creecher
Blood Oath
The Dead of Winter
Tales of Terror from the Tunnel's Mouth
Tales of Terror from the Black Ship
Uncle Montague's Tales of Terror
New World
Redwulf's Curse
The White Rider
Death and the Arrow

– CHRIS –
PRIESTLEY
SUPER
POWER
LESS

HOT
KEY
BOOKS

First published in Great Britain in 2017 by
HOT KEY BOOKS
80–81 Wimpole St, London W1G 9RE
www.hotkeybooks.com

A CIP catalogue record for this book is available
from the British Library.

ISBN: 978-1-4714-0497-9
also available as an ebook

1

Typeset in Berling 10.5/15.5 pt by Palimpsest Book Production Limited,
Falkirk, Stirlingshire

Printed and bound by Clays Ltd, St Ives Plc

Hot Key Books is an imprint of Bonnier Zaffre Ltd,
a Bonnier Publishing company
www.bonnierpublishing.com

For Adam

Chapter 1

If Only Any of Them Knew

David is halfway to the shop when he spies a group of girls he knows from school. He doesn't usually employ his super-powers for such trivial things, but as they draw near he engages his power of invisibility and they walk on past as though he doesn't even exist.

He smiles to himself. They move away, chatting and laughing, oblivious. But as that sound dies away, he hears another. He comes to a stop and tilts his head like a bird, straining to hear, pushing the trailing locks of his long hair away from his ears.

A voice. He can hear a voice. Only just. Only him. Only with his super-hearing. He is picking up cries for help – distressed cries coming from about four miles away or so, he guesses.

David looks around to see if anyone is watching. Just Mrs Harper walking her dog, and Mrs Harper wouldn't see a T. rex if it wandered by.

He runs along the pavement, picking up speed all the time, his feet drum-rolling, and then, with a final bound, launches himself into the air, pushing his hands flat out in front of him like he's diving into a pool.

Mrs Harper barely registers him as anything but a gust of wind, a blurred smudge at the edge of her vision – just another loose, half-formed thought among many that drift, unmoored, around her mind of late.

David twists in the air and changes direction, shivering the upper leaves of the big chestnut tree on the end of Mill Lane, squinting into the onrushing air, listening all the time – homing in on the source of the sound.

He flies to the top of the church tower, gripping the flint with his fingers, standing with one foot on one of the carved faces sprouting from the ancient walls; getting a better bearing on the direction of the cries. They sound more panicky now.

He climbs in through the little arched window near the bells, strips and stashes his clothes in the usual place, emerging after a moment in his costume – a dark metallic grey of an almost indestructible material, the surface bristling all over with spikes. He dives into the air once again, rushing down over the roof tiles then out across the deserted graveyard, heading for the fields beyond.

A flock of rooks scattered across the moist, cake-brown earth rise up at his passing, cawing and flapping languorously in the strengthening wind. It begins to rain. How can it be so cold on a summer's day?

David slows down, lets his feet drop until he is 'standing' in the air and then hovers there, motionless. He can see the road ahead, over and through the tangle of tree branches, bending, snaking; the dampening tarmac beginning to shimmer darkly, almost as dark now as the river that runs alongside it.

Ember-red rear lights shine in the gloom below, heading away from him. A white van on the road. David hears the voices again. Screams. Muffled screams. He sees the brake lights of the van flare up. The source of the cries is close. But it's not the van.

He flies on, focusing on the voices until the wind, the rain, his own heartbeat are shoved behind a wall of silence as he blocks everything else out and concentrates his whole mind onto that fine point.

There. Below. A car has lost control and skids up the grass verge, leaving a dark curving wake of muddy tyre tracks as it crests the bank and slides sideways into the rippling black water.

David hangs in the air for just a moment before hurling himself downwards past the low electrical hum of a pylon as the car begins to rock and sink beneath the bubbling surface. The white van drives on, unaware.

David can never understand it. It surely ought to be easier to fly downwards. It had to be. With gravity and everything? But it always feels as though he's towing a whole bunch of helium-filled balloons. He wants to fall, to plummet, but he has to claw his way through the air. It's more like swimming to the bottom of the ocean, like diving underwater.

Underwater. The car is almost submerged now as David lands, feet first – *thud* – on the bonnet, crouching down on his haunches, one palm slapping down on the wet metal, to stare through the windscreen at the screaming man whose terrified face is blurred by the rain and river water streaming over the glass.

The look of terror on that face turns instantly to confusion and amazement and then excitement and hope as the wiper clears the windscreen and he sees David, who now rams his hands into the metal of the car, forcing his fingers through until they grip the frame of the chassis and then he heaves, leaning back into the air, straining, his face upraised and contorted by the effort.

It takes most of his super-strength to pull the car free from the water's murderous grip, but free it comes, with a great vomiting *whoosh* and David carries it through the air towards the road and then, *bang*, in comes a blinding flash of light in human form.

The blow seems to hit his entire body like a massive electric shock and he is hurled sideways, unable to maintain his grip on the car, which bounces once against the grass of the embankment and then splashes back into the water.

David himself drops to the ground, dazed, and it's a few seconds before he come to his senses to see the car sinking once again. He gets up and launches himself through the air.

'Ow! Watch where you're going!'

David just manages to stop himself falling over and taking Mrs Harper with him. Her tiny dog starts barking and jumping around on the end of the lead, like a white woolly fish on a hook.

'Sorry,' he says. 'I'm so sorry.'

'David?' she says, peering at him, her eyes narrowing. 'Is that David?'

'Yes, Mrs Harper,' he says.

'Well, what are you doing? You walked straight into me.'

David rubs his eyes. He apologises again and says he was miles away.

Mrs Harper shakes her head.

'You always were a dreamer,' she says. 'Just like your father.'

Her face twitches as she realises what she has said.

'Sorry, my love. I didn't mean to –'

'No. It's fine,' says David mechanically.

How many times has he heard those words – or words like them? So many that they have become sounds and nothing more. But it was what people wanted to hear. They wanted to be reassured.

'Stop barking, Sammy, you silly dog. It's David.'

David smiles down at the dog, but that just seems to excite the ridiculous creature even more and it snaps at him, an incongruously fierce expression on its cuddly-toy face. Sammy has never liked David. Mrs Harper chuckles, happy to have this distraction from her faux pas.

'He's very protective. Aren't you, Sammy? Yes, you are.'

David nods.

'Well, sorry again, Mrs Harper,' he says. 'I'd better get on.'

'Try to stay awake this time,' she says, wagging her finger. 'I was saying to Holly only the other –'

'I will. Bye.'

David smiles as he walks away. If she only knew. If only any of them knew. But then that was the whole point of having an alter ego – no one was meant to guess you were a superhero. You had to look like you could never be anything more than the nobody you were. The more unlikely the better in fact.

Maybe – just maybe – a superhero's girlfriend might guess, but only after a long while or after some crisis of one kind or another – and it was never a good idea because, sooner or later, supervillains seemed to always get their hands on a superhero's girlfriend.

Luckily David doesn't have a girlfriend, so that isn't a problem.

Chapter 2

To Be or Not to Be

The next day David is lying on his bed, his window open just a little so that a light breeze is, every now and then, tickling the fine hairs on the back of his hand and playing across the pages of the comic he is reading.

It's hot. It's the middle of July. Midday midweek noises drift lazily in – a distant jackhammer, the wheezing air brakes of a delivery truck stopping on the high street, birds chattering in the roof gutter, someone in one of the gardens whistling thinly.

David's bedroom is at the very top of his house. It had been his dad's office when they first converted the attic – it still had his old desk, his chair – but David had moved his bed up there after his dad died.

There was no real need for it – this room is actually smaller than the room he vacated – and it annoys his mother on some level, David can tell; although she's never said anything about it. He tells himself he doesn't care what she thinks. He tells himself that a lot. Often it's true.

David has made the room his own – and not just by the

mess that his fastidious father would never have allowed. No – he has decorated the walls with posters he himself has made: drawings of his favourite superheroes in their typical poses, coloured up on Photoshop with their names above, in just the way they're written on the covers of the comics.

All apart from two, that is, who are nameless.

David turns his head as his mother walks in, but immediately returns to the comic he's reading. He hopes, by doing this, he's making it crystal clear that he finds this imaginary world more deserving of his attention. She doesn't seem to get the hint.

'Why don't you at least just open the blinds?' she says, her voice muffled and muted by the fog wall of David's aggressive disinterest.

'It just seems a shame to spend such a lovely day inside,' she says, looking towards the window.

David follows her gaze, squinting into the light. A honeyed glow is seeping in horizontal bands through the slats of the Venetian blinds and then striping its way diagonally across the wall. A birdwatching scope stands silhouetted on a tripod pointing out through one of the gaps.

They used to go to wildlife reserves, David and his dad. They were always jealous of the guys in camouflage who had scopes, when they only had binoculars. David's father always promised him they would get one, but they never did. Then, one birthday, he bought David this. That was the last birthday before . . .

That was the last birthday that mattered.

'Seen anything interesting?' says his mother, approaching the scope.

David tells her there was a blackcap in the Johnsons' pear tree.

'Really?' says his mother, leaning towards the eyepiece.

'Please don't move it!'

His mother flinches and tells him she was only going to have a quick look.

'Well, it's hardly going to still be there,' mutters David.

She frowns at him and grinds her teeth.

'It's so gloomy in here. Why lie around in semi-darkness? I'm surprised you can see to read.'

He mumbles that he likes it like that and does so with a pained expression, eyes still determinedly fixed to the page. Leave me alone. Leave. Me. Alone.

'You like it gloomy? Is that what you're saying?'

'It just doesn't bother me.'

'But it's like an oven in here.'

'Look, I'm trying to read!' he says with a sigh.

'Read?' she says witheringly. 'They're comics, David. Don't make it sound like I'm interfering with your enjoyment of Dostoyevsky.'

'Who?'

His mother closes her eyes for a moment.

'Well, Shakespeare then,' she says.

'You expect me to read Shakespeare?'

'You know what I mean,' she says. 'And anyway, don't say it like that. You loved doing *Hamlet*. Don't pretend you didn't.'

13

He had enjoyed *Hamlet*, it's true. To be or not to be? That is the question.

'Why are you so snooty about comics anyway?' says David. 'You're an illustrator. Comics are full of pictures.'

'I'm not snooty. I admire a lot of that stuff. I loved how you used to copy from them and make your own versions. But you don't draw any more.'

'Yes, I do.'

But not much, she was right. Not often.

'You just read them mostly, you know you do. And nothing much else.'

David didn't respond. What would be the point?

'I thought you were going to get a job,' continues his mother, determined to at least try to have a conversation of some kind.

'I know you did,' he replies, looking back at his comic.

'Would it be so terrible?' she says, cocking her head. 'To get out of the house? To meet some new people? To earn some money?'

'Money!' says David. 'That's all you ever think about.'

'That's just not true,' she says, frowning. 'Why would you say that?'

He mutters to himself.

'Do you have to be so rude to me all of the time? I know things –'

'I know – I'm sorry, OK,' says David without looking at her. 'I'm sorry.'

He knows she is staring at him. He knows the hurt look she'll be wearing. He feels a faint twinge of remorse but it is quickly smothered. His mother turns and, grabbing the handle, says over her shoulder, 'I'll be making a cup of tea in a while. Do you want one?'

'No,' says David. 'Thanks.'

His mother leaves, her footfalls dying away as she descends to the ground floor of the house and to the kitchen. Upstairs, David shakes his head, puffs out his cheeks and blows the door shut with a slam before returning to his comic.

It is a *Silver Surfer* comic – *Silver Surfer* #18 to be precise, entitled 'The Surfer Fights Alone Against . . . The Unbeatable Inhumans'. The cover art is by the great Jack Kirby and shows the Surfer getting zapped by Black Bolt.

It's one of David's favourite comics. The artwork is amazing – especially the last spread, which has the Silver Surfer escaping Black Bolt and zooming away at cosmic speed to land on some barren planet, dejected and alone, rising up at the end to say that he's done with love and mercy. The last page shows him yelling in rage – 'Let mankind beware! From this time forth . . . The Surfer will be the deadliest one of all!'

Sometimes David will lose interest in the story halfway through, but never the artwork – or never if it was by one of the greats – Kirby, John Buscema, Gene Colan, Jim Steranko, Steve Ditko, Neil Adams. He can just fall headlong into that stuff and never come up for air.

No one David knows has any time for this old-school stuff. There are some kids he knows who read comics – even comics featuring the same characters. There is a superhero movie coming out every other week after all – but they are all the new versions and re-boots and David just doesn't get the same buzz out of any of that.

These were his dad's comics and David knows how much he loved them. It was a special connection they had. A bond. So his mum can moan as much as she likes, but when he reads these comics he's closer to his dad and he's not going to stop. Not for anything.

He drops the comic on the bedspread and stares up at the pitched ceiling above him and then over at the window, cut through by the blinds. He gets up and stands peering out through the slats the way he's seen detectives do in old movies, prising them apart with his fingers.

His house stands at the end of the block and his elevated position up there in the attic gives him a god-like view over almost all the back gardens in the street.

Not that it isn't a view of deadening dullness: a grid of long thin gardens separated by brick walls and panel fences, overgrown by climbers, shaded by trees and hedges.

Mostly the gardens are laid to lawn. Some have a shed; some new, some rickety. A couple of people have little wooden offices. Trampolines and swings and climbing frames mark those houses with small children – or the memory of them. David's own garden has a swing hanging from the tree, though no one uses it now and the rope is so old it would probably snap if anyone tried.

Some gardens celebrate the green-fingered talents of their owners, others are overgrown or under-loved. David's own is a mix of both and he stands for a while, gazing down in a kind of stupor, not really thinking about anything in particular, but letting the present and the past run together, unchecked.

And then Holly Harper steps out into her garden in a bright sky-blue bikini.

David feels his whole body quiver for a second – like he is a bowstring, plucked by the sight of her. He steps carefully to the scope standing on its tripod, waiting. He raises the blinds a fraction to clear the view in front of the lens.

David has already focused the scope onto Holly's lounger. He did that two days ago – the first time he saw her sunbathing. It really is breathtaking, the sharpness, the clarity. It is super-vision. He has actual super-vision, but he has decided that it would be wrong to use it for this. Very wrong.

Holly is a tiny doll with his naked eye, but with the scope he can read the label on the bottle of suntan lotion she is squeezing into her cupped hand.

Holly lives round the corner, down the street. She is five and a half years older than David. She has dropped out of university and is back at home. She is earning money babysitting and cleaning for people in the neighbourhood while she 'gets her life back together'.

David has always found her a bit scary. Not that she has ever really spoken to David for years – and even then . . . He's just always found her to be the kind of girl who makes it plain in every curl of her lip and arch of her eyebrow exactly how low an opinion she holds of you.

Holly is, however, in David's considered opinion, spectacularly – supernaturally – gorgeous.

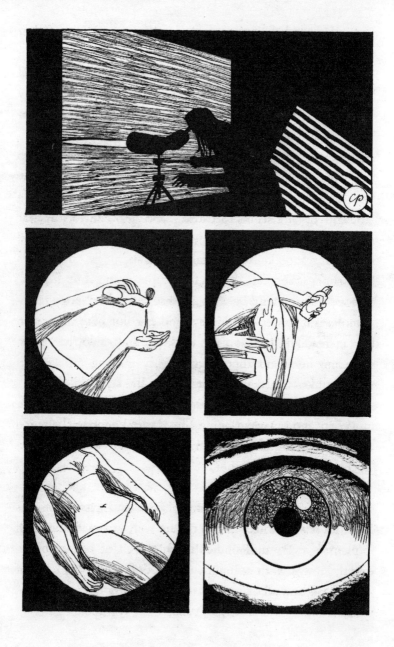

She sits on the edge of the sunlounger, kicks off her flip-flops and bends forward, rubbing the lotion into her feet and ankles and shins. She moves up her body, higher and higher – and David follows the movement with his eyes. Now her smooth stomach, now her chest; her fingertips disappearing inside her bikini top.

A banging pulse at the back of his eyes makes it hard to concentrate. Holly looks up warily, some sixth sense seemingly spooking her, peering up at the windows of the surrounding houses – or so it seems to David – and her gaze does appear to sweep round like a lighthouse beam, making David recoil even though he knows she can't see him.

Can she?

He presses down onto the eyepiece. His throat is dry. Holly puts her sunglasses on and lies back, her skin glistening from the cream. He lets his gaze track up and down her body, lingering here and there, breathlessly gorging on what is revealed, feverishly imagining what is hidden.

'Anything interesting?' says his mother.

'What?' says David, standing up, almost knocking the scope over, fumbling, grabbing. His mother puts a cup of tea down on his cupboard.

'I said I didn't want one.'

Holly's beautiful body is not altogether excised from his mind. It sticks to his brain like a cobweb. His own body still pulses with the thought of her. It's like she's here in the room. His mother's searching gaze hits him like a bucket of cold water and all at once she's gone.

'Sorry,' she says. 'I forgot. What were you looking at?'

Did she forget? Does she suspect?

'I . . . I thought I saw the blackcap again.'

David can hardly speak. His throat seems to be closing up. He sounds like he is stoned. His own voice seems distant to himself.

'Lovely,' says his mother, walking over.

'I was wrong though,' says David, picking up the scope and hurriedly moving it to one side.

Chapter 3

You Will Remember Nothing

David hears the doorbell's ding-dong chime far below. He sits up and realises he's sweating. His mother was right about the room. It gets so hot in summer. Hot and stuffy. His father used to complain about it all the time.

He looks towards the direction of the sound. He can just make out the sound of the front door slamming shut. After a few moments delay, he hears his mother's voice calling up the stairs.

'David! Joe's here.'

He waits a while, expecting to hear Joe's footsteps on the stairs, but all he can hear is his mother and Joe talking in the distance. Eventually, reluctantly, he gets up from his bed and goes downstairs.

'It's alive!' shouts his mother in mock alarm.

This is an old joke and David does not deign to dignify it with a reaction. Joe laughs. Of course. David frowns. How he hated it when his mother showed off – and he hated it even more when Joe gave her encouragement.

'Hi, Joe,' he says, stifling an extravagant yawn.

'Like I said,' responds his mother, turning to Joe and

21

rolling her eyes, 'he's on sparkling form. I'll leave you to him.'

Joe laughs again and slaps David on the shoulder. David flinches and moves away.

'Your mum's just been showing me that book she's been working on. Her pictures are brilliant.'

'I know.'

What is this? Has David's mother put Joe up to this?

'So?' says Joe.

'What?'

Joe lifts his tennis racket and waves it in David's face as though trying to hypnotise him.

'You will remember nothing . . .'

He remembers.

'What? Oh! Was that today?'

Joe shakes his head.

'Yes. But if you're not up for it . . .'

'No,' says David. 'I'll get some balls.'

'About time,' says Joe.

'What's that supposed to mean?'

'Nothing,' says Joe. 'It was a joke. Jesus. Lighten up.'

David peers at him and then walks away to get his racket and a tube of tennis balls.

'We're off, Mrs D,' shouts Joe.

'OK!' she calls, coming back into the kitchen. 'Have a good game. Be gentle with him, Joe.'

They have been walking down the street towards the park for about five minutes when David comes to a halt and puts out his racket to stop Joe. Joe asks if he's forgotten something.

'"We're off, Mrs D?"' mimics David. 'What the hell?'

'What?'

'Who does that?' says David. 'Who shouts that to someone else's mother?'

Joe shrugs.

'I don't know. Me, I suppose.'

'Well, it's weird.'

'Is it?'

'Yes, it is.'

'I don't see why.'

'Well, it just is.'

'OK then,' says Joe.

'It is,' insists David.

Joe says nothing more despite David giving him room to. This is perhaps the character trait in him that David finds most irksome – his ability to simply end any kind of argument by a tactical show of agreement and move on, seemingly without a care in the world.

If he was agreeing that he was wrong, that would be one thing. But he isn't actually agreeing – David can tell – he is just saying the words that made any continuation of the argument seem aggressive and petty. He isn't even agreeing to disagree. He is fake-agreeing. He is disagreeing to disagree.

But whereas such regular infuriation might have been expected to kill off their friendship, there seems to be some unbreakable bond between David and Joe – an unspoken contract – that surprises both boys, but which both feel obligated to respect.

They are certainly an odd, unlikely couple: David pale and languid, long-limbed, long-haired; Joe black, stocky, hair always close-cropped. Joe is sociable, David not. Joe can move seamlessly through most of the factions at school, whereas David, as much through choice as anything else, remains doggedly on the outside of everything. But they had formed their friendship early at primary school – and it had stuck, surviving the difficult times of recent years.

David and Joe play tennis every now and then during the holidays. They have done this for years. Neither of them is very good but that has never really mattered, because they are fairly equal in their lack of tennis skills.

They play in an unloved tennis court at the local park. It's free, but so badly maintained that no one with any ability or money would want to play on its pockmarked, fractured and leaf-strewn surface, so it is mostly available whenever they turn up to use it.

As they approach the court on this occasion, however, they can see it is in use. A group of four boys aged about ten years old are playing there already.

'We won't be long!' shouts the nearest of them without looking round, concentrating on returning the serve that is about to head his way.

'OK!' shouts Joe, and he and David put their rackets down and stand watching through the high chain-link fence.

They recognise the boys. They've seen them on the court before and also seen them watching, waiting for their turn to play. Joe and David remember all too well being bullied off the court by older boys when they were that age and are disinclined to chase the younger ones off too quickly. The boys on court nod their appreciation of this benevolence.

Something about the look and feel of the day – the light, the mood – whatever it is that triggers these wormholes in the memory – sets off a wave of nostalgia in David and before he knows it he is tumbling back to a day he had spent here years before. It is hallucinatory – hyper-vivid.

'Do you remember,' he says, quietly, as though anything but a hushed tone will spook the mood, 'you know – when we played doubles with Ellen and Violet?'

'Yeah,' says Joe, turning with a crooked smile, nodding. 'Weird. I was just thinking about that too.'

They both return to their separate reveries, each in a kind of trance, their minds freely flowing back in time to replay that match.

Now it is two years earlier. He and Joe are at school and they're talking about playing tennis that coming weekend when Violet, who sits at the same table, says she wouldn't mind playing and then Joe says, 'Why don't you come along on Saturday?' and David is annoyed that he hasn't run this past him first until Violet says to Ellen that she should come along and then they could play doubles and she says, 'Sure. OK. Why not?' and then she gives David this kind of secret look and David can't stop thinking about her for days after-wards.

Ellen had long been a focus of David's thoughts, waking and asleep. She is almost as tall as he is and rounded in her figure. She has a great smile too – dimples and big brown eyes that go from sweet to naughty in an instant.

David looks forward to that tennis match with a manic intensity that shocks him. He feels super-sensitised. The only thing he's ever had that had taken him over in that way previously is the flu. But this is the reverse of that. Where that deadened and stifled, this enlivened. It is like anti-flu.

The presence of the two girls changes everything. Everything. David and Joe have been to that crappy tennis court so many times and yet suddenly it's like David is wearing 3D glasses – everything takes on a hyper-real realness. He feels like his body has been in sleep mode all his life and only now – only now has someone found the remote and switched him on.

They play mixed doubles. Violet partners Joe, and Ellen partners David. David can't recall much about the game except that he and Ellen win and when the final, winning ball is hit, Ellen shouts 'Yay' and leaps at him, throwing her arms round his neck and they hug and jump up and down and her soft breasts are pressed against his chest and her bare arms slide across his shoulders and if he has ever felt better or more alive in his whole fucking life, before or since, he can't remember. He can't remember.

After the game they go to the shop, they buy drinks and take them into the woods by the river and hang out all the rest of the morning, talking and laughing and David tries to keep as physically close to Ellen as he possibly can, and whenever her skin pulls apart from his he feels it as keenly as a slap.

Then as he and Ellen talk – what the hell did they talk about? He can't remember – they both turn to see Joe and Violet wrapped in a long kiss, arms round each other, hands clambering, and Ellen turns to him with a half-smile of an invitation and David wants so much to reach out and pull her towards him, but the world just seems to freeze and Ellen's half-smile slowly fades and Joe and Violet pull apart and then suddenly it starts to rain and everyone is heading home.

'That was such a great day,' says Joe. Then almost immediately he adds, 'Sorry. But you know what I mean.'

'It's OK. I wish it was that day again,' says David. 'I wish I could go back to before, you know? Pretty much all the time.'

'Yeah,' says Joe.

Because he knows that was not the only thing that happened that day . . .

'How come you and Ellen never ever went out?' says Joe eventually, in a desperate urge to say something. David says he knows why. All the joy of the recollection is draining away.

'Later I mean.'

David shrugs. What was there to say? She was different now. He was different now. Everything was.

The boys finish their game and leave the court to David and Joe. They play for an hour or so but the memory of that day has ruined David's concentration. He suffers a resounding defeat.

Afterwards they sit on a bench, sweating and panting and drinking water. Neither of them mentions that day again.

'Look who it is,' says Joe, nodding towards a group of teenagers sitting on the grass in the distance.

David looks and sees that they're all kids from school. Not just any kids, but the higher echelons of school society. The elite. A couple of them turn round and look in their direction. Someone waves.

'I suppose we ought to go and say hi,' says Joe.

'What?' says David. 'Why?'

Joe laughs.

'Because that's what people do, you weirdo.'

David looks away.

'They're not that bad,' says Joe, smiling, annoyed with himself for calling David a weirdo. 'Harry's OK. Ben's not that –'

'Yeah – and Matt McKenzie is a bastard,' says David. 'Why are you even sticking up for them anyway?'

'I'm not sticking up for them. They just don't bother me as much as they do you. You used to hang out with them yourself. You used to play football with Ben. Remember?'

David snorts and shakes his head.

'You need to just relax a bit, you know?' says Joe.

'Do I?'

'Yes!'

David takes a deep breath and lets it out with a sigh.

'I'm not going to pretend I like those people,' says David.

'Ellen's there,' says Joe with a grin.

'So?'

'Don't pretend you're not still interested in her.'

David looks away. It's true, but how does Joe know? Has

David made it that obvious? His whole body is racked by an involuntary cringe.

He's barely spoken to Ellen in ages. Everything has changed – and not just David's world. She barely even looks the same. She's thinner now. Her hair is longer. She even sounds different. It's not the Ellen sitting over there he's interested in – it's the old Ellen. It's a memory he fancies.

'They've seen us. We can't just ignore them.'

'Why not?' says David.

Joe sighs and gets to his feet.

'Come on,' he says. 'Don't be such a misery.'

'A misery?'

'Yes – a misery!'

'No.'

'Come on. It's only –'

'Look, I'm not going, OK?' says David. 'And what was that dig about getting some balls?'

'It was a joke! Jesus!'

'If you want to go and stick your head up their arses then go ahead. Maybe they'll let you be their mascot.'

Joe shakes his head wearily.

'See you later, David,' he says, walking away. 'Text me if you fancy doing something.'

He keeps walking, getting smaller and smaller until he merges right in with the group on the ground and David soon can't really distinguish him from any of the others. He finds this troubling.

David wishes he hadn't made the jibe about Joe being a mascot. He could see he was upset. He gets up and heads home. Alone again, his thoughts immediately return to that day two years before – to Ellen and to the softness of her body next to his.

He had been dazed by the time he got back home. He had been exhausted too. His body had been on turbo-boost. He keeps seeing Ellen's face in his mind's eye, and each time he sees it he knows for sure that he would grab her and pull her forward and they would kiss and kiss and why couldn't he have done that in real life when it mattered?

But it didn't matter, because he saw a spark in Ellen's eye that even his painful ineptitude had not entirely extinguished. He would have another chance, he remembered thinking. There's always tomorrow.

He had walked a deliberately long way home, despite the rain, and his mother had called him into the kitchen when he walked in, soaked to the skin, cold from the rain, asking him why he never took his phone with him.

His dad's friend Mark Miller had been there with her. They'd sat him down at the kitchen table, neither seemingly able to actually broach the subject – whatever the subject was. His mother's red-rimmed eyes had been leaking tears.

David had assumed it was about him – that he had done something wrong. He had done a quick scan of all his recent activity, none of which had contained anything that merited this degree of gravitas. His mother bursts into tears.

'There's been an accident, David,' Mark had said. 'Your dad . . . I'm so sorry, David. Your dad – your dad has been killed.'

Chapter 4

His Radioactive Spider

David squints into the onrushing wind and rain, twisting his body and changing direction with the effortlessness of a falcon. The cloud below him is patchy and each break reveals a map-like view of the town below.

His super-vision homes in on the road and the river, the one dull and dark, the other catching the light and shimmering like a curved sword.

He sees the car too; sees it leave the road and career up the embankment, sees it launch itself off the edge and hit the surface with a firework splash, the water shining in the headlights.

David forces his way down, never taking his eyes from the car as it begins to sink. The screams of the driver are in his ears as he launches himself towards the car. But out of nowhere he is struck a massive blow and is knocked sideways, smashing into a field on the other side of the river.

He gets groggily to his feet and looks up, trying to see what hit him, and is dimly aware of a dazzling white shape heading towards him once again when it hammers into him like a train.

He is sent tumbling over and over in the dirt of the ploughed field. He crouches down and soars into the air, heading back towards the water and the car. He has to get to the car!

David hurtles through the trees at the river's edge and bursts out above the water where he can see the roof of the car just slowly disappearing beneath the surface.

He throws himself down, but before he can reach the water he is intercepted and smashed into again. He falls into the water and shields his eyes from the light now shining above him. It lets him flounder and look for the car, but only because it knows he will never find it. He hears a banging and turns to see where it might be coming from.

'David!' says his mother, opening the door. 'I thought you were asleep. Did you not hear me knock?'

'What?'

He squints, adjusting to this new reality.

'Look at the state of this place!'

David raises himself up on the bed and looks around. It is a mess – even by his standards: clothes strewn everywhere, empty mugs, wrappers, comics.

'It's not that bad,' he protests.

'Just get this room cleared up,' she says after a moment. 'Pick these clothes up and put the comics you're not reading back in the boxes. You know how upset you'd be if they got damaged. Holly is here to clean – not to tidy up after you.'

David does a double take.

'What? Who?'

He sits up so quickly he bangs his head on the wall behind him.

'Ow! Fu—'

'Holly Harper,' says his mother, scowling. 'She's here to –'

'What are you even talking about?'

'I told you,' she says. 'Holly is going to be cleaning for us now.'

'No, you didn't.'

'I'm sure I did.'

'You didn't!' he yells.

His voice fills the room like an animal slamming against a cage. His mother flinches and steps back. She hesitates before responding.

'What on earth is the matter?' she says quietly. 'What difference does it make to you?'

David swallows hard and tries to calm himself.

'Why do we even need a cleaner anyway?' he mutters.

'Ha!'

'Why her then?' he says.

'Why not her?'

David returns to his comic. Or rather he turns his face in that direction. But his brain is fizzing. Holly? Holly in his house? In his room? How? What?

'So if you could just tidy up like I asked,' says his mother, shaking her head.

'OK, OK,' he says.

'If you could do it *today*, I'd appreciate it. I can see you're very busy, but Holly will be here tomorrow. So . . .'

'Tomorrow?'

'Yes – tomorrow,' she says, waving her hands in the air in exasperation. 'What has gotten into you?'

She leaves the room, sighing, and heads downstairs. David gets up from the bed and goes slowly to the window, peering through the blinds. Holly's sunlounger is there but it's empty.

He starts to gather up the comics from the floor and find the appropriate bags and boxes for them to be filed away in. He likes having them lying around and the act of putting them away always makes him sad. But he promised he'd look after them. He promised.

His father had bequeathed these comics to him and David wonders if he has gifted some secret knowledge of himself that might be decoded in their pages. These comics – they are all David has of him that is not transient or mutable.

This room – his father's old office – is a reliquary now. The desk, the chair, the scope, the comics – they are objects of devotion. His mother will never understand that. How can she?

His mother, their friends, Joe, Dr Jameson – they all want David to move on but he's not going to pretend that he is the same as before. He isn't the same. Nothing is the same. He isn't going to betray his father like that.

He isn't going to forget – how can he? – and smile and laugh just to make them all feel better; to give Dr Jameson the satisfaction that he's cured him. He isn't ill. He's different. He's changed. Fundamentally. For good.

It was after his father died that the superpowers came. All comic-book heroes – and villains – have a moment when they stop being an ordinary human being and are transformed. The Fantastic Four were exposed to cosmic radiation, Wolverine and Captain America were experimented on,

Spiderman was bitten by a radioactive spider and so on. Well, for David, the trauma of his father's death was his radioactive spider.

Before that the world of the comics and the rest of his life had been separate things. It was obvious where one stopped and the other began. But now it's much more difficult.

Having superpowers is a blessing and a curse. Everyone who reads comics understands that. You have great gifts but with them comes a huge responsibility and the need to have a secret life. David hasn't chosen this life – it has chosen him.

He can't tell anyone about his powers. They wouldn't believe him anyway. To reveal his alter ego would endanger all those around him. That's the deal. There is nothing to be done about it. At least he only *seems* boring. So many people really are.

Chapter 5

Winkers Are Wankers

David gets to the top of the steep, narrow stairs up to his attic bedroom and opens the door. To his eye-popping astonishment, there is Holly with her back to him in her tight sky-blue bikini, bent over, dusting the scope.

'Hello!' she says with a grin, turning round. 'Don't mind me. You won't even know I'm here.'

David wakes with a start. The whole night seems to have been filled with dreams of Holly – restless, breathless dreams from which David emerges sweating and gasping as though from a fever or a fight.

His body is still twitching and he feels both thrilled and disgusted by the breadth of his imaginings and urges. Holly. Holly. Holly . . .

He slides out of bed, reluctant to leave its grip, and walks over to the window to peer through the slats. A blanket of pale grey clouds smothers the sky. This dull and unremarkable view seems to bring him to his senses and he yawns and gets dressed.

He goes downstairs, realising as he does so that he can hear his mother talking to someone. He almost turns round to go back upstairs, but instead walks into the kitchen to find his mother standing, holding a mug and talking, although there seems to be no sign of anyone else.

Then he hears a clanking noise and realises there is someone, obscured by the table, with their head and shoulders stuffed awkwardly into the cupboard under the sink. It isn't until this person comes out that David sees that it's Mark Miller from down the road.

Mark had been David's father's best friend. They'd played squash together most weeks. They'd gone to the pub most weeks too and they even went to the cinema together on what his mother had referred to as 'man-dates'.

Mark has been around for as long as David can remember, and with both his parents being only children, he thinks of him as an uncle. David likes him. He is one of the good guys.

Mark feels that familial attachment too, David can tell. He is a lawyer. He dealt with everything after his father's death and has been a massive help to his mother. He still is. Him and his wife, Marie.

'This is so good of you Mark,' says David's mother.

'Ah – it's nothing,' says Mark, his voice straining as he tightens something under the sink. 'To be honest, I really enjoy doing this sort of thing. It's a sickness really. Although don't tell Marie, for God's sake.'

'I'm useless,' says David's mother. 'I always mean to learn but then I never do. They do courses, don't they? Adult-education courses, I mean.'

'Marie is firmly of the opinion that this is the whole point of having a man about the place.' He groans to himself. 'Sorry – that was a stupid thing to –'

'It's fine. As you know, Daniel didn't know a hammer from a spanner, so we'd have called you anyway. He wouldn't have been offended in the slightest.'

David feels a momentary urge to spring to his father's defence, but it's true and he knows it. His father was not the do-it-yourself kind at all – and was happy to admit it. He designed buildings, but he had no interest in putting shelves up. But all the same, it doesn't feel right. It feels disloyal, and everyone in the room seems to sense it. There is awkwardness all of a sudden.

'OK,' says Mark, sliding out from under the sink and sitting up, wiping his hands on a cloth. 'That should do it. Any more trouble, give me a shout and I'll take another look. I'm pretty sure it'll be fine though.'

'We can't thank you enough,' says David's mother. 'Can we, David?'

'Er – no,' says David.

Mark nods at him.

'You're welcome, mate. That's what friends are for.'

'Would you like a cup of tea, Mark?' says David's mother. 'There's cake.'

'Absolutely. But can I just wash up first?'

'Of course – you know where it is.'

Mark went off to the downstairs toilet and David's mother put the kettle on.

'How about you, sweetheart?' she says. 'Tea and cake.'

David shrugs.

'I haven't had breakfast yet.'

There is something going on, David can tell. Why are they

involving him in the conversation? Why is Mark calling him 'mate'? Why is there cake? There's never cake.

Mark comes back, takes the mug of tea that is offered to him and sits down at the table. David's mother puts the cake on the table and tells David to sit down.

'Why?'

'Because it's what people do,' she says, with one of the infuriating non-answers that David finds so annoying. But he sits down anyway. David's mother cuts the cake and gives him and Mark a slice each. Then she rubs her hands together as though she intends to warm them over a fire.

'I'm . . . going to leave you to it, if you don't mind,' she says. 'I've got to make a phone call.'

David catches sight of an odd exchange of glances between Mark and his mother before she heads off, closing the door behind her.

It? What exactly is the 'it' she is leaving them to?

'How are things?' says Mark before he bites into the cake, nodding approvingly.

David shrugs.

'OK,' he says, taking a mouthful of cake himself.

Mark smiles and takes a sip of tea. He is already wishing he hadn't agreed to do this. David can see he is trying to shepherd some words into the right order. He stretches and eases himself back in his chair. It creaks. Get on with it. Get on with it.

'Worried about the old exam results?' says Mark eventually.

David shakes his head.

'Well, good. You're confident then?'

'I've done OK, I think.'

Mark nods, having seemingly exhausted that topic.

'Your mother tells me that you're always in your room,' says Mark at last. 'What's that all about?'

'Well, no, I'm not, actually,' says David. 'I played tennis only the other day.'

'Excellent,' says Mark. 'We'll have to have a game sometime. You any good?'

'Nah,' says David.

'Me neither, so that's perfect.'

David knows for a fact that this is untrue. Mark is one of those people who is passably good at any sport he tries. He's seen him play tennis. David wouldn't stand a chance. Mark sips his tea again.

Waiting for whatever it is that Mark is about to say is making David tense. What is it? Jesus – is it the scope? Does he know about David spying on Holly?

'But I'm guessing it must be true that you spend a lot of time in your room, or your mother wouldn't have mentioned it.'

David puts his mug down and sits back in his chair. It's not the scope. It's something else.

'I don't know why she's been talking about me at all,' says David.

'She's your mother,' says Mark. 'She's worried about you, that's all. Besides, she isn't talking to strangers in the street or phoning in to the radio.'

'I don't like being talked about.'

Mark nods and smiles.

41

'I can see that, David,' he says. 'Sorry. But I'm glad she feels able to tell me. And it's not like I'm a stranger after all. You have to understand that she has a lot on her plate. It's been hard for her.'

'Because my father's dead, you mean?'

'Yes,' says Mark. 'If you want to put it that way.'

David chews his lip.

'You're a teenage boy,' says Mark. 'You should be out there having some fun, not in here talking to me.'

'I just want to be left alone.'

Mark nods.

'Maybe what you think you want is not what you really need,' says Mark. 'Maybe you need to talk to someone. Someone who doesn't know you. Someone you can open up to. You were seeing someone, weren't you, for a while, and your mum tells me you stopped going. Dr Jameson, wasn't it?'

'I don't want to open up,' says David. 'I don't want to talk about it. I'm fine.'

'I don't think you are.'

David shrugs.

'When I was your age I did some crazy things,' says Mark, chuckling at some recollection. 'I'm not saying you should do anything quite so crazy – in fact I would strongly advise against it – but you want to look back, don't you, and see more than the inside of your room or the pages of a comic.'

'For God's sake. I knew we'd get on to comics eventually.'

'No need to be like that,' says Mark. 'No need for that tone. We're friends.'

David stares at his plate and at the half-eaten cake. Mark smiles and leans over to tap his arm.

'Come on,' he says. 'We are friends, aren't we?'

'Yeah. Of course. But I'm OK. Honest.'

'Are you sure?' he says. 'Because you don't have to pretend if you aren't. It wouldn't be surprising now, would it? Your mum's worried.'

David sighs and pushes the plate away.

'She just doesn't get me at all,' says David.

'Well, explain it to her,' says Mark. 'Explain it to me. Because as far as I can see, you're wasting hours of your life reading old comics.'

Can he explain it to Mark? Maybe. Maybe he can. But the words won't come.

'You'd both rather I was on Facebook or Twitter?' says David.

'Frankly I would,' he says. 'At least they're social. At least they let people in. You seem to want to shut everyone out.'

'No, I don't.'

But it now occurs to him that he does. And what's more, he does not in any way feel bad about it. He does want to shut them out. He just wants to be left alone. Where is the harm?

'Good,' says Mark with a warm smile. 'Because your dad wouldn't have wanted you to be miserable.'

'I'm not,' says David.

'You often look kind of miserable, if I'm being honest.'

'So do lots of people,' says David.

Mark laughs.

'Fair point. Indeed they do.'

He puts his mug down and gets to his feet.

'I hope you don't mind me butting in,' he says.

David shrugs. He does mind. He minds a lot.

'Just try and give your mum a break,' says Mark. 'She seems tough, I know, and together and everything, but I know she feels lost too, sometimes.'

Did she seem tough? Or together? David tries to imagine if this is true. Mark reaches out. David thinks he wants to take something from him but he is reaching out to shake his hand. David takes it and Mark squeezes it, manfully.

'OK, mate,' he says. 'I'm going to get going.'

He goes to pick up his toolbox.

'Mark,' says David's mother, stepping into the kitchen a little too casually, 'all done? How was the cake?'

'It was very good,' he says, looking at David with a portentous expression. 'It was very good.'

'Excellent,' says David's mother, beaming and clasping her hands together – as she always did when she was nervous and didn't know what to say.

'Say hi to Marie,' she says eventually. 'Ask her to text me to let me know if we're still on for Wednesday. She'll know what I mean.'

'I will. Bye. Bye, David,' says Mark, winking at David.

David frowns. What does that wink mean? He doesn't like being winked at. He objects to it strongly in fact. Winkers are wankers, everyone knows that.

But Mark isn't a wanker – is he?

44

Chapter 6

X-Ray Vision

David lies on his bed, headphones on, watching movie clips on YouTube on his laptop. It's hot and stuffy and he's a little groggy. The sleepless night is catching up with him. He doesn't even register that Holly has come into the room until she puts her hand on his foot.

He flinches and looks up to find her leaning towards him, hair tied back in a ponytail, wearing a tight white vest top and black tracksuit bottoms. Is this real? It feels like another dream beginning. But yes. It's real. She's here to clean.

'Sorry to interrupt your porn-watching, but I've got to hoover in here.'

'What? No – I'm not watching por—'

But she has already switched the hoover on and is putting her earbuds in. She turns away and sets about her work, her face a neutral mask that could have signified concentration or boredom or just about anything. David wonders what she's listening to.

Holly looks more at ease in David's room than he does most of the time. She seems to just immediately own the space, running the brush-headed nozzle of the hoover along

45

the corners of the walls and ceiling as if she had always done that and that her being in David's bedroom isn't in the least bit incredible.

She glides round the room with a kind of casual efficiency and, while feigning a renewed interest in his laptop, David studies her every movement, his mind constantly and feverishly switching to the memory of her in her bikini, superimposing that image onto the one in front of him, stripping her clothes away as though he had X-ray vision. But that isn't one of his superpowers.

X-ray vision is always problematic to David, because how would you control it if you had it? How can you see through walls but stop at the flesh of the people on the other side? How can you see through a person's clothes but not their skin and bones? If Superman could see through people's clothes, then why wasn't he constantly undressing Lois Lane with his super-eyes?

There were adverts for X-ray specs in some of the comics. The picture showed a big pair of glasses with concentric circles in the lenses and 'X-RAY VISION' written on the frame. They said they were a scientific wonder, which David kind of doubted as they were only ninety-five dollars. 'Girls will never trust you with these, but let them look for themselves and apparently see legs right through your pants.'

Holly turns the hoover off and it whines nasally, shutting down. Without its roar a new, soft intimacy seems to shrink the room and David shifts uneasily. It feels weird. He has imagined having a girl in his room so many times, but it never felt quite like this.

Not that Holly notices. She appears utterly oblivious to David – or no more aware of him than of the desk or the chair. She picks up the various items from the top of his chest of drawers, dusting them and the surface they had been standing on before replacing them.

David takes every chance he can to watch her as she goes round the room, studying every inch of her – the lacy yellow bra straps visible beneath those of her vest, the way the material of her tracksuit bottoms stretches when she bends over – so close he could have reached out and . . .

'What are you doing?' says David as Holly yanks the cord on the Venetian blinds, pulling them up and clattering them clear of the window.

'Excuse me? I told your mum I'd try and clean your windows. The window cleaner can't reach up here from outside.'

'But . . .'

'But what?' says Holly, carrying on regardless. 'I'm not asking you to do anything. A bit of air in here wouldn't go amiss . . .'

David has already taken the precaution of putting the scope and tripod in his wardrobe, but there is still something very disturbing about having Holly looking out of the very window he uses to spy on her.

'It's quite a view you've got up here,' she says, opening the casement and leaning out to spray the outside of the pane.

'I suppose,' says David.

She sets about rubbing the glass in concentric circles and this activity sends a series of rhythmic movements through her whole body and David watches them all, spellbound.

'You can see every garden in the street,' she says above the squeaking of her cloth.

'Sorry?' he replies, pretending not to hear.

Holly doesn't bother repeating. Either she knows he's heard or doesn't care that he hasn't. She simply finishes that window and turns to do the other. When she's finished she closes the windows and sprays the inside.

'There,' she says, when she's finished. 'You can actually see out of them now.'

She doesn't seem to have noticed the patch that David had cleaned specifically for the scope to look through. She wipes her hands on her vest, leaving two smudges across her stomach.

'Filthy,' she says, with a grin.

David smiles awkwardly and nods, opening his mouth to reply but unable to come up with anything. Holly isn't looking at him in any case. She is walking back to the hoover, putting her earbuds back in.

'Just got to finish the floor,' she shouts, changing the attachment, and the hoover roars back into life.

David puts his own headphones back on and returns to his laptop, casting furtive glances at Holly as she pushes the hoover round the carpet.

'All done,' she says eventually, as she turns the hoover off.

And that's that. She's gone. She clumps down the stairs and then a mighty, melancholy silence settles on the room, like the soundless void that follows a firework display.

Chapter 7

More Himself?

David grabs hold of the front bumper as the back of the car disappears beneath the espresso-coloured water. The driver glances behind him as water begins to fill the car, and then stares out in panic at David.

The light is fading as though day is being sucked under with the car. David grits his teeth and digs his fingers through the metal behind the bumper. It screeches and groans as it buckles and twists in his grip.

He strains and heaves. He has to generate all the power because he's not standing on anything to brace himself against and every muscle and sinew bulges in his arms and neck as he gives a great yell and pulls the car up into the air.

The driver's face shows astonishment now, rather than fear, but his knuckles are still white as he holds tightly to the steering wheel – as though it's the only thing stopping him tumbling backwards into the water.

David has control of the car now and begins to carry it to the bank. The driver finally exhales the breath he has been holding and a weak smile appears on his face as he realises he is safe.

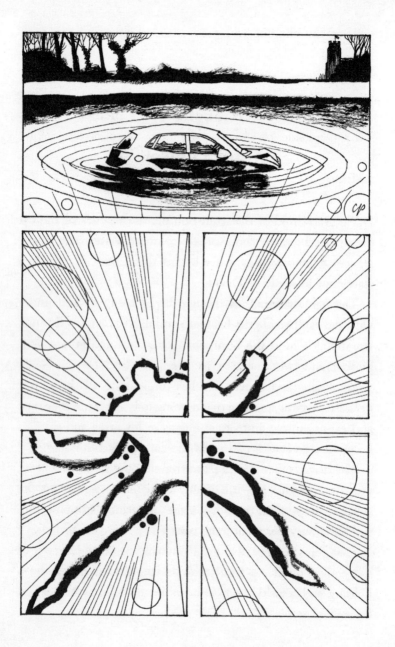

Then the blinding whiteness smashes into him.

'David?'

'Huh?'

'Hello? David?'

It's Mrs Jardine – Dr Jardine – Joe's mother. David is standing outside Joe's house; standing on the doorstep looking lost.

'Erm . . .'

She chuckles.

'You're always in a dream world, aren't you?' She turns away and yells over her shoulder. 'Joe – David's here to see you.'

She stands aside and ushers him in with a wafting motion.

'Don't just stand there,' she says. 'Come on in.'

'Thanks,' says David. Then, as an afterthought, 'How are you?'

'I'm all right,' she says as they walk into the kitchen. 'Thank you for asking. How about you?'

David shrugs.

'OK.'

She looks at him with an expression David has seen many times on many faces – a look of sympathy mixed with awkwardness mixed with frustration. Do we still have to be gentle with you? they seemed to be saying. Do we still have to tread softly? Are you not over it yet? Give us a break.

And David is always aware that Joe must talk to her about him – that she knows more than he might want her to know. It has always made him feel both closer to her and wary of her, at the same time.

'How's your mum?'

'She's good,' says David. 'Really busy. She has loads of work on.'

'She's so talented, your mother,' says Dr Jardine. 'I can't draw to save my life. Such an amazing way to earn a living.'

David nods. He knows. Dr Jardine has told him this many times – pretty much every time his mother gets mentioned.

'My mum says everyone else's job always seems more interesting than your own.'

Dr Jardine smiles. David wonders if they haven't had this exact conversation before – with the exact same words – and thinks Dr Jardine is thinking the same. She had been kind when his dad died – really kind.

'Believe me – no one is ever jealous of me being a GP!'

Joe comes in. He says nothing – he just nods at David, and Dr Jardine leaves them to it with a parting smile at David. He sits on the sofa, Joe on a nearby armchair.

'How come your mum's not working?'

'I don't know. She's got some meeting in town – she did tell me what it was about but . . .'

David nods, only half listening to the reply.

'Sorry,' says David, eager to get his apology out of the way. 'About the other day.'

'What do you mean?'

'You know – not going over to see Matt and Ellen and the others after tennis.'

Joe shrugs.

'I don't mind.'

But David knew he did.

'It's just that they really wind me up. I shouldn't have said you'd be a mascot.'

Joe nods. He wants to say more. He has planned to say more. But it doesn't come.

'Gah – it doesn't matter. Forget it.'

'You'd make a rubbish mascot anyway.'

'True,' says Joe.

'What did you get up to?'

Joe shrugs.

'Not a lot really. We had a kick-around for a while, but I was a bit knackered after tennis to be honest. We just sat around mostly. Talking. You know.'

'About?'

'I don't know – if you're that interested you should have come over.'

David smiles. He has a point. But he carries on anyway. He suddenly has a very clear and persistent image of Ellen in his head.

'Did you – did they – talk about me?'

'Ah – is that what this is about?'

'Well, did you?'

David's stomach knots itself. Why is he even asking this? Time was when all he wanted was to not be talked about, not be stared at, pitied.

'Not really,' he says. 'A bit – at the beginning. They wanted to know why you hadn't come over.'

'And?'

'And I said you had to shoot off.'

'Did they ask why?'

'No.'

'What would you have said if they had?'

'That you were having your hair done.'

David grins.

'My hair done?'

'I don't know what I'd have said. They didn't ask. So . . .'

'OK, OK.'

David can tell this version of events is not perhaps the entire truth – or not a comprehensive description at any rate – but what is the point in picking away at it? He trusts Joe. Joe has stuck by him through everything. He knows Joe would never say anything bad about him when he wasn't there. Who cares what the others said?

Except he does a bit. He hates himself for it, but he does care. He doesn't care what they think exactly – he just cares that they are talking about him at all. He hates the idea that they say his name out loud. He doesn't even want to be in their thoughts.

Except maybe Ellen's.

'Actually, we talked a bit about college next year and how school already feels like ages ago.'

David nods. It's true, it did. Maybe they are a bit worried too – given that other schools feed into the college and they will go from being top dogs to being just one of many top dogs, each of them having to justify its place in the pecking order all over again. No such issues for David and Joe of course . . .

'I can't wait to get started,' says Joe.

'I know what you mean,' says David. 'I'm pretty bored with the holidays already.'

'That too,' says Joe. 'But I mean it's exciting, you know? A chance to be something different. To start again.'

'You're going to reinvent yourself?' says David with a quizzical arch of his eyebrow.

Joe frowns.

'Would that be so bad?'

David laughs. Joe scowls at him.

'You're happy just the way you are, is that it?'

David didn't like the sarcastic snort that followed this statement.

'Hey,' he says. 'I'm certainly not going to let Ben and Matt and those others convince me I need to change to suit them. Definitely not. Is that what you want? To pretend to be something you're not?'

'I didn't say that,' says Joe. 'I'm not talking about pretending to be someone you're not. It's a chance to become more yourself. That's all.'

More himself? More himself. He's totally himself – more than himself. If only he could explain to Joe, but he can't. It hurts to have him think that all there is to David is what he sees in front of him, but that's all part and parcel of having a super-identity. It goes with the territory.

'So – are you going to be more yourself?' says David.

'Maybe,' says Joe.

David mutters under his breath.

'Forget it,' says Joe with an irritated sigh and suggests they play FIFA on the Xbox. David's mind returns again and again to the thought of being discussed at the picnic.

He realises he is being stupid. What does it matter what they think or say? And yet he has horrible imagined glimpses of them all – including Ellen Emerson – mouthing his name and laughing.

So distracted is he in fact that he finishes the game with only nine men, having had two sent off for hideously mistimed tackles, and he does not even manage a single shot on target.

And he's still chewing it over on the way home, torturing himself with invented conversations and then beating himself up for being so ridiculous. Why hadn't he just gone over with Joe? Why does he have to make life so hard for himself?

It's a question he's asked himself so many times since his father died. Why couldn't he just be sad like his mum? Why did he have to start acting weird?

That's when the lying had started. He'd started lying about all kinds of things, even when he didn't have to. He couldn't stop. It felt weirdly powerful – like he was in control when he was anything but. Like he was making his life up as he went along.

But no one likes a liar. He got into trouble at school. He went from everyone feeling sorry for him to everyone feeling pissed off with him. It was quite an achievement.

Chapter 8

Positively Cold

David's mother is rushing around the house frantically when he comes back from Joe's. He's in a bad mood, but his mother fails to acknowledge or even notice it, and this makes it worse.

She has just finished packing her work up when the doorbell rings.

'Go and get that, David,' she says. 'It'll be the courier. Tell him I'll be a couple of minutes.'

David answers the door and does as he's been told. The courier fidgets on the doorstep, scrolling through his phone, with David unsure about whether he is supposed to stand there or invite the man in.

His mother arrives in any case and hands the package over to the courier, who thanks her and heads off.

'And don't bloody bend it this time,' she mutters to herself as the van moves away.

David follows her down the hall and is about to head upstairs when she calls out over her shoulder, 'You haven't forgotten that the Millers are coming over tonight, have you?'

He has no recollection of this whatsoever.

'What? When? What time?'

'About seven thirty. Does that give you time to get your make-up on?'

'That's very funny, Mum,' says David. 'A bit homophobic, but never mind.'

'Homophobic?' says his mother, rolling her eyes. 'Don't be ridiculous.'

'If I did wear make-up? Why should that bother you?'

'It wouldn't bother me,' says his mother. 'Well, it might a bit. But not because I'm homophobic. I'm just not sure you would . . . That it would . . . It would freak me a bit, I have to say.'

'But if I was gay you'd be fine with it?'

She walks back towards him and stares at him.

'Are you?' she says, her voice almost sounding pleading, wishful. Is that what this is about? Is that why you're like this? 'Are you gay? Because if you are, you know –'

'I'm not gay,' replies David.

'Because if you were –'

'I'm not gay, OK,' he says. 'I was just making the point. I was just wondering how cool you'd be with it if I was.'

'I'd be very cool with it,' she says in a hurt voice. 'I'd be really cool. I'd be positively cold. I mean – you know what I mean.'

'Really?'

But he knows she would.

'Yes,' she says. 'Why would you even ask?'

'You don't have any gay friends,' says David anyway.

'What?' she says. 'I do!'

'Who?'

58

'I don't know,' says his mother. 'But I do. I know I do. I just can't think. In any case what's all this about? Why the sudden interest in my attitude to gay people? Are you sure –'

'Mum, I'm not gay, OK?' he says, though even he can see why she might think that after this outburst. 'I like girls. Women, I mean. Older girls. Young women.'

'Oh,' says his mother, sounding more uncomfortable at the idea of talking about his interest in the opposite sex than she had been about the idea that he might be interested in his own. 'Well, good.'

'You see,' says David.

'What?'

'Why did you say "good"? If you don't mind me being gay.'

'You just said you weren't.'

'I'm not!'

His mother takes a deep breath.

'Shall we draw a line under this conversation and move on? I haven't got the time.'

David shrugs. He's made his point. If he had one. He's made some kind of point, he's sure.

'Do you think you could give me a hand?' she says.

'Doing what?'

They both seem eager to move on.

'Could you just go round and tidy everything away – just neaten things up a bit.'

David nods and does as he is asked, although there isn't really a tremendous amount to do. He is the only one who makes a mess and he spends less and less time downstairs. His mother is obsessively tidy.

David lays the table and then leaves his mother to get on with the cooking, ambling back down as the Millers arrive.

After a drink and a pre-dinner chat, which is mercifully short on the usual probing into David's life, they all sit down to eat. David is only half listening to the conversation most of the time, but his ears prick up when, as he is helping to clear the dishes away, Holly's name is mentioned.

'Obviously it's very sad for her and her parents that Holly's back home,' says Marie in a voice that does not suggest great sadness, 'but to be honest, she's been a godsend to us.'

'I know,' says David's mother. 'It's great to have her as a cleaner.'

Marie screws up her nose.

'Marie!' says Mark.

'What?' says David's mother.

'Well,' says Marie, dropping her voice as though she thought Holly might hear from their house, 'she's OK, I suppose. As a cleaner. If you keep an eye on her. Lovely as a babysitter though – the girls adore her.'

'I think you're being a bit unfair,' says David's mother. 'She does her best.'

Marie takes another swig of wine.

'Yes,' she says, swirling the wine in her glass. 'I'm just saying her best isn't that good. Only the other day –'

'Anyway,' says Mark, 'I was –'

'Don't do that!' hisses Marie.

'What?' says Mark with a sigh.

'Don't shut me up when I'm saying something you don't like the sound of. It's very annoying.'

There is a tense silence. David taps his fingers on the tabletop. His mother stares at him. Marie laughs a little too loudly.

'Sorry, Donna,' she says. 'Look at David. He doesn't know what to do, poor thing.'

David blushes. His mother grimaces. Marie reaches across to touch David's hand. He jerks it away and Marie knocks her glass over, wine flooding the table.

'I'm so sorry,' says Marie.

'It's fine,' says David's mother, frowning at David, leaping up to get some paper towels. 'Don't worry.'

'Maybe I'm a bit tipsy,' says Marie, making a funny face at David as though they were in it together. 'I'm so sorry.'

'I think maybe we ought to go,' says Mark.

'Why?'

'Because you're embarrassing yourself.'

'No,' says Marie coldly, 'I'm embarrassing you.'

David would be happy to admit that they were, all of them, embarrassing him. He gets back up and puts the rest of the dishes in the dishwasher and asks if it's OK if he goes to his room. This seems to lance the tension and Mark and Marie's stony faces crack into smiles as they wish him goodnight.

David climbs up to his room. He tries to read a Doctor Strange comic but he just can't concentrate – something he takes as a serious indictment of his mood, because, well, if you can't concentrate on a Doctor Strange comic then what the hell – and so he gets up and walks over to the window – and to the scope.

He zooms in on the Miller house straight away. Mark and Marie are saying their goodbyes downstairs, but he isn't looking for them. The curtains to their lounge are open. The room is empty. David moves up the side of the house and sees that the light is on in the bathroom.

The window glass is textured – rippled and distorted – but he can see a vague shape moving about and then the light goes out. He moves back down to the lounge and sees Holly walk in and sit down on the sofa. David gulps back an unsteady breath.

From his angle he can't see her head, only her body from the shoulders down – her arms, her hands, as she clicks through the channels on the TV remote and pulls her legs up onto the sofa.

David watches her for a while as she settles down to watch TV. It isn't like watching her sunbathe somehow. It ought to be less exciting because she is fully clothed, but it is more intimate somehow. He knows the Millers' lounge. He'd played there as a child. He feels as if he is there in the room with her. He can imagine himself actually sitting beside her, putting his arm round her, sliding his other hand up inside her T-shirt. And she would turn and –

Holly suddenly puts her legs down and turns to face the door as Mark and Marie walk in. She stands up and they talk for a while before Holly picks up her jacket and leaves. The lounge light is switched off. Mark and Marie head straight up to bed. David wonders whether they will have sex. In movies, he's noticed that people sometimes have sex after an argument – to make it better. He speculates briefly about the Millers naked and passionately interlocked, but only briefly.

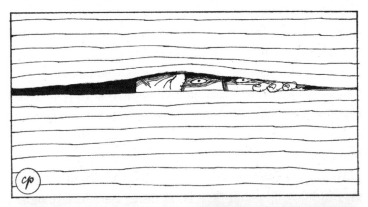

David stands up and looks out through the slatted blinds, at the dark, at the night, at the black houses with their coloured windows picked out here and there.

He thinks of all the people – all the lives – behind those windows, bright and black, and feels more keenly than ever a kind of jealousy in the back of his mind towards the normality of the lives they conceal. He grips the scope and for a second imagines himself taking it from its tripod and putting it away in a cupboard, perhaps for good. That, he says to himself, would be a good thing; a healthy thing – a sane thing.

But he doesn't. Of course he doesn't. And the shame of this inability to do the good and healthy thing stabs him and stabs him until he can take no more and he has to let go of the scope, tears filling his eyes.

He has to let go and leave the thing where it is.

Chapter 9

Permission to Be Happy

If it's possible, David is becoming more reclusive. He just wants to be somewhere else – someone else. His super-self seems to possess an authenticity his real self struggles to match. He has been using his power of invisibility more and more, particularly when he comes downstairs. Most of the time his mother doesn't even know he's there.

He spends his time watching films or reading comics. He does not want to give his mind room to think because, when he does, those thoughts are invariably barbed and poisoned. His mind has become his enemy. He has to tame its imagination by giving it enough to feed on – enough to keep it busy.

David's shrink, Dr Jameson, had asked him if he thought he would ever give himself permission to be happy again and David had been annoyed at the question but had also seen very clearly in that instant that he would never be happy again. Not truly. And people didn't like that. It's a kind of sin.

It isn't even as though people want you to be really, truly happy. They would be content with a convincing pretence.

They just didn't want you to make them feel unhappy, or awkward or whatever. It's always about them really. But screw them.

So David is not going to give himself permission to be happy. Not now, not ever. His dad deserves better than that, and if his mum can't see it, that says more about her than it does about David.

This very thought is in his head as he walks into the kitchen one evening to find Marie and his mother laughing and busying themselves getting ready for a night out. He scowls at them. Particularly at his mother.

'Hello, love,' says Marie, either not noticing the scowl or seeking to cheer him up. 'Have we woken you up?'

David smiles, but sarcastically, to let her know he understands she is joking, and walks over to the sink to pour himself a glass of water.

'Are you hungry?' says his mother. 'I can –'

'Just thirsty,' he says.

'You're sure?'

David nods, pouring himself another glass. He sees Marie make a face. The 'oh dear, he's in a bit of a mood' face. That was the partner to the 'oh dear, poor David' face. And just as annoying. Maybe more annoying. They go back to talking as though he isn't there. Which is fine by him, by the way. Totally fine.

'Holly may as well move into our place,' says Marie. 'I feel like she's a proper employee rather than a bit of extra help. I don't know why Mark has to be out the same night as me. It's not like I didn't tell him ages ago that we were going.

66

And then yesterday he suddenly announces he has this works do he simply has to go to.'

Marie rolls her eyes.

'Still – it gives Holly some work,' says David's mother, always reluctant to join Marie in criticising Mark. 'It's not like you can't afford it. She's trying to get on her feet again.'

'I know,' says Marie. 'I know. You're right.'

'If David would get off his backside, he could babysit for you,' says David's mother, loudly, for his benefit.

David ignores her.

'Aww – bless him,' says Marie. 'No offence, David, but I've never been keen on the idea of boys babysitting. It's not natural, is it?'

'Not natural?' says his mother.

She doesn't normally pick Marie up on this kind of thing in front of David – but she doesn't stop herself in time. Or smooth the aggressive tone out of her voice. Marie does not notice.

'I just mean, girls are more suited to it,' continues Marie blithely. 'You know, if the baby wakes up.'

'Really?'

'I know our kids aren't babies any more but they can still be a handful sometimes. And Morag's been having terrible nightmares recently.'

'Oh?' says David's mother, not altogether ridding herself of her frown. 'Poor little thing.'

'She's so nervy,' says Marie with a sigh. 'I hope it's just a phase.'

'I'm sure it is.'

David had hung about deliberately when they were talking

about Holly, but his interest has expired. He says goodbye and walks towards the stairs to go back to his room.

'We won't be that late,' says his mother.

'I'll bring her back safe and sound,' says Marie. 'If we can find the way!'

'Don't say that,' says his mother in exasperation. 'That sounds like we're going on a drunken spree. We're going to the cinema and maybe we'll have a drink –'

'Or two!' says Marie with a chuckle.

'I mean it, Marie. Stop.'

Marie rolls her eyes at David, but David looks away.

'Bye, David,' says his mother. 'There's a pizza in the freezer. Don't forget to turn the oven off.'

'I know,' he says. 'I'll be fine.'

The door slams behind them and David stands a moment, mentally taking possession of the empty house. It's not an entirely pleasant sensation.

He always imagines that he is going to enjoy being in the house on his own. After all, he spends so much time in his room, and with his mum working, that he may as well have been alone mostly. And yet he doesn't.

Instead, a terrible melancholia descends on him when he is in the house alone. It is the melancholia that others ascribe to him all the time and which he always denies. But it becomes true when no one else is around.

When his mother is in the house he doesn't feel the absence of his father nearly so much. He himself had been busy and was out a lot, and so as long as his mother was around David could at least pretend there was some kind of normality still

68

in existence – that his father is just busy somewhere – held up, on his way home.

But with his mother out, David's thoughts are uniformly dark. The certainties of his superhero comics and the lurid thoughts of sex flee his mind and all available space is filled with a cloying blackness.

David wanders around the deserted house, unable to settle, unable to calm his mind enough even to watch TV. It had taken his mother a while to feel comfortable with leaving David alone for extended periods. David could sense her reluctance to let him out of her sight.

It isn't just that though. It is a sense that she does not know him any more and so does not really know what he might do when left alone. She never quite voices it in these terms, but David has overheard her talking to Marie, expressing these kinds of concerns. He had been cross – hurt – to hear it.

But now he isn't sure she doesn't have a point – that in fact he isn't entirely safe to be left alone for very long. He feels overtaken by a great wave of despondency. His super-senses seem to magnify everything, making it impossible to read or watch TV.

He hears conversations from a street away. He feels the draught from a passing moth. It's like he's tuned to every channel at once. He wonders if one day his mind will simply overload. Maybe it already has.

David stands at his bedroom window. It's close to ten and his room is as dark as the night outside. The gardens are a mysterious confusion that his memory of them by daylight can not entirely disentangle.

David peers through the slats of his blind. The houses all around are now a black fortress, roofs and walls combining to make one dark mass against the green-blue-black of the night sky.

Many houses are solid black but others have squares of colour as room lights shine through curtains and blinds like fragments of stained glass inside a dark church. The scaffolding on the house opposite is just visible, as is the shiny fabric the builders have put down to protect the roof.

Night sounds drift by from far away, audible only because of David's super-hearing: a distant burst of a police siren and the eerie baby-crying whine of a cat on heat. But mostly it is quiet. No wind. No rain. The black cut-outs of the trees are frozen. If anything is moving in the gardens below, only the darkness knows.

But there are signs of movement at the illuminated windows. David pans from one to another. Mrs Davison is washing something up at her kitchen sink. The dark blue blind is only half pulled down and David can see her hands busily moving among the suds.

There are trees between his house and the Millers', but there are breaks in the leaves and through one such large break David has his clear view of the window to their lounge.

There she is, on the sofa. He would recognise those legs anywhere – those legs he has scanned with the scope so many times while she was sunbathing. But even while he is thinking about her bikini-clad body, David realises she isn't alone.

70

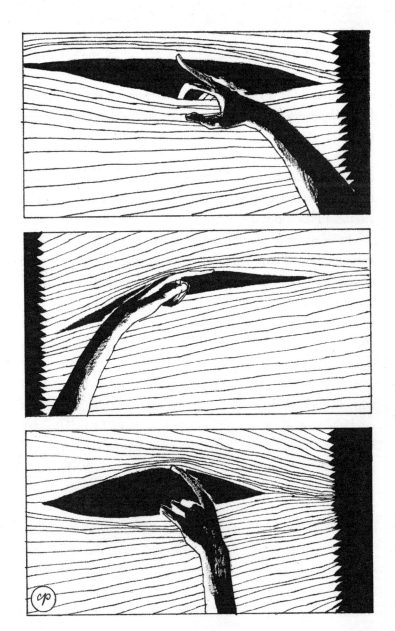

Someone else walks into the room – a man. David can't see who it is because his top half is cut off by the top of the window but, his heart racing, he sees the stranger's hand move across Holly's shoulder then her breasts, as David himself has so often wanted to do, as she lies back on the sofa.

The man walks forward towards the window. The house isn't overlooked by any other, but he is obviously feeling cautious, so he grabs the curtains and pulls them closed, shutting David out.

David gasps as though a screen has gone blank while he was watching a film. He slaps the wall angrily with the palm of his hand, staring at the curtains, willing them to part.

Chapter 10

Super-Sensitive

David pretends to be asleep when his mother gets back – even when she clumsily opens his bedroom door to whisper goodnight. But how is he expected to sleep?

He has lain awake for hours thinking about what he'd seen – and not seen – through the scope, the view already enhanced and edited to add content not actually glimpsed other than in his imagination.

What are the facts? Holly has a boyfriend. They are secretly screwing in the Millers' house while the Miller children are asleep and while Mark and Marie are out. Not just kissing or cuddling – that seems pretty clear – but actually doing all those things that David obsesses about on a daily basis.

And not just that, exciting though all that certainly is. No – now David knows about it! It's a secret he has unearthed by chance. He feels complicit somehow – as though he himself is involved. It has been one thing to spy on Holly sunbathing, but to spy on her with a man seems to bring David closer to her in his imagination – to bring sex closer to him.

'Ah,' says his mother, when he finally goes down for breakfast. 'Good morning.'

'Morning,' mumbles David, slumping down onto a chair. He's exhausted. He feels properly weak.

'Are you OK?'

He nods.

'Seriously, David,' she says, coming over and putting a hand to his forehead, 'you look terrible.'

He shrugs her away.

'I'm OK. Honest. I'm just tired. You must have got back late.'

'Sorry,' she says. 'You know what Marie's like. I popped in to see you but you were fast asleep.'

'It's fine,' says David.

Don't talk. Don't feel you have to talk. His mother smiles, mistaking his reluctance to engage in chatter as an attempt to put her mind at ease.

'I was about to make a coffee,' she says. 'Do you want one?'

She moves around the kitchen to the tune of clinking crockery and rattling cutlery drawers. Holly. Holly. David's mind has become uncontrollable now. He worries that he is projecting these lewd, disgusting thoughts – that his mother will see them leaking out of him. He closes his eyes tightly shut but it makes no difference.

'David?' says his mother, more worried now. 'Are you sure you're all right?'

'Just a bit of a headache,' he says, opening his eyes and blinking through the blur.

'Do you want some paracetamol?'

'No. Thanks.'

She stands and scrutinises him for a moment or two, but David speaks before she can say anything else.

'Did Marie come back here?' says David, hoping that talking will, after all, make him think of something else.

'No – I dropped her off at her house. She's so noisy. I knew she'd wake you up.

'I was serious about the babysitting, you know,' she continues. 'Marie gave Holly fifty quid! Fifty quid! The kids slept right through apparently. She basically got fifty quid for sitting watching TV.'

'I don't want to babysit, Mum,' says David.

'You don't want fifty quid either, I suppose?'

David shrugs. What would he do with fifty pounds?

'Well, I don't see why not,' says his mother, putting his mug of coffee in front of him. 'You're just as sensible as Holly as far as I can see. I hope you didn't agree with all that tosh Marie was saying about boys and babysitting. Honestly! She makes me so cross sometimes. It's like she –'

'I don't want to do it anyway,' says David, frowning. 'So what difference does it make?'

'OK,' says his mother. 'No need to get grumpy. I was just saying.'

'Why do you have to go on about everything?'

His mother sighs.

'Do you know what?' she says. 'You're right. Do what you like.'

David expects more, but his mother has already turned away to drink her own coffee and read the paper. David goes to the cupboards and pulls out a box of cereal and a bowl.

He pours milk in and begins to read the comic he's brought down with him.

'David,' says his mother when he's finished his cereal and taken himself off to the sofa to carry on reading – or at least pretending to, because his mind has not finished playing with the images from last night. 'I have to wait in for this call from the ad agency. Do you think you could pop out to the shops for me?'

David sighs and puts the comic down.

'Jesus, David,' she says. 'I haven't asked for one of your kidneys. You say I make such a big deal of everything.'

'I didn't say anything.'

'There isn't much,' says his mother, shoving a note towards him across the table. 'But make sure the butter is unsalted. Unsalted. Remember.'

'OK, OK,' he says. 'Unsalted.'

'And don't –'

The phone rings and his mother leaps to grab it.

'Don't what?' says David.

'George,' says his mother, frowning and shooing him away. 'Hi. Good of you to call. I appreciate it. How's the weather over there?'

David shakes his head, picks up the note, shoves it in his pocket, puts on his shoes and jacket and leaves the house, slamming the door behind him.

He moves along the aisles methodically, grabbing items from the list and putting them in the wire basket, but all that he can think about is the next time Holly will be in his room.

'Hey,' says a voice behind him, and he turns to see Ellen Emerson, baffled a little, seeing her out of context – and by her acknowledging him at all. He struggles to remember the last time she did that.

'Hi,' he says.

'You jumped!' she says.

He smiles. He had indeed jumped. Inside he still was.

'Nervous?' she asks.

David shrugs.

'Why would I be nervous?'

'Guilty conscience? Exam results?'

David has not given the exam results a single second's thought. He knows he's done OK. He smiles at the guilty-conscience thing though to make it look like it is a joke and not the actual truth which is what it is.

'You don't live round here, do you?' he says.

'Me?' says Ellen. 'No. But my dad does. I call him my ex-dad to wind him up. He doesn't live at home any more.'

'Oh.'

Ellen shrugs.

'Old news. They divorced a couple of years ago. Now he has this girlfriend who's not that much older than me. It's really creepy actually.'

She grimaces and shudders.

'Do you miss having him around?'

Ellen shakes her head.

'Not really. That sounds really bad, doesn't it? But it's true. I don't.'

She clamps her hand over her mouth and looks pained.

'Oh shit – sorry, David. I wasn't thinking.'

David shakes his head.

'It's fine,' he says. 'Don't worry about it.'

And weirdly, it is fine. He isn't just saying it to make Ellen feel better. Although he is also doing that – he is saying it to make her feel better. He surprises himself that he cares.

'But you do miss him, I bet?' she says. 'I bet he wasn't an asshole like my dad.'

'Yeah,' says David with a half-smile. 'I mean no. Yes – I miss him. No to the asshole bit.'

No one ever actually talks about his dad. This feels weird. Good weird.

'I remember when they told us in class,' she says, looking at him with eyes that sparkled suddenly, her voice faltering. 'Everyone was like . . . But maybe you don't like people talking about it?'

He hates people talking about it. Usually.

'No – it's fine.'

And it is.

'I did want to say something. You know – at the time. But I didn't know how. And then you were . . .'

She doesn't know how to finish the sentence.

'Weird?' suggests David.

She laughs.

'Yeah. A bit.'

'I went a bit crazy, you know?'

She nods and is clearly happy to leave it there, but for once David wants to continue.

'I was an idiot. I started making stuff up all the time – lying when I didn't even need to.'

'Why though?' says Ellen. 'Not that it's any of my business.'

He shrugs.

'I don't know. I suppose the real world just seemed so shit. I pissed a lot of people off. Joe was the only one who stuck with me. And my mum . . .'

'Do you get on with your mum?'

'She's OK,' says David. 'It's been tough for her. I've been . . . I don't mean to be, but . . .'

'You don't have to explain to me.'

'I just wish I could hit the rewind button sometimes. You know what I mean?'

'Tell me about it. Does she work, your mum?'

'Yeah. She's an illustrator.'

'A what?'

No one ever knows.

'She's an artist – an illustrator. She does all kinds of drawings and paintings for books and magazines and even packaging stuff. She's just been doing these adverts for someone in America – you know, like massive billboards.'

'Cool.'

She's right. It is cool. He wishes he could feel that more when he's with his mother – like he used to. He used to really love that she drew and painted and they'd spend ages doing that together. The memory troubles him and he shakes it off.

'So that's where you get it from. You were always really good at art.'

'Yeah – I suppose.'

'Are you going to do art when you . . . ?'

They realise that they are blocking the aisle and move aside to let a woman go by with her trolley. David realises with some surprise that he is extending the conversation deliberately.

'How come you didn't come over the other day?' she asks. 'In the park?'

David shrugs. Some of the easy-going air evaporates.

'Joe came over.'

'I know.'

'I thought you and Joe Jardine were like best buddies.'

Has Joe said something?

'We are,' says David. 'I don't know why I didn't come over.'

'Yes, you do,' she says. 'You don't like us, do you?'

David shrugs. Is this why she was talking to him. Were the others around? Is this a trick? A test?

'I don't dislike everyone.'

She leans forward and whispers conspiratorially.

'But some. Matt for instance.'

David looks away. She's right. He hates Matt. But Matt is Ellen's boyfriend now. What is he supposed to say? Ellen chuckles. She seems to enjoy his discomfort. David rocks back and forth on his toes and heels, preparing to walk away.

'It's OK,' she says. 'He rubs a lot of people up the wrong way. Me too, a lot of the time.'

'It's nothing to do with me.'

'What?'

'Nothing. It doesn't matter.'

'OK then . . .' says Ellen. 'Are you done? Shall we pay?'

'Yeah.'

Ellen stands next to him. They queue and pay and then stand outside for a moment. David waits for her to say something.

'You aren't a big one for the small talk, are you?' says Ellen with a grin.

'No.'

She smiles and David feels he needs to say something else. So he says he has something on his mind. Which is true – but having said it he wasn't sure why he had. Why is he confiding in Ellen? A girl he barely knows.

'You want to talk about it?'

Ordinarily he would say no, but maybe he does want to talk about it. Maybe it's good that he barely knows her. Isn't that what Mark had said – talk to someone who didn't know you? Maybe it makes sense. Mark isn't really a wanker. Mark is a clever guy.

'I don't know,' says David.

But yes – maybe he does.

'That's OK,' she says. 'I should be getting back anyway.'

Suddenly he knows that this, at least, is something he doesn't want. If he has to talk to make her stay, then OK. How bad can it be? To just talk?

'No!' says David, grabbing her bare arm. 'Don't go. I want to tell you.'

She looks at his hand on her arm and David suddenly becomes super-sensitive to the fact that he is touching her smooth skin. He can feel her pulse beating against his palm. He feels the microscopic movements in her muscles, the goosebumps gathering on her flesh. He lets go, checking her face for any sign of annoyance, but she seems OK. Better than OK. She is smiling even.

'So?' says Ellen softly. 'Come on – let's sit down.'

There is a bench opposite the shop, near the bus stop. They cross the road and sit, David unnerved at being so on view.

'What's on your mind?'

'There's this girl,' says David. 'Well – a woman – I don't know.'

'OK . . .' says Ellen with a grin.

'No – it's not like that,' says David.

Not like what? What was it not like?

'She lives round the corner. I've known her since I was little. She cleans for us now. She had some kind of trouble at uni and had to drop out and come back to live with her folks and . . .'

'And?'

'And I saw her, you know – with this guy. She was babysitting for friends of ours and she let him in and they were – you know . . .'

'Ah – I get it,' says Ellen. 'You fancy this woman. What's her name?'

'Holly?' says David. 'No – Jesus. No. Of course I don't.'

Why had she said that? David shifted uncomfortably.

'OK,' says Ellen, all woman-of-the-worldly. 'It's OK to have the hots for someone.'

David wishes he hadn't told her now. He also wishes he hadn't sounded quite so outraged at the idea of fancying Holly.

'How did you see them anyway?' says Ellen. 'Were you skulking around in their back garden?'

'No,' says David.

What kind of person does she take him for?

'I can see their house from my bedroom window, that's all.'

'But they couldn't see you?'

'I'm a long way away,' says David.

Which was true. She peers at him.

'You must have good eyesight.'

David shrugs.

'But if you don't fancy her,' says Ellen, 'why are you even thinking about it? I don't get it. What's it got to do with you?'

'Nothing,' says David. 'It's just that, well, I'm worried about her . . .'

Ellen raises her eyebrows.

'You're worried about her?'

'Yeah,' says David, genuinely wondering what was going to come out of his mouth next. 'She's had a rough time of it lately – you know, with dropping out of uni, like I said – and I don't want to see her get into trouble.'

'That's so sweet.'

Ellen puts her hand on his thigh, squeezing it gently. It sends a delicious spasm pulsing through David's entire body. Sitting there with Ellen, talking about Holly. He is suffering a kind of sensory overload. He is losing any facility to edit the information coming through his ears, his eyes, his flesh. Everything – near and far – floods into him. It's too much. And then . . .

'I'd better go,' she says, getting up and stretching as though nothing had happened.

David stands up too.

'Yes – me too. Thanks.'

What was he thanking her for? For listening? For squeezing his thigh?

'You're welcome, David,' she says with a smile. 'Maybe we can talk some more sometime?'

'No – yeah – that'd be good.'

She smiles and claps her hands together. Her hands are small, pale – the fingers delicate and thin. David can't take his eyes off them.

'How about Ben's party. Are you going to come?'

David screws his face up. Ellen laughs.

'Come on!' she says. 'You have to.'

'I really don't.'

'Listen,' she says, grabbing his hand. 'I know what it's like – being sad. But you can't make a life out of it. You have to let yourself snap out of it sometime. You're not a bad person if you enjoy yourself.'

David nods. He has received versions of this bullshit for years but somehow from Ellen it seems to make sense. Well, not exactly sense – but he didn't care.

'I know.'

'Things will get better.'

'I know.'

He doesn't know. He doesn't know. He doesn't fucking know that at all!

'Well, then? The party?'

David takes a deep breath. On the one hand he would rather pull his own testicles off than go to the party, but on the other hand Ellen was lovely.

'OK,' he says. 'I'll think about it.'

'Good,' she says. 'Bye, David.'

'Yeah,' he says. 'Bye.'

And she is gone. David walks back to his house, his thigh still tingling from her touch; his mind, now struggling to cope with competing images of Holly and Ellen, has already started to merge them both.

Chapter 11

A Different Kind of Super-Wrong

Ellen, Ellen, Ellen. David walks home washed by successive waves of emotion. A couple of times he has to stop himself taking off and floating away in front of people. His feet won't stay on the ground. He has to physically shove them downwards to make sure they keep contact. It makes his walk look a little weird as he forces each foot down in opposition to the anti-gravity at work. People stare at him, but he doesn't care.

'I thought you were never coming back,' says his mother when he walks in. 'I texted you. Did you not get it?'

'Didn't have my phone with me,' says David. 'Sorry – bumped into Joe.'

'Joe?'

'Yeah.'

Why was that so unlikely? David hates it when a lie is just randomly disbelieved for no good reason. His mother shakes her head. David carries the shopping into the kitchen. There is someone sitting at the table.

'Hi, David.'

It's Marie. She waves, grinning.

'Oh – hi, Marie,' says David.

'Sorry I kept your mum out so late. Look at you. You've got a bit of a rosy glow about you, handsome.'

David can feel all the store of excitement from his meeting with Ellen draining away.

'My God,' says David's mother. 'Are you flirting with my son now? What is the matter with you?'

Marie laughs. But David can tell that his mother had been serious. Marie shakes her head and smirks.

'There's nothing wrong with flirting,' she says. 'You should try it yourself sometime. That man last night might have been more –'

'Shut up, Marie!' says David's mother. David can hear a real edge of irritation to the tone.

'What man?' says David.

'Do you see?' she says, looking at Marie.

'What's she talking about?' says David.

'Nothing. We went for a drink after the movie and a couple of men came over and tried to chat us up. Marie encouraged them for some reason.'

'Ha!' says Marie. 'They only came over because that very good-looking man wanted to speak to you. He was too shy, bless him.'

David's mother grimaces at Marie, but she just frowns back. Marie has never been one to take a hint. A hint is like a red flag to her – she sees it as encouragement.

'David's all right,' she says. 'Aren't you, sweetheart?'

'I'm fine,' he says, scowling. 'I'm going to . . . I'm just off to my room.'

'David?' says his mother.

'I'm fine. Honest.'

'You see?' says Marie. 'He's fine.'

This is what is to be expected. David understands that. His father is dead so they all have to move on. His father is dead so his mother can do what she likes now. She can see other men. She might remarry. Everyone just has to move on.

David notices something on the table next to Marie – a pack of cards, but strange ones.

'What's that?' says David pointing to the top card as he walks by.

'Oh, don't get her started, for God's sake,' says his mother.

Marie smiles up at him.

'Tarot cards,' she says. 'I was going to read them for your mum, but she's too scared.'

'I'm not scared,' says his mother. 'I just think it's rubbish. Not the same thing. I'm a little bit scared that you think they make sense though.'

Marie rolls her eyes at David. David frowns.

'How about you, love?' she says.

'No,' says David. 'Thanks. I don't . . . It's not my thing really . . .'

His mother chuckles.

'He's being unusually polite,' she says to Marie, then looks at David. 'Don't be embarrassed. You don't have to pretend.'

'I don't know anything about it really,' says David, still staring at the top card as Marie moves her hand back and forth, gripping the pack.

'It's very old,' says Marie. 'Tarot.'

'That doesn't make it true,' says his mother. 'Loads of ideas are old and they're still nonsense. Lots of the very worst ideas there are happen to be very, very old.'

'You seem interested though,' says Marie, looking at David, ignoring his mother.

David is interested. In one card in particular.

'That card,' he says. 'That one on the top . . .'

'The Tower?'

She passes it to him to have a better look. It shows lightning hitting a tower, fragments falling off. It looks a lot like the church tower.

'What does it mean?' he says.

'Oh – well, it's very complicated. All the cards have all kinds of meaning depending on what cards they follow, but this one means change – a huge, dramatic kind of change. Are you sure you don't want me to do a reading for you?'

'No,' says David, handing back the card. 'Thanks.'

It's so hot in David's room that he walks over to the window, raises his blinds and opens the window. The room seems to audibly gasp as the fresh air floods in.

He looks out across the gardens, letting his eyes roam aimlessly across the view – or so he pretends to himself. But Holly's garden is empty and so his eyes do not linger there.

The roofers across the way are holding some meeting at the top of the scaffolding they erected the week before, pointing to various parts of the roof and to the dormer window they are working on.

David's super-hearing means he can hear every word of their conversation – but they're not saying anything he's interested in. He enjoys the fact that they are oblivious to Holly when she sunbathes because the tree in Mr Dewhurst's garden entirely blocks their line of sight. If they only knew what they were missing.

A boy's head keeps appearing over a fence further down the street as he bounces on a trampoline. Mr and Mrs Wentworth are having tea outside at their little table in the shade of an umbrella. A flock of small birds flies past.

David smiles. Then smiles at himself for smiling. How quickly Ellen seems to have changed his outlook. A scene that only hours ago might have seemed tedious and dull, seems now to have a kind of familiar charm about it.

But no sooner does he register this change of heart than he is struck by a twinge of guilt for letting himself so easily be deflected from his secret super-destiny. Is this all he has been waiting for to lighten his mood – the attentions of a girl?

He knows that on some level he has been waiting for a sign – a signal that it is OK for him to stop being unhappy, and maybe this is it. Maybe Marie's card was for him.

His mind flickers between the scaffolders, the card and the church tower it so resembles. Maybe there's something in all that crap. Maybe it is telling him that there is about to be a cataclysmic shift in things and that Ellen is the thing that makes it all happen.

The roofers are arguing now. The voices are louder and one of them flicks the air with the back of his hand and storms off, climbing down the ladders noisily and at speed, shaking the frame of the scaffolding.

Then Holly steps out of her house. She isn't wearing a bikini this time though – she is wearing jeans and a grey T-shirt. She has a white mug in her hand. David grabs the scope.

Holly walks slowly over to the lounger and sits on the edge, cradling the mug in her hands and taking a sip. David zooms in, panning up from her candy-striped flip-flops, rising up her legs to her hands and then her face.

She is crying.

Her face is frozen, mask-like, but tears fill her eyes and spill down her cheek, leaving a glistening trail on her face.

David recoils from the scope and pushes it away. It has always been wrong to spy – the wrongness was part of the excitement, part of the thrill. But this – this feels a different kind of super-wrong.

Chapter 12

It's a Free Country

David surprises his mother with his willingness – downright enthusiasm even – to go to the shop for her, given his traditional reluctance, but what she can't know is that David wonders if he might see Ellen there. The concept of shopping has now become inextricably linked to the idea of Ellen.

He hopes that in casually meeting her they might talk further about the things that have been playing on his mind. He registers momentarily that he seems to have gone from never wanting to talk – to avoiding anything but the most cursory conversation – to actively seeking it out. All he knows is that it feels right.

He can't talk to his mother. He won't talk to Mark. He wishes he could have talked to Joe, but that was never what their friendship was about. That's hardly David's fault. Or not just his. Is it?

But there's no sign of Ellen, no matter how long he dawdles in the aisles, drawing the suspicious glances of the woman stacking shelves in the toiletries section. He refuses to make eye contact with her and goes to the tills, pays and leaves.

It was a long shot but even so – he can't stop himself from being disappointed. He has the vague emptiness he always feels in the pit of his stomach when expectation is smothered. He tells himself he's being stupid, and the emptiness just gets a little emptier.

He had walked to the shop with his face upraised, admiring the pool-chalk blue of the sky and the dusty wisps of clouds blowing across it. He walks back looking at his shoelaces. If he had not been so downcast he might have avoided meeting Matt McKenzie.

'Well, look who it isn't,' says Matt. 'It's David Dickhead.'

David has already looked startled before his brain has had time to stop his face looking startled.

'Oh, hi,' says David.

'What brings you round here?'

What the hell brings you round here, more like.

'Oh – yeah,' says Matt, not waiting for the reply, if indeed he ever wanted one. 'You live round here, don't you?'

David nods. First Ellen and now Matt. Too much of a coincidence.

'Ellen's dad lives over there,' he says with a nod. 'So . . .'

David bristles at the mention of her name. What does Ellen see in him? He looks Matt up and down. He's taller than David, a tousled mop of mousy hair tumbling over his face like a cloud.

'You look jumpy, David,' he says. 'You'd think I was going to hit you or something.'

This hasn't occurred to David until now. That doesn't make it any less likely. A quick glance side to side shows there is no one around, and Matt likes to hurt people. He doesn't even pretend otherwise.

But this lack of witnesses works in David's favour as well. With no one to see, there is nothing stopping him hitting Matt. He would have to hold back of course – hit him just hard enough to knock him out. That might be a lot of fun. But Matt would wake up of course, and it would all start again.

'So,' says Matt, 'what are you doing for the holidays?'

Nothing. He is doing nothing. His mother says she is too busy and they will have to wait until Christmas to go away.

'I'm going to . . . er . . . New York,' says David, for no other reason than that he has always wanted to go and his mother is doing a job for a design company there.

Matt laughs.

'You are so full of shit,' he says, and walks off.

David waggles two fingers at Matt's back before setting off home. With every step he feels more and more of a pathetic weakling for letting Matt push him around and humiliate him. But what can he do?

His mother is at the table with a coffee, doing the crossword, when he comes back.

'Hi,' she says, smiling and looking over her glasses at him. 'Thanks for doing that, love. You OK?'

'I'm fine.'

He puts the shopping down on the kitchen floor and starts to unpack it. He never does this normally, but he is still thinking about Matt and forgets.

'Where does the mustard go?'

'In the cupboard – middle shelf.'

When he's put everything away he goes over to the sink and pours himself a glass of water and then turns round to notice the jacket on the back of the stairs. He feels a little dizzy.

'Wait,' he says. 'Is that . . . Holly's?'

'Yes,' says his mother, tapping her pen on the newspaper. 'She sent me a text asking if it was OK if she came a day early. I said it was fine. What's the matter?'

David puts the glass down and bolts for the stairs.

'I checked to make sure your comics were safe!' calls his mother, but David isn't listening. He's taking the stairs two at a time, bursting into his room gasping for breath.

It's OK. It's OK. The scope is at the window where he left it. Holly is at the other end of the room by his bookcase.

'Hi!' he says.

His voice sounds casual. He hopes.

'Hello there,' says Holly.

She smiles. Maybe she hasn't even noticed the scope, or if she had maybe she hadn't noticed where it was pointing. He sits down on his bed and picks up a comic. Try as he might, he cannot even feign an interest in it and looks up to find Holly leaning towards him. She's not smiling any more.

'I wonder what your mother would say if I told her what you were really looking at through that thing?'

'I don't know what you mean.'

He does know what she means, and hearing her say it is sickening. His stomach feels like it flips over.

'Oh, you don't?' she says.

'No.'

His voice cracks and almost gives out. Holly smiles at him.

'I knew you had a good view from up here the very first day I came up,' she says. 'And I don't mind you having a look from up here. It's a free country. I doubt you're the only one. But peering through that thing is just plain creepy. You've crossed a line.'

'I don't even know what you're talking about,' says David. 'I don't –'

'It was still bloody focused on the sunlounger, you little pervert,' snaps Holly. 'Right where my arse would be, I'd imagine. I could see every crumb from the toast I had this morning. Every crumb! So don't bloody lie to me!'

David opens his mouth, but all the many things he had practised in his head for just this eventuality now seem like the silly protestations of a child – a stupid little child.

'What is your mother going to say?' says Holly, shaking her head and leaving, letting the threat trail behind her.

Then David does find some words.

'Well, what would Marie say if she knew you had a boyfriend in her house when you're supposed to be babysitting?' he blurts out just as Holly closes the door behind her.

She had begun to descend the stairs, but she stops and now David hears her slowly come back and the door open. Her face looks transformed. He is genuinely scared.

'What did you say?'

David coughs before jabbing his finger towards her.

'I said, what would Marie say if I told her about you and –'

Before David can finish, Holly has crossed the room and grabbed him by the throat, pushing him back against the wall.

'Are you threatening me?' she hisses. 'Are you fucking threatening me, you little shit?'

Her face is flushed. Her eyes are wild, twitching, scanning his face as though for some sign. Just as suddenly as she had grabbed him, she lets him go and he scrabbles away, clutching at his throat.

'You're crazy!' he mutters.

'You better believe it!' she spits. 'I'm bad. Don't you understand? Don't mess with me, David. You'll regret it. I promise you. I will chew you up.'

David says nothing. What is there to say? She stares at him for what seems like a long, long time and then she turns and walks away, slamming the door behind her and clattering down the stairs.

He hammers both fists into the bed. He feels guilty – he always feels guilty – but he also feels angry: angry at himself for being caught, angry at Holly – that she has exposed him in this way.

The irony is not lost on him but it doesn't stop him feeling indignant about having his private self laid bare. It is ridiculous, he knows it is. How can a voyeur demand privacy – but it doesn't stop him from feeling like a hermit crab plucked from its shell.

It would be the last straw for his mother if she found out. He's seen the way she looks at him sometimes – like he's in need of pills or worse. She might even send him away.

For treatment or something. Can she do that? Maybe she can.

'Did you say something to upset Holly?' says David's mother when he finally comes down to eat.

She doesn't know. Holly hasn't told her.

'What? Me? No.'

'She seemed upset when she left.'

'Did she?'

'She's had a tough time, David,' says his mother. Again. 'We need to be kind to her.'

'Tough time how?'

Even as he says it, he wonders why he would ask that. Why talk about Holly at all. He is an idiot, he thinks. An absolute idiot.

'I don't want to go into details,' says his mother. 'As a matter of fact, I don't really know the details. But I know she had to drop out of university and she's trying to get her life back on track. I know she's had a tough time.'

'What's that got to do with me?' says David.

'All I'm saying is – oh, never mind,' she says. 'Not everything is about you, David.'

David walks tentatively over to the window when he returns to his room after dinner. It seems wrong – it is wrong – but he can't stop himself looking out or looking towards Holly's garden. He has given up even trying to pretend to himself that he is anything else but lost to this addiction.

But David recoils when he sees Holly sitting there on the

lounger. Even without the scope he can see that she is looking straight up at him – and she's holding something.

He pulls back from the window and stares at the slats of the blinds. Is this some kind of trap? He leans forward again, puts his eye to the scope and zooms in. There is Holly's blurred face filling the viewfinder. He focuses and pulls back.

The thing she is holding is revealed to be a large piece of white card on which is written in black pen:

MEET ME IN THE PARK
AT THE BENCH BY THE
SWINGS AT THREE O'CLOCK

Chapter 13

A Kind of Thrashed Electric-Guitar Chord

David looks at his watch, looks away, sniffs – looks back. It is a quarter to. He turns towards the gardens but Holly is gone. She has seen the blinds move – he is sure of it. She knows he's seen the sign. No question about it.

But should he go? The look on her face when she lost her temper – she looked capable of anything. What does he know about her really? Nothing good. David finds himself wondering exactly what trouble she got herself into at university – so bad that she had to leave. She has always intimidated him – right back to when he was a little kid and she and her friends would shoo him away – now she actually frightens him.

This amuses him momentarily and he smiles despite himself. Some superhero he is. All he has to do is stay put. He can say he never saw the sign. She can't prove he did. And what can she say or do really?

But David can't stop himself. For good or ill, he has relinquished control of the part of himself that might have decided otherwise. He simply feels compelled to see where this new turn will lead.

A fascinating new intimacy has entered his relationship with Holly and it is too unsettling and exciting to ignore, however unpredictable she is. Because of how unpredictable she is. He is a moth and he is going to flap towards that flame whatever the consequence.

His thoughts do briefly touch on Ellen as he opens the front door, but only briefly. Holly's lure is just too bright, too intense. It drowns everything else out. Besides, Ellen is with Matt; stupid, annoying Matt.

David leaves the house and walks to the park, aware that he has the theatrical air of someone trying hard not to attract attention – like a secret agent or a private detective from a straight-to-DVD movie.

He sees Holly in the distance and stops. Still time to change his mind. She is looking down into her lap, her face in shadow. He looks at her for a while, swallowing drily, and then she looks up and there is a kind of thrashed electric-guitar chord and David has no choice but to carry on towards her, feedback ringing in his ears.

'Hi,' says David, sitting down next to her – or at least near her.

Holly sighs. Talking about this – talking about this and/or talking about it to David – is clearly an effort; an unpleasant and unwanted, painful necessity.

'Look – I won't say anything to your mum,' says Holly, her eyes half shut. 'About you spying on me. Annoying though it is. I shouldn't have said that.'

'OK,' says David.

This ought to be good news, but it is delivered in a voice that gives little comfort. Even so, sitting there beside her in the park, David's memory of her wild temper slowly evaporates. It is more like a dream he's woken from than something that has actually taken place not long before.

'I shouldn't have grabbed either. I get angry sometimes. Just crazy angry. I'm sorry.'

'It's OK,' says David as though being choked and threatened is something he has encountered on a regular basis. 'I shouldn't have said anything either.'

She turns to look at him.

'Not that you should be spying on people.'

'I know.'

Holly turns away and stares at her own hands for a long time.

'Fuck, David,' she says finally. 'You can't say anything. To anyone.'

She looks up at him with tears trembling in her eyes.

'I know.'

He is surprised at how emotional she is. She is shaking, he can see that clearly now. David can't see why it is such a terrible secret. Embarrassing maybe – but deserving neither of the fury nor this fear, surely? She seems to read these thoughts and attempts an explanation.

'Marie would go apeshit – absolutely apeshit – and she'd tell my parents and they'd get all freaked out. I've put them through a lot, you know? I just . . .'

David nods, hoping this will look like he understands when he doesn't really understand much at all.

'I won't say anything. I promise,' he says.

She nods back and something like a smile appears fleetingly, but only fleetingly. Her face is visibly quivering – every muscle taut and trembling under the skin.

'Thanks,' she says finally, barely opening her lips. 'I won't forget it.'

Then she is shaking her head again, her hair falling across her face. She hugs herself, leaning back against the bench. David feels some of her rage return and edges away.

'Why did you have to be spying on us anyway?' she whispers, frowning at him.

'Look, I couldn't help seeing what I saw,' says David, taken aback by this sudden lurch in mood. What happened to grateful? Holly raises a quizzical eyebrow.

'OK, OK – so I could have helped seeing it,' says David. 'But I saw it and I can't un-see it. I never wanted to see it. I just –'

'All right!' says Holly, slapping both hands on the wood of the seat and making David start. 'For fuck's sake.'

David leans back further away from her. She sees him move and puts up her hands, as a peace gesture.

'Sorry,' she says. 'But I really don't need this shit.'

'Then why . . . ?'

David doesn't know how to finish the sentence, and the look on Holly's face makes him certain he shouldn't try.

'Don't you start judging me. Mr Peeping Fucking Tom.'

'It's not like that,' says David.

Although it is a bit like that.

'What would you call it then? Spying on people? Spying

on people in their private moments. Staring at my tits through that . . . that . . . thing.'

She waves her hand in the general direction of David's house. They both look off that way for a moment. He says nothing.

'What's the matter with you?' says Holly. 'Why can't you just watch porn on the Internet like a normal kid or go out with a girl or something?'

'Look, I've said I'm sorry.'

'What did you see anyway?' she says. 'The other night.'

'Not much,' says David. 'He closed the curtains, remember.'

'Well, I'm very sorry,' says Holly. 'I'll get him to leave them open next time and you can get an eyeful.'

David decides that anything he says will probably make things worse so opts for returning to saying nothing at all. Holly just sighs. How long is he expected to sit here? he wonders. Is she going to say anything else? David eventually looks up from studying his feet and notices, with a puzzled double take, that Ellen is walking towards them.

'Hi,' she says.

'Er, hi, Ellen.'

David shuffles back and forth on the bench. Holly frowns. Ellen casts a quick glance at her, then back to David.

'I just saw you over here and thought I ought to say hello,' she says. 'I'm with a few of the guys.'

David can see them looking their way from the other side of the park. He forgets to reply.

'I hope I'm not disturbing anything,' says Ellen.

'No,' says David. 'No. No.'

'OK then,' says Ellen with a smile.

Holly shakes her head and makes a little noise in her nose that his mother sometimes makes.

'Oh. This is Holly,' says David, taking the hint. 'Holly, this is Ellen.'

'Hi,' says Ellen. 'David's mentioned you.'

'Has he indeed?'

David flinches and refuses to meet Holly's stare.

'Anyway,' says Ellen, 'just saying hello. Catch you later, David. Don't forget about the party. Bye, Holly.'

Holly and David watch her walk back to the group.

'Pretty,' says Holly.

'I suppose.'

Holly leans towards him.

'What the fuck did she mean – "David's mentioned you"? You haven't spoken to anyone else about this, have you?'

'No!' says David. 'Of course not!'

'Because if you did,' she says, peering at him, 'I'd have to do something very unpleasant with that telescope of yours.'

'I haven't said anything about you!'

Holly grimaces at the idiocy of this clear untruth.

'All right. I just mentioned that you clean for us. I may have mentioned you were hot.'

Holly raises an eyebrow and smiles.

'Hot?'

'Yeah,' says David, blushing a little. 'Maybe.'

'Let's hope she agrees,' says Holly.

'What?' says David. 'Why?'

'Because the hotter she thinks I am, the hotter she'll think you are, my friend.'

David furrows his brow.

'Really?'

Holly chuckles. She is clearly chuckling at his lameness – something that David usually hates more than anything – but he doesn't mind her laughing at him because she looks so good when she laughs.

'She's got a boyfriend,' he says.

'So?' says Holly. 'What's he like, this boyfriend?'

'He's an idiot.'

'Well then.'

David smiles. What is he supposed to do? Just grab Ellen and say, 'You're mine now!'? Maybe that's how Holly does things, but then she looks like . . . well, she looks like Holly.

'So are we OK, David? You know – about everything . . . ?'

David nods.

'It's nothing to do with me. None of it. I honestly don't care. What other people do is their own business, right?'

Holly smiles. She narrows her eyes as she looks up at the sky, then closes them altogether. David waits for her to say something else but she is silent. He just sits and marvels at her profile – wonders at how close he is to such an amazing creature. It's like sitting beside a tiger.

'Do I know him?' says David.

'Who?'

She opens her eyes and turns lazily towards him.

'Your boyfriend?'

'Why would you know him?'

David shrugs. He can tell he's said the wrong thing, but it's too late.

'No reason. I was just wondering.'

'What happened to it being none of your business?'

'Yeah – right. Sorry.'

Holly relaxes again and smiles.

'OK then,' she says. 'So we're cool?'

'Sure,' says David. 'Of course.'

'Thank you.'

Holly leans forward and kisses him on the cheek. David shifts uneasily and stares at his feet. She smiles. Then she gets up and leaves without even glancing back, and David looks over at Ellen and the others as they turn away and pretend not to have noticed.

Chapter 14

Kindness Doesn't Get You Laid

David looks out across the gardens. A cloud shadow crawls sluggishly across the roof tiles opposite. Below, Holly is in the garden lying on the sunlounger. She lies on her back, her arms above her head. She is wearing round tortoise-shell-rimmed sunglasses.

There is no one about. There is no one but him. And her. He pulls on the cord and raises the blinds. He opens his window, standing on a chair to climb through, gripping the frame before letting go and launching himself out over his garden.

Even though there's no one around, he employs his power of invisibility before leaving so he has no fear of being seen. This takes more effort though – it drains him and makes him feel a little light-headed. He swims through the air, up and over the big birch tree and hovers above Holly's garden and above Holly, lying far below. She turns over onto her stomach.

He lays out flat in the air, a copy of Holly's prone body below him, and then sinks slowly towards her until he comes to rest about ten feet above. He hovers there, arms outstretched, cruciform, as though he is floating in the sea, looking down under the water at some beautiful species of fish or coral.

Holly seems to be asleep. Maybe she's dreaming. Maybe she is dreaming of him. Why would she dream of him? But maybe she does. We don't have control about who we dream of. She stirs and shifts her position, turning over. Her breasts rise and fall a little with each breath. She moves her face to one side. She has a mole on the line of her jaw.

David moves closer still. He drops his arms and reaches out his hands towards her but flinches as she suddenly takes off her sunglasses and stares straight at him.

He is invisible. He knows that. She can't see him. And yet – and yet she lifts herself onto her elbows and stretches out her lovely pale neck, frowning, peering up. Then she suddenly reaches out a hand to grab him.

David jerks back from the scope.

He still feels dizzy and clings on to the windowsill for a moment. Things have changed. Holly knowing that he watches her has not – as he thought it might – cured him of wanting to watch. If anything, it has made him want to watch more.

It isn't like she has expressly forbidden it. Has she? She hasn't exactly given him permission either, but it feels more consensual – two-way now: a game – a sexy game. His phone pings and he walks over. It's Ellen. Ellen? How did she even have his number?

The text says: 'You around? I'm at the shop.'

David replies: 'OK. See you in 5.'

Is this a date? It feels like kind of a date. Kind of. They

have arranged a meeting. Isn't that what a date is? Whatever it is, it's a definite step, David is sure if it. A big step. Of some kind. Or other.

'So are you coming to Ben's party?' says Ellen as they sit down.

'Ben who?'

David knows exactly who she means. Ellen knows he knows and smiles at his attempt at nonchalance.

'Something tells me I'm not invited,' says David.

Ellen nods.

'Yes, you are – I'm inviting you.'

David grimaces. He just wanted to talk to Ellen, be with her – why do they have to talk about some stupid party he doesn't want to go to? Maybe this wasn't such a good idea.

'OK – but I'm not sure that Matt and his friends are going to be OK with that. And to be honest I don't really care whether I go, so . . .'

'Well, it's not their party,' says Ellen. 'I've known Ben for ages. Much longer than them. Our mums know each other. They've known each other since college. In any case, you can come with me.'

'Really?' says David, grimacing again.

'Charming!'

'No – I mean, won't Matt mind?'

'Stop worrying about Matt.'

'I thought you and Matt were . . .'

She raises an eyebrow.

'I wonder where that sentence was going.'

'Going out,' says David. 'I thought you and he were a thing.'

'A thing?'

'Come on – you know what I mean.'

She laughs.

'Well, the thing is dead,' she says. 'It has been for a while. It just didn't know. Like those movies where the ghost doesn't know they're really dead. It was like that.'

'Oh,' says David. 'Sorry.'

'Are you?'

'No – not really,' he says. 'I've never liked Matt to be honest. It's mutual.'

'He's not so bad,' she says. 'When you get to know him.'

'Says the girl who dumped him.'

'Did I say I dumped him?'

'Well, didn't you?'

She laughs.

'Yeah,' she says. 'Matt's not the dumping kind. We'd still be trying to work things out when we're sixty if he had anything to do with it. But if it doesn't work, you can't force it, you know what I mean?'

'Yeah,' says David.

Of course he didn't know what she meant. How could he know what she meant? He'd never dumped or been dumped or ever had the chance to discover whether he was the dumping kind or not.

'I always had a bit of a thing for you, you know,' she says matter-of-factly, as though she is telling him she liked the colour blue or bacon sandwiches. 'Even before we played tennis that day.'

'Have you?' says David, trying to hit the same tone but sounding short of breath. She nods.

'Remember that field trip we took? With the school. Ages ago.'

'To the Lakes?'

He knew.

'Yeah,' she says. 'Remember we had to walk up that stupid great hill?'

'Yeah,' says David with a chuckle.

'It's all right for you – you were like a mountain goat or something. But then you stopped and looked back and saw me dragging my sorry arse up and watched as I slipped and fell face first in the mud.'

'I remember,' says David.

'I was sure you were going to laugh, but you didn't. You came back – you held your hand out and you helped me up.'

David shrugs. He was pulled back to that day – to the feel of her hand in his, her crooked smile, the red sail of a yacht on the sparkling lake way off in the distance behind her head. It was time-travel vivid.

'Anyone would do that,' he said.

She shakes her head.

'Well, no one did – only you. I've never forgotten it. You're kind. Kindness doesn't really get you noticed much, does it, though? Kindness doesn't get you laid.'

David blushes. Ellen laughs. She never used to talk like this. She sounds so sure of herself. He tries again to connect this new Ellen to the old one and fails.

David smiles but it's a bittersweet memory, the memory

of that school trip. David's father had picked him up from the bus when it dropped them off outside the school. As they drove away David watched Ellen saying goodbye to her friends, hugging them and squealing. It was the start of feeling un-included. That was why it had been so amazing when, out of the blue, she'd agreed to play tennis that day.

'So you'll come? To the party?'

David grimaces and shakes off the memory. She stands up and he stands with her.

'Come on!' she says, slapping him on the arm. 'Please!'

Then she reaches her arm round his waist and pulls him towards her. Not all the way. It was just a kind of grabbing gesture, her fingers digging into the flesh at the small of his back, but it made David feel as though the ground had suddenly tilted. The whole world now sloped towards Ellen.

'Yeah,' he hears himself say. 'OK.'

He would have agreed to go anywhere at that moment. Ellen lets go of him, having got her way.

'Good,' she says, as though ticking something off a list.

With that she begins to walk away, but turns back after a few steps.

'So that was Holly?' she says. 'In the park the other day.'

David can see the nonchalance is contrived. That's interesting, he thinks. Maybe Holly had been right.

'Yeah,' says David, feeling a little taller. 'That was her. Why did you have to say I'd mentioned her though?'

'Well, you did.'

'I know – but she thought I'd told you about her and her boyfriend.'

114

'You did. You did tell me that.'

'I know – but she can't know that.'

'I'm sure you handled it very well.'

'I got away with it – just.'

Ellen nods, smiling. Again she turns to walk away and again she is unable to resist saying just a little more.

'I thought she'd be better-looking.'

'Oh?' says David.

Why was that? Had he even described her? He can't remember.

'Yeah,' says Ellen, flaring her nostrils a little. 'I don't know why. I imagined someone sexy.'

'And you don't think she is?'

'What – you do?'

Wait. Wait. Careful.

'What? No – I just . . .'

Ellen flares her nostrils before speaking.

'She seems a bit slutty to me.'

'Slutty?'

'A bit, yeah,' says Ellen, screwing up her nose. 'Some men find that sexy, I know. But then . . .'

David waits for the rest but it never comes. Ellen is always so self-assured – or seems so self-assured – but David can see that she is bothered – bothered by Holly and bothered by David knowing her; but bothered in a way he's never seen before. The skin of her neck is a little red. She is tapping the toe of one foot.

Holly was right: she has made him seem more interesting than he is and that feels good. It feels surprisingly good.

'OK then – I'll see you at the party if not before,' says Ellen with a little wave and a tight smile. 'You know where it is?'

He nods.

Then, to his surprise, she walks back towards him, leans forward and kisses him on the lips. David is so surprised, in fact, that he doesn't move and just stands there, feeling the soft collision of her lips on his.

'Bye,' she says.

'Bye,' says David, every nerve ending crackling and fizzing.

Chapter 15

A Fresh Wound

David stands at the top of the church tower, one hand holding on to the window's edge, his foot on the moss-crowned stone head, listening into the wind. There! He'd know the sound of that engine anywhere. And then the cries for help.

He launches himself into the air, as though pushing off from a rock into the sea. The wind feels cold, damp. The first spots of rain strike his face. The graveyard and the boundary trees pass by beneath him.

He swoops out over the fields, kicking his feet every now and then like a swimmer, urging himself onwards, faster and faster, the air rushing past his ears and over the slippery grey suit he wears.

He flies over the top of the rookery, the spikes of his suit whistling, birds taking flight noisily as he passes over. The road snakes away below him – slicing through the earth, glinting like a fresh wound.

Then the screech of brakes and there is the car swerving to the left, bumping up the kerb with a thump and crunch, smashing through the flimsy fence, careering up the embankment, tyres spinning, mud spraying.

David changes direction, throwing himself downwards, diving down, down – come on! come on! – until he is only a few metres above the embankment.

The car has already plunged into the water and David races to grab it before it is submerged. The driver is yelling and banging on the inside of the glass as David digs his hands into the metal and heaves with all his might.

The burst of light comes out of nowhere and hits him round the side of the head. David is dazed but he shakes it off and holds on and keeps pulling. The light creature begins to uproot a nearby tree.

It is almost impossible to look at, but through the glare David can see the human form at its core. He turns back to the car, the image burned onto his eyes in negative. The driver stares out through the windscreen as David strains to pull the car free of the water.

The tree smashes across David's back, knocking him onto the bonnet of the car which crashes into the water and begins to sink again. Pain rips through his body.

The light creature strikes again, the tree missing David by a fraction but smashing the side windows of the car, letting water flood in and the driver's screaming voice out.

David's spiked costume is battered and scarred across the back, the supposedly indestructible fabric torn through and several deep cuts in his flesh. He knows that he will heal in no time – that's part of his gift – but for now it hurts like hell.

He turns just as the thing leaps at him, punching him twice before David can block the onslaught and hit back. It

119

takes three of David's strongest punches to knock the creature free and send it tumbling into the river, where it sinks, glowing eerily underwater.

The car too is submerged now and David dives after it, grabbing at the door to pull it open, but no sooner has he done so than the light grabs him from behind and begins to choke him. David watches as the car begins to sink into the blackness below them.

He tries to prise free of the light creature's glowing fingers but the grip is too strong. David can feel himself getting weaker. He gathers all his remaining strength and leaps back, smashing the back of his head into whatever face the thing possessed.

Now free, he lunges to the surface for breath. There is no sign of his enemy. David dives down again in search of the car, but with increasing panic he realises he cannot find it anywhere. The river seems impossibly bottomless and he can see nothing – nothing at all in the murk.

David launches himself out of the water, erupting like a champagne cork, and throws himself onto the bank, sobbing and gasping for breath. He is aware of a glow to his right. The light thing hovers above the river, pulsing, but makes no further attempt to attack him.

'Bastard!' yells David. 'I'll kill you!!'

But before he can even stand up, the thing has turned and flown away at such unfathomable speed that David knows he will never, ever, be able to catch it. He clenches his fists and howls at the wind and the rain and the rippling surface of the water.

Chapter 16

A Superhero Has to Have a Name

It's decidedly odd when Holly comes to clean again. She and David eye each other nervously as she enters the room, like cats meeting on a garden fence, not quite knowing how to adjust to the new boundaries of their relationship.

Holly sets to cleaning after their brief hellos, just as before, and as before David sits on his bed, his eyes moving from comic to Holly and back again. Ellen or no Ellen, Holly's presence – and the proximity of her much-fantasised-about body – is a magnetic distraction.

But the difference is that whereas Holly usually finishes up and leaves with barely a word, this time she clearly feels that she needs to acknowledge David – to talk to him – to keep him sweet perhaps. She sits down at his desk.

'So what's the story with all the comics?'

She leans down and picks one up from the end of the bed. It's *Fantastic Four* #129. It has Ben Grimm aka The Thing being pulled between Medusa, who has her red hair wrapped round one arm, and Thundra, who has a chain wrapped around the other. Holly smiles and flicks through.

'Lots of buxom women in skintight Lycra. Now I see what's going on.'

David shrugs.

'They belonged to my dad,' he says, running his fingers through his hair, taken by surprise by this new requirement to converse with Holly.

'Right,' she says, nodding.

'He brought them back to ours from his mum and dad's house. His dad – my granddad – had just died and he was clearing the house. I could tell they were really special to him. I'd never been that into comics, to be honest, but I saw him looking through them a little bit after and he was crying.'

'Crying?'

'Yeah,' says David, realising he has never told a single soul this story. 'He pretended he wasn't but I could see that he was. He was wiping the tears away when I came over and he put his hand on my shoulder and said – in this really quiet voice – that he wanted me to keep them – to look after them.'

'That must have been weird for you,' says Holly. 'To see him upset like that.'

'It was – a bit – at first,' says David. 'But then it was kind of cool because it just made this bond between us. He was never really that kind of a dad, to be honest. Not a big one for showing his feelings. So it felt like we were closer because of that – because of the comics. My mother doesn't get it.'

'Maybe she's jealous,' says Holly. 'Maybe she's jealous that you still have this bond.'

'No – I don't think it's that. She's not like that.'

'Maybe you haven't explained it properly,' she says.

'Yeah, well – maybe she hasn't listened.'

'I wish I hadn't asked now,' says Holly.

'Sorry,' says David after a moment. 'It's just . . .'

But he isn't really sure he can explain. To anyone. Holly doesn't seem to care. And he likes that. He hates it when people make you finish a sentence – like you were short-changing them if you didn't give them the whole thing. Like you owe it to them.

'He suggested that we go to Forbidden Planet – the comic shop, you know – and get individual archive bags and boxes to file them all away in. They're like antiques now, all those seventies comics. It was fun actually.'

David pauses a bit at the memory and is aware how geeky this sounds. He feels the need to try to defend himself – and his father.

'He wasn't a collector – he just used to buy them at his local shop and would get whatever they had, so there are little runs where they follow one after another and there are loads of gaps and then series just come to a halt. I might try and fill the gaps, buying them second hand. You can find them online now.'

Holly looks at the walls and the drawings stuck to them. She is already regretting asking about the comics. David can see that and blushes a little.

'And you did all these?' asks Holly, unable to think of anything else to say.

David nods and follows her gaze as she looks from one to the other: Captain America, the Hulk, Wolverine, Sub-Mariner, Batman, Spider-Man, Thor, the Silver Surfer . . .

'Yeah,' says David. 'I just copied them.'

'They're good though. You must get that from your mum.'

'I suppose.'

'What about these?'

She points to two drawings with no names above them: one of a figure in a metallic grey costume covered in spikes, the other a figure that is human shaped but blank, with rays of light bursting out.

'They don't have names,' she says. 'What are they called?'

'I made those up myself,' he says. 'I haven't thought of names yet. Most have already been taken. Names, I mean.'

'Yeah – but still – they've got to have names. A superhero has to have a name.'

'I suppose.'

Holly goes a little closer, peering at the drawings.

'What superpowers do they have?'

'Well, that one – the one with the spikes – he can fly and he has super-hearing and super-strength and a kind of super-sense a bit like Spider-Man's spidey-sense.'

'Spidey-sense?'

David shrugs, smiling.

'You're not a Spider-Man fan then?'

'I've seen the movie.'

'Which one?'

'The one with Kirsten Dunst.'

He nods. This is nice. They're chatting like normal people.

'What's the business with the spikes on his suit? Do they shoot out or are they tipped with poison?'

124

'Tipped with poison? No! They're just . . . I don't know –
he just has spikes.'

'How about Spiky?'

'No.'

'Spikyman?' she says with a chuckle.

'OK, OK – very funny.'

'Sorry. And the other one – the one that is just a burst of
light?'

'He's super, super-strong. He can fly too. I don't really
know all his powers.'

She smiles and raises an eyebrow.

'But you made him up, didn't you?'

'Yeah – but even so . . .'

This talk of superpowers is almost unbearable. To have
them spoken about with the images of his super-self and
arch-enemy right there in front of them . . . The urge to say
more is overwhelming. But he can't. He can't.

She turns back to the pictures.

'You're really good,' she says, and David can tell by her
voice she isn't just saying it to please him.

'Thanks.'

'Is that what you'd like to do? Be a comic-book artist?'

He shrugs. He had wanted that once. More than anything.

'I don't know. I don't know what I want to do.'

She nods. He nods. There is a silence that edges towards
awkward before Holly says what's on her mind.

'I've got to thank you again for not blabbing about
you-know-what.'

David nods again.

'If I can ever do anything for you,' she says, adding with a suggestive smirk, 'within reason.'

David blushes. Did she just say that? Did she just hint at some kind of . . . ? She laughs at his visible discomfort and he laughs in a failed attempt to hide it.

'Anyway – I better go,' she says, getting up.

'I'll see if I can think of anything,' blurts David as she is heading out the door.

'Sorry?'

'I'll see if I can think of anything – you know, that you can do for me.'

Holly nods and smiles and leaves and David lies back on his bed. A broad smile spreads across his face. He knows exactly what he's going to ask her to do for him . . .

Chapter 17

Seeing Other People

David slumps down next to Joe on the bench. Why had they chosen to play tennis on such a blistering hot day? David finishes off the last drop of water in his bottle and gasps, tongue lolling like a dog's.

'You worried about the exam results?' asks Joe, head back, eyes closed.

David shakes his head.

'Nah – not really.'

'Me neither,' says Joe, opening his eyes and looking up at the one cloud in the sky. 'Although my mum clearly wants me to be.'

'Mine too. If you don't look worried they think you don't care. If you look too worried they think you've screwed up.'

Joe nods.

'You decided what subjects you're going to do next year?'

David shrugs.

'You're doing art though, right?'

David grimaces.

'I don't know. Probably not.'

'Why?'

'What's the use of it?' says David. 'What's the point?'

'The point is, you're good at it. That's what the point is. I can't understand why you wouldn't do it.'

David crushes his water bottle and throws it in the litter bin nearby. He doesn't want to talk about it. Why does Joe even care what he does or doesn't do?

'It's just because your mum did art, isn't it?' says Joe. 'You don't like the comparison. She is really good. But she'd be able to help you and stuff.'

'So?' says David. 'I don't see you becoming a doctor like your mum.'

'I'm not clever enough.'

'Yes, you are,' says David.

'All right – but I don't want to be a doctor,' says Joe.

'I don't want to be an illustrator,' says David with a shrug.

It's not exactly true. Whenever he sees his mother at work he gets a twinge – a kind of regret, a sense of loss for something he never really even had. It's like he is looking at a future he is denying himself.

'You don't have to be. You could be something else. They do loads of stuff at art college. You could be a sculptor.'

David laughs.

'A sculptor?'

Joe laughs too.

'I don't know – something. A photographer.'

'Then what would be the point in me being able to draw?' says David.

'All right, not a photographer. A painter then.'

'I don't want to be a painter.'

Joe lets out an exasperated growl.

'Well, OK – what do you want to be?'

David has no idea. Not any more.

'I don't know,' he replies. 'I really don't know. What about you? Do you still want to be prime minister?'

They both grin at this reference to an incident from primary school when their teacher asked who knew what they wanted to be when they grew up and Joe had rammed his arm into the air like he was trying to touch the ceiling.

'Miss! Miss!'

'Joe?' she had asked. 'Tell us what you'd like to be when you grow up.'

'Prime minister, miss,' he'd said.

There had been the briefest of pauses before the whole class broke out into laughter – including David, who then turned to see a look of tear-filled outrage on Joe's face.

'Yeah – I do,' says Joe.

He is deadly serious and his face still carries a trace of the little boy sitting on the floor buffeted by laughter that day all those years ago.

'Do you know, I wouldn't be surprised,' says David.

And he wasn't just saying that.

'Listen,' says Joe. 'I'd better shoot off. Me and my mum are taking Fuzz to the vet's.'

Fuzz is Joe's cat.

'Is she OK?'

'Just old mostly,' says Joe.

He picks up his racket and bag.

'Did Ellen get in touch?'

'Ellen?' says David.

'How many Ellens do you know? Did she call you? She asked for your number.'

'And did you give it to her?'

'Yeah – why wouldn't I?' says Joe with a smirk.

David shrugs.

'Why is she after your number then?'

'I don't know. When did you see her?'

David recognises the urge to lie on Joe's face – the almost imperceptible flicker of the eyes as he tries to concoct something but gives up.

'There was a picnic the other day,' he says. 'It was Tilly's birthday. You know Tilly?'

'Yeah, of course.'

He likes Tilly. She is one of that crowd that actually seems OK. He is surprised to feel a pang of regret that he was not invited, but mostly he is surprised by a kind of jealousy – not for Joe's invite, but for Joe having this other life outside of their relationship.

'I shouldn't have said,' says Joe, seeing the look on David's face.

'What? Don't be daft. I don't give a monkey's what you do.'

Although he does.

'OK then,' says Joe. 'It's just you looked a bit hacked off.'

'Rubbish. Don't flatter yourself.'

'OK.'

'Why would I care?'

Joe nods.

'Look – Ben's having a party,' says Joe. 'Everyone's going. You should come too.'

David screws his face up like he's just bitten down on a piece of chilli.

'I don't know,' he says. 'I'm not really a party person.'

Joe laughs.

'No shit.'

David smiles.

'You know what I mean.'

'Not really,' he says. 'You don't have to be wild and crazy, you just have to come along, have a couple of beers and have a laugh. There'll be people there you like. Ellen will be there for instance . . .'

'What is this with Ellen?'

'I don't know,' says Joe. 'You tell me.'

'All right, all right,' says David. 'We bumped into each other the other day and got talking. That's all.'

Joe nods approvingly.

'Look at you – talking to a girl and stuff.'

David blushes.

'I know, I know.'

'Good for you, mate. Anyway – like I said, I'd better get going. Got to get Fuzz to the vet. Think about the party.'

'Yeah – sure – see you around.'

'Text me if you want to come over.'

David nods and waves his racket and Joe waves his back and walks off at speed after a glance at his watch.

David tortures himself with images of the picnic – everyone lazing around in the perfect sunshine, a cloth laid out across the grass covered in paper plates and bowls filled with sand-wiches and crisps and cupcakes.

He's not sure where he is getting these preposterously idyllic images from because he can't remember ever being present at a picnic like it. Maybe it's a movie he's seen – or even a comic.

Wherever it's from, it hurts. The pointlessness of the pain doesn't make it any less acute. He wouldn't have gone even if Joe had invited him, but even so . . . It feels like Joe is becoming less his friend and more theirs.

Which wouldn't be so bad if David was better at friendship, but he is happy to concede he's rubbish at it. That's why he only has the one real friend.

Chapter 18

Like a Frog in a Box

Time seems to slow down. It gets hotter and hotter. David feels becalmed in some kind of equatorial limbo, too hot to do anything but lie marinating in his own sweat, counting the days until Holly returns, phrasing and rephrasing the conversation he intends to have with her.

This sultry, fevered air of expectation only intensifies when the actual day arrives, with David fidgeting, unable to settle in one position, totally incapable of following the *Silver Surfer* comic he has been trying to finish for the past two hours, when Holly bursts in like a guitar solo.

'Hi, there,' she says, dragging the hoover through the door. 'How're things?'

'OK!' says David, trying to not to look as if he has been waiting for her. 'How about you?'

'I'm good, thanks.'

He tries to summon up the courage there and then, but he can't. The anticipation has made things worse. He's not prepared, he's just mentally exhausted and a little wired. The hoover roars into life and David slumps back on the bed.

Holly finishes and is almost out of the door before David finally, in desperation, gulps and says what's on his mind.

'You know how you said if there was ever anything you could do for me?' he says, the words still a lot harder to get out of his mouth than into his head.

'Uh-huh?' says Holly, a little warily, putting the hoover down.

'Well – I do have something to ask you . . . It's a bit embarrassing though.'

Holly raises an eyebrow.

'I'm not sure how grateful you think I am,' she says.

David blushes.

'No – it's not . . . No – I wanted to ask . . . to ask you something. I wanted to ask you about kissing.'

Holly folds her arms.

'Kissing?'

'Yeah?'

'You want me to kiss you?'

Yes. Yes. Yes.

'What?' says David. 'No . . . I mean . . . I was more meaning that I wanted to ask you how. You know – how to do it.'

'You don't know how to kiss?'

David shrugs. This isn't going to be easy.

'You've never kissed a girl?'

'Of course I have!' says David indignantly.

Holly stares at him.

'OK – not properly,' he says.

'No tongues?' says Holly with a smirk.

She seems to be enjoying this more than David had expected.

134

'Once,' says David. 'At school – ages ago. But that doesn't count.'

David gets a vivid replay of the event in his mind – an older girl he didn't really like pushing her face into his, her tongue jabbing into his mouth, the breathlessness, the giggles of those around.

'Doesn't count?' says Holly. 'Why?'

'Because she kissed me,' he replies.

'And that's wrong because . . . ?'

'Not wrong exactly,' says David. 'Well, not wrong at all. It just doesn't help me, does it? Because I want to be the kisser – not the kissee. I need to make the moves and I don't have any.'

Holly nods.

'I see.'

'Ellen – that girl you met,' says David. 'She kissed me. The other day. On the lips.'

'And?'

'And I just stood there like an idiot.'

Holly smiles. It is a kind smile but it makes David feel like a child and he frowns and slaps the bed.

'Stop beating yourself up about it,' says Holly. 'There'll be a next time.'

'That's the point,' says David. 'There is going to be a next time. She's asked me to a party.'

Holly shrugs.

'OK then. That's good.'

'No – that's what I mean. She's going to want me to kiss her. Isn't she?'

'Let's hope so.'

'So I want it to be good. Really good. You know? She's really popular.'

Holly raises her eyebrows again.

'Popular, huh?' she says. 'You're worried about the competition.'

'Yes,' says David, 'I'm worried I'll look like an idiot. That she'll laugh at me.'

'She won't laugh at you.'

David groans like he is in real pain and he does feel pain – he feels like he is being pulled apart.

'Please,' he says.

Holly smiles at him.

'I don't know,' she says, looking towards the door. 'It feels a bit weird.'

'I know. I know. But still. Please.'

She sighs and shakes her head.

'I don't know what you want me to say, but I'll try. If you think it'll help.'

David sits up, looking her in the eyes.

'OK, OK. So how would you – you know – want to be kissed?'

Holly puffs out her cheeks and her breath whistles out. Then she chuckles and sits back, studying him.

'Do you know, no one has ever asked me that,' she says. 'So I've never really had to think about it.'

'But you must have been kissed loads of times,' says David.

'Because I'm such a whore, you mean?'

136

'No!' says David, wide-eyed. 'Jesus. I just mean . . . Fuck – no! I meant because you're, you know . . .'

'No,' says Holly 'What? "Popular"?'

'Hot,' replies David. 'You must have been kissed loads of times because you're really hot.'

She smiles at him. A different smile altogether. His heart leaps about like a frog in a box.

'And you say you have no moves.'

David blushes. She continues.

'But yes – I have been kissed a few times, it's true. I can't pretend I haven't.'

'And what makes a good kiss?' says David.

'Hmmm,' she says. 'That's a very good question.'

Holly puts her hand to her jaw and looks up quizzically as though pondering a philosophical conundrum. She taps her chin with her finger, deliberating about what she'll say next.

'Sometimes it's the person – you know, you've wanted to kiss them for so long and then you do and there's a sense of excitement in finally getting there.'

Her face changes after saying this and David senses her falling back into some filed and locked-away memory, her eyes flickering, sparkling. But only for a moment.

'Sometimes it's the occasion – it feels extra special because it's your birthday or Christmas or a lovely sunny day or you're drunk or whatever . . .'

'You're drunk?'

Holly chuckles.

'Hey – don't knock the power of intoxication to make something feel better than it is.'

137

'So I should get her drunk, is that what you're saying?'

Holly sighs.

'No – I wouldn't suggest that.'

David is no nearer to understanding what made a kiss memorable or not – what made it the kiss of someone who could kiss rather than someone who couldn't. He needed facts. Details.

'Tell me something practical,' he says.

'OK then,' she says. 'No one wants to kiss someone with rank-smelling breath.'

'I brush my teeth!' says David defensively.

But his mother is always saying he doesn't do it properly or enough. David has an image of himself going in for the kiss with Ellen. He cringes.

'Look, if you're going to take everything personally then don't ask,' says Holly frowning. 'Jesus.'

'OK, OK,' says David. 'Sorry. OK. No smelly breath – OK. What else?'

'I don't know,' she says, scratching her head. 'This is a bit weird.'

'Come on,' says David, moving closer. 'Imagine I'm your boyfriend and I'm going to kiss you. What would you want me to do?'

This appears to amuse Holly greatly, but after a moment she claps her hands together, pulls a very serious expression and answers.

'Well,' says Holly, 'I would want you to look at me.'

'Look at you?'

'Yes – but not like I was a difficult crossword puzzle. Or

like I was some photo you're drooling over. I mean, really look at me. Me. Just me.'

David remains confused.

'A kiss can be the sexiest thing in the world, you know,' says Holly. 'It mostly isn't, but it can be. Mouths are sexy. Lips are sexy. Tongues are sexy. We use our mouths to breath and to talk. It's a big thing, to join mouths. We just piss and screw with the other things.'

'What? Oh – right . . .'

David gulps at the mention of those 'other things'. The room suddenly seems to shrink.

'A girl wants to feel like you're looking at her – just her – and really seeing her. Do you understand? She doesn't want to feel like you're just kissing someone – anyone. She wants to feel like you're kissing her. Just her. Only her.

'You want to feel like you are the only person that matters in the world to that other person – for that shared moment. Can you understand that? Can you imagine what that might be like – to shut the world out, to stop time and just focus on that kiss?'

David tries to do that – to imagine that he and Holly are indeed the only people in the world – and to his surprise everything else does seem to fall away in his thoughts and a kind of peace sweeps in until they sit in a kind of sparkling bubble adrift in a void. It is surprisingly easy.

'Good,' says Holly.

She can see it in his eyes. He can see it in hers too.

'What then?' says David, his voice now hushed. 'What would happen then?'

'Well,' she says, her own voice now barely a whisper. 'I like hands.'

'Hands . . .' says David, mesmerised.

'Yes. Hands. I'd like him to touch my hair maybe.'

'Like this?' says David.

He lifts his hand tentatively to Holly's hair and runs a few strands between his fingers.'

'Kind of. But less like you're my hairdresser,' she says.

David drops the hair. Holly laughs. The world begins to seep back in. The bubble doesn't burst but it certainly loses some of its sparkle.

'Sorry. Don't give up,' she says, kindly, quietly. 'Move inside the hair . . . put your hand on my neck . . .'

David does as he is told. Her neck is smooth and warm and he lets his hand glide up towards her ear.

'That's good,' says Holly. 'You need to get a balance between rubbing and tickling. You're not giving a massage, but the last thing you want is for her to squirm and pull away giggling. Although that can break the ice. Oh – you know there's no one rule for all this.'

David nods, still entranced. He is listening and not listening. Something has been set in motion and David does not want it to stop.

'And now my face,' says Holly. 'Again, you're touching something precious, not stroking a dog. And look into her eyes all the time. That eye contact is sexy. You aren't embarrassed to look at her. You want to look at her. She's beautiful.'

David looks at Holly. She is beautiful. She is. She really is. Not just hot – but beautiful. He lets his hand slide round

140

behind her head and he pulls her towards him and leans in. The door clicks. Holly is standing at the window by the time it opens.

'You've been up here a long time, Holly,' says David's mother. 'I wondered what had happened to you.'

'Oh, David was just telling me about his comics,' says Holly.

The speed of Holly's lie and mood change impresses David a lot.

'I didn't know you were interested,' says his mother.

'I'm not really,' says Holly. 'But you know what he's like.'

David's mother laughs. David frowns. That almost-kiss is still clinging to his thoughts. He's be happier if they both just left him alone to savour it if all they're going to do is take the piss.

'Seriously though,' says Holly, 'I do like the movies – some of them. I like Iron Man – what's that actor called?'

'Robert Downey Jnr,' says David's mother. 'He's great, isn't he?'

'God, yes,' says Holly. 'So sexy.'

'Absolutely,' says David's mother.

David frowns again.

'We're embarrassing him,' says David's mother.

'Aww!' says Holly. 'You're not embarrassed, are you, David?'

'What? No . . . I don't care . . .' he says.

Holly laughs.

'Anyway, I'm finished now, so I'll be on my way. Bye, David.'

'Oh – yeah – bye,' says David, picking up a comic.

Holly follows his mother out of the room and he can hear the diminishing patter of their feet on the stairs, their voices in the distance, the slam of the front door as Holly leaves the house.

David looks down at his hand; at a sparkling strand of Holly's hair trapped between his fingers.

Chapter 19

Superpowerless

David can't stop thinking about kissing. He thinks about it when he's awake and dreams about it when he's asleep. Sometimes he'll be kissing Ellen, but mostly – mostly – he is carrying on that almost-kiss with Holly, rerunning it and re-editing it in different ways as though his mother hadn't come in and they had been left alone.

Would she have kissed him? Would she have let their lips meet. David tells himself that this is just another fantasy but it doesn't feel that way. It feels inevitable. Maybe that's just wish-fulfilment on his behalf. He's almost sure that's what it is. Almost. Probably.

But in any case, kissing or not kissing Holly is not really the issue and he knows it. It's the kissing or the not kissing of Ellen that really matters. Isn't it?

His mind drifts to thoughts of superheroes and their girl-friends. It's OK for a girl like Pepper Potts because Iron Man is only really a superhero when he wears his suit, or Invisible Girl from the Fantastic Four because she's a superhero just like Reed Richards is.

But when Superman kisses Lois Lane, does he have to pull

back like when he's Clark Kent and hits someone – does he have to only give a fraction of his super-kiss for fear of crushing Lois's face?

As the day of the party nears, David can't decide what he dreads more – the idea that he might make a fool of himself in the kissing or just the very idea of going to a party filled with people he has spent his whole school life avoiding like the plague.

The party would be teaming with the 'popular' people. David isn't popular. He isn't close to being popular. He is a kind of marker for those who are popular. The popular people know they are popular, in part, because they aren't people like David.

What the hell will they make of him suddenly turning up at a party after all these years? Will they even notice him? Or will they tell him to get lost? Or worse. Just the thought of it makes him cringe. And yet he can't stop himself going.

He wishes now that he'd made more of an effort with these people – even if it had been a fake effort. He's seen that in operation – that fakery – and despised it – but he also knows it works.

David has never made any secret of his contempt for the golden ones at school over the last few years – even if they had been mostly unaware of it. But his refusal to play the game has won him enemies, he knows that. You are expected to know your place and accept it. Then you are deemed to be 'OK'. Being 'OK' was the best people like him could hope for. That's what Joe did. That's what David will not – cannot – do.

144

Or so he has always told himself. But maybe he just needed an incentive. He had never wanted to be friends with any of those people, and even before his father's death had been content with Joe and his own company.

But now – now everything is different. Or it seems to be. All because of Ellen. Or the thought of Ellen. Her lips, her lips against his or her tongue in his mouth. Her tongue in his mouth. His in hers. Lips. Tongues. Tongues. Lips.

The usual barriers are in place in his mind but they seem not to be able to withstand the flood of images crashing against them like waves over a sandbank. He is helpless; inundated.

So the next time Holly comes cleaning, David is waiting to continue where they left off on their kissing masterclass.

'I've got an idea for your comic-book character. The one with all the light rays coming out of him.'

'Yeah?' says David.

'What about . . . Lightforce?' she says, jazz-handing as she does so.

David nods appreciatively.

'Actually that's not bad. Lightforce . . .'

'Really?'

'Really.'

'You see – every superhero has to have a name.'

'Strictly speaking he's a supervillain.'

'Same difference.'

David nods. It's true. They all had to have names. Villains too. Maybe villains even more so. That's part of what's cool about them.

'I watched Iron Man again after our last conversation,' says Holly.

'It's good,' says David.

'It goes on a bit,' she says. 'But I do like –'

'Robert Downey Jnr,' says David. 'I know – you said.'

Holly smirks.

'What can I say – he's cute. It's weird though. I hadn't thought about it before but he's kind of like a battery-powered toy.'

David laughs.

'I don't think he'd appreciate you calling him that.'

'No,' she says. 'But he made himself into this kind of part machine. He seems really powerful, but he's also really weak, when you think about it. He's either superpowered or super-weak – weaker even than you or me.'

David nods.

'A lot of superheroes are like that,' he says. 'They have some kind of disaster that changes them and then they are trapped being superheroes.'

'Trapped?'

'Yeah – I mean they can't have a day off. They have to do it whether they like it or not, don't they? Bruce Banner never wanted to be the Hulk, the Fantastic Four never asked for their powers. Tony Stark makes the best of having to save himself from having shrapnel in his heart. He creates Iron Man because he chooses to have superpowers rather than be . . . superpowerless.'

Holly nods.

'Superpowerless?' she says. 'Yes. I can see that. Without

the suit he's actually weaker than a normal person; without that thing in his chest that keeps him alive.'

'Exactly. It's a curse and a blessing at the same time. Lots of superheroes are like that. A lot of them would swap with a normal human being if they could.'

'But then what's normal?'

David nods.

'Happy then. They'd give it all up to be happy. You can't be happy and be a superhero.'

'Can't you?'

David shakes his head. A bitter passion comes into his voice.

'How could you be? However powerful you were, you could never fix everything, protect everyone. There will always be more supervillains out there. You're always going to feel like . . . like you've failed.'

Holly frowns, taken aback by the intensity of this little speech.

'That's a pretty gloomy way to look at it.'

He shrugs. He smiles, trying to lighten the mood he has created.

'It just seems like how it is.'

'I'd take having superpowers over being superpowerless any day of the week.'

David nods.

'About last time,' says David, 'you know – the kissing thing –'

Holly laughs.

'I know!' she says. 'Your mum coming in like that. Ha! What would she have thought?'

'It's just that the party is coming up this weekend, so . . .'

'So what?' says Holly.

'I thought we could – you know . . .'

She stares at him.

'I think we covered everything we could,' she says. 'You're on your own.'

'But –'

'Seriously, David – you'll be fine. I've got to get on.'

He opens his mouth but the hoover has already roared into life and Holly is in work mode, earbuds in. David settles back on the bed and picks up a comic.

It's *Daredevil and the Black Widow* #106. Daredevil, aka lawyer Matt Murdoch, is another superhero whose gift masks a curse. Blinded by radioactive material that heightens all his other senses. He is weakened and strengthened by it. Made less and made more.

David thinks about this for a while but soon he finds himself looking from the curvaceous Black Widow to Holly and back again as she works her way round the room. He wishes he had a sexy superhero sidekick.

Chapter 20

Sociable and Yet Not

David has worried that his mother might not be OK with him going to a party across the other side of town but she seems delighted – although she tries hard to hide it.

She is so transparently pleased, in fact, that David has the strongest urge to cancel.

'Just text me when you're leaving and try not to be too late. You know I won't sleep properly until I hear you come in.'

And that is pretty much it.

David gets a text from Ellen saying she hopes he's still coming and he texts back to say that he is. They're texting. Just like normal people. David has never really texted anyone in his life apart from his mother and Joe. She ends hers with a smiley face and a heart.

David did used to text his dad. His name sits there on the list on his phone, a constant reminder that there will never be another text from him. Not ever.

The party is at Ben's house. His parents are away on holiday. This made David nervous for a start – worried that he was going to be involved in one of those news items where teenagers trash the house while parents are out of town. But Ellen has explained to him that Ben's parents know all about it and are completely cool with it. And of course Ben would have parents like that. Of course he would. Tosser.

But the thing that has really swung it for David is the fact that Ellen says that Matt has said he's not going if Ellen goes because it would be too embarrassing, and as she is going and has told him she is, then Matt won't be there.

Ben's is a big house – much bigger than David's, and David's is pretty big. It's a tall Edwardian villa, detached and at the end of a dead-end road backing on to the park. David has been there before, years ago when he and Ben mixed in the same circles – or when no one really had any circles. He'd gone to Ben's tenth birthday party. So had Joe. And Ellen. Matt too. Although Matt was a dick even then.

David could hear the whump, whump of the music when he turned the corner from the main street. He has arranged to meet Ellen on that very corner, but there is no sign of her and no reply to his text so he sets off towards the house wondering if she'll be hanging around outside or might even have arrived early, popped in and lost track of time. Just then his phone pings.

It's Ellen. A text. Something has come up, she says. She will be there, but she'll be late. She apologises profusely and says she'll see him there. Smiley face. Smiley face. Smiley face. Heart. Heart. Kissy lips.

David's face is not smiley. He seriously considers turning round and going home there and then. He is only going to the stupid party because of Ellen and now she isn't even there – and who knows if she'll ever actually turn up. Maybe she is having second thoughts about being seen in public with someone like David. Who could blame her? The fantasy is starting to curdle.

If anyone had asked, David would have said he hated parties, but in truth he can't really remember the last one he'd been to and suspects that it may even have been that tenth birthday party of Ben's at the same location.

Apart from parties his parents had had, that is. Or rather his mother. His father had disliked parties as much as David. But it's not like he doesn't know what a party is. Or that's what he tells himself anyway, as he walks more and more slowly towards Ben's house.

But Mark is right about that at any rate – David has spent too much time on his own in his room. Hard as it is, dull as it may turn out to be, maybe he does need to start talking to people again. All the same, he realises that he has absolutely no idea what to say.

He had hoped for a group of people to arrive at the same time as him, so that he wouldn't be noticed, but after standing outside for a few minutes he feels like he is sticking out more by loitering and so, with a deep breath and a cold sensation in his guts, he pushes at the open door and walks in.

He needn't have worried about the reaction. There isn't one. He isn't noticed at all. At. All. The music is loud but almost drowned out by the sound of people shouting over the top of it to be heard.

He uses his super-hearing to double-check that there is no whispering about him, but he detects nothing at all. Maybe they've forgotten who he is. That seems preferable somehow to that they simply don't care.

There are some kind of flashing coloured lights coming from one room, pulsing to the beat, and he heads in what he assumes is the direction of the kitchen to drop off the bottles of beer he's bought. Or that his mum bought, on the last trip to the supermarket.

'Excellent!' says an older boy he's never seen before, who takes the bottles from him and puts them in the fridge – which looks entirely packed with other bottles.

'I'm Blake!' he says.

'Oh – David.'

'You're at school with Ben?'

'Yeah,' says David. 'Er . . . How do you know him?'

'I don't,' he says. 'I just like parties. Don't tell anyone.'

David nods. Blake laughs uproariously.

'I'm his brother. It was a joke.'

'Yeah – of course. Right. Ha!'

Blake looks at David for a while, but neither of them can think of any reason or way to prolong this encounter so Blake moves off, beer in hand.

David opens the fridge and takes out a cold beer, finds a bottle opener and opens it. He takes a swig and squeezes through the crowd into the corridor.

He has been there barely ten minutes and he is already baffled by what he is supposed to be doing. How did you get to know what to do at parties? Grown-up parties – where there was booze and dancing and groping in the corners.

Where did they all learn? Everyone around him seems to

153

be borderline hysterical, cackling and whooping and leaping about. He can't understand why.

He stands in the doorway of the room set aside for dancing. It looks like it had been the lounge but it has been cleared of furniture for the duration of the party. Blake is with a girl called Willow from David's English class. He is enthusiastically grinding his hips into hers to the beat of the music. She looks decidedly less enthusiastic, but he grinds on oblivious.

David finds that his bottle is already empty and returns to the kitchen for another – at least it gives him something to do for the next few minutes. He drinks that even more quickly and is most of the way through the next beer when he becomes aware of someone standing beside him.

'Look at you – drinking beer and hanging out at a party just like regular people.'

It's Joe.

'Oh,' says David. 'What? Hi.'

Joe smiles and leans back a little unsteadily against the wall, beer bottle in hand.

'I've been watching you,' he says.

'Oh?'

'Yeah. I always thought you were putting it on, but you really are a bit weird, aren't you?'

'Cheers.'

'You're welcome . . . So you must be interested in Ellen if she managed to get you to a party,' says Joe. 'Not really your thing, surely?'

'Don't underestimate the power of alcohol to enhance an experience,' says David, waving his beer bottle.

'Who said that?'

'Me – I just said it.'

Joe nods and smiles. He clinks his empty beer bottle against David's. But there is a coolness there. Would Joe rather not be seen with him? Is it because David has come for Ellen when he wouldn't come for Joe?

'Listen,' says Joe. 'I'm going to get another one. You?'

David shakes his head.

Joe moves off, merging with the crowd, and David stands alone. He takes another swig of beer. He feels more relaxed. Maybe it suits him, this party life. Sociable and yet not. Surrounded by people and alone.

There is just one thing wrong. There is an absence of Ellen and it is this Ellenlessness that David notices most of all, despite his attempts to manufacture an air of what he hopes will look like moody disregard. He wanders from room to room in the hope that he will bump into her. He doesn't. He checks his phone and walks straight into someone.

'What the fuck is going on with the hair, David?' says Matt McKenzie, grabbing a couple of locks and holding them out.

David pulls away. Not too quickly. Not fast enough for it to be perceived as aggressive. He doesn't want to start anything. Superheroes don't fight civilians like Matt. It wouldn't be fair and it would mean his cover would be blown. Restraint. That was the key.

'Yeah – what kind of a look are you going for?' says his sidekick, Rory. 'Sad schoolgirl?'

Matt laughs.

'Anyway,' says David, starting to walk away.

'Whoa,' says Matt, blocking his path. 'Where you going?'

'I just –'

'Well, that's not friendly, is it?' says Matt, turning with a look of mock hurt on his face.

'It really isn't,' says Rory.

'Look, I don't want –'

Matt suddenly grabs David by the jaw, squeezing his cheeks together, shoving him back against the wall. A small group has gathered now.

'Let him go.'

David sees Joe shove through to the front.

'Stay the fuck out of it, Jardine,' says Matt without turning to look at him.

He is staring into David's face, his eyes bulging. He knows. He knows that Ellen has invited him. She's told him. David clenches his fists but what can he do? He has the power to break every bone in Matt's body with one punch, but he has to control himself. He has to rise above such pettiness. With great power comes –

'Say, "I'm a pretty girl",' says Matt.

'I'm a pretty girl,' says David in a monotone.

Rory laughs. His breath stinks of tobacco.

'That was good,' says Matt. 'But now say it like you mean it.'

'I'm a pretty girl,' says David in exactly the same voice as before.

Rory laughs even louder.

'For fuck's sake, David,' says Joe. 'Come on – leave him alone, Matt.'

'And I said, keep out of it, you bla—'

Joe steps closer.

'What was that?' he says. 'Where was that going? Black, was it? Black what? Huh?'

The crowd mutters and Matt loosens his grip on David's face and licks his lips, looking uncomfortably from face to face. David wriggles free and rubs his jaw. Someone turns the music off.

'David!' says Ellen, pushing her way through. 'What the hell are you doing, Matt? Don't be such a jerk.'

'Really?' says Matt. 'You're really going to go out with this prick?'

'It's all about pricks with you, huh, Matt?'

'I didn't hear you complaining.'

Ben shoves his way through.

'No fighting,' he says. 'I mean it. Matt – stop being an idiot.'

Matt bites his lip and stares at Ellen, who is hugging David. Grudgingly he taps Rory on the arm and they head towards the door. As he passes Joe he jabs out an elbow and catches him in the nose, knocking him backwards.

'Hey!' yells David, and rushes forward, spinning Matt round and throwing him up against the wall. He pulls his arm back, ready to punch him. Time seems to slow down to a crawl and he sees a look of genuine panic on Matt's face. David crunches his hand into a fist and hurls it forward, but before it hits home Ben grabs his arm.

Ben's brother Blake lurches in and yanks Matt sideways by the scruff of the neck and frogmarches him to the front door. There is a hush following the slamming of the door and then a muffled shower of abuse from the street outside. Joe stands nursing his nose. David is facing the wall where Matt had been, thinking about the punch that never landed.

'Arsehole,' says Blake as he came back. 'Why do you hang out with people like that?'

Ben ignores him. He is staring at David.

'Leave it a few minutes and then you can go too,' he says.

'What?' says Ellen. 'Why has he got to go? It was Matt who was causing trouble.'

'It's fine. I'll go.'

'You see?' says Ben, still looking at David. 'He's happy to go. Which is cool, as I didn't invite him!'

Ellen blushes.

'What? So? And I suppose you invited everyone personally, did you?'

'It's fine,' says David. 'Really.'

So they leave – he and Ellen. David is painfully aware of everyone watching.

'You OK, Joe?' asks David as he goes.

Joe nods, holding a tissue to his nose. Then the music is turned back on and the house returns to party mode.

Chapter 21

Full of Surprises

Ellen hooks her arm through David's and cuddles into his side as they walk. When they get to a small park they stop and sit on a low wall under a buzzing street light.

'Why did you tell me you'd checked with Ben?'

'I meant to. I was worried he'd say no, if I asked before. He wouldn't have been bothered if it hadn't been for the trouble. I might have known Matt would do something stupid. He's honestly quite sweet when you get to know him. But he does have a macho thing going on.'

'Not like me, huh?' says David.

Ellen smiles.

'Oh, I don't know,' she says. 'You looked like you were going to knock his head off.'

'I don't normally . . . I mean, I'm not really . . .'

'What?'

'I don't know. I'm just not like Matt, I suppose.'

'Don't compare yourself to him,' she says. 'Don't compare yourself to anyone. There's just you. And then there's other people. I never compare myself to anyone. We're all just random.'

'Trouble is, most people don't think like that,' says David.

'Screw most people,' says Ellen.

David smiles. This is the moment. If it was a movie, then this would be the moment the music started up and everything in the background would fade to a blur.

He puts his hand to her hair and then her face and strokes it and she leans into his hand and closes her eyes. He tries to remember what Holly said.

David moves his hand to the nape of Ellen's neck and then round behind her head and she is already leaning forward by the time he pulls her gently towards him, her eyes half open now as their lips meet.

He tries to heed Holly's advice about being in the moment, but thinking about Holly's advice is taking him out of the moment and back to his bedroom and he finds himself wondering again about whether or not he and Holly would have kissed had his mother not walked in.

Not that this kiss with Ellen – this kiss that is taking place right now – in this particular moment – is not fine . . . better than fine. It is. It is. It so is. But David is aware that he is kissing both Ellen and Holly at the same time, one in the flesh and one, possibly even more amorously, more passionately, in his imagination.

Ellen seems happily oblivious to David's divided attentions, and when they finally come up for air, she pulls back with a smile on her face and an appreciative twinkle in her eye. If there has been a test, David seems to have passed it.

He had expected that he would feel giddy with excitement

but his main emotion, apart from a strange floating sensation, seems to be more a kind of breathless relief verging on exhaustion.

'You're full of surprises, aren't you?' says Ellen, a mischievous curl to her smile.

Am I? thought David. Am I? But he knows what she means. He has surprised himself. Why would a person like him have any kind of finesse when it came to kissing? That was a man's kiss and he is very much a boy. He feels a fraud all of a sudden. It feels wrong.

'Look,' says Ellen, 'I know this sounds crazy, but some of us are going to stay in a cottage on the coast in August – after results. To celebrate, hopefully. It's owned by Tilly's dad. I was going to go with Matt but . . . well . . . I wondered if you'd like to go.'

'Yeah,' says David, without pausing to think. 'Of course. Would the others be OK with me going? I don't want a repeat of what just happened.'

'Absolutely,' she says. 'They didn't like Matt – so they'll be overjoyed that I'm coming with anyone that isn't him.'

'Oh – thanks.'

She laughs.

'You know what I mean.'

'I'd really like to go,' says David.

'Your mum will be OK about it?'

'Sure.'

He thinks about it for a moment.

'Maybe.'

Ellen smiles.

'Maybe don't tell her any more than she needs to know,' she says with a smirk. 'You know?'

David nods. Lie. She means lie. He can do that. He's good at that.

'It's going to be great.'

'Yeah,' says David.

'We can get to know each other a bit better,' says Ellen, putting her arm around his waist and pulling him close.

'Absolutely,' says David.

'It'll be romantic,' says Ellen. 'No sneaking around.

'Listen,' she says, 'would you mind if we called it a night? All this crap with Matt . . . I'd just like to start again, you know?'

'Yeah,' says David. 'I'll walk you back.'

'Don't be daft,' she says. 'I'll be fine. I only live a couple of streets away. But thanks.'

She didn't want him at her house. She didn't want her family to see him. So what? he thinks. His mother didn't even know Ellen existed.

'OK,' he says. 'If you're sure.'

'I am.'

They kiss again. Not passionately this time – a gentle, soft parting kiss that if anything was more thrilling than the first because it hinted at an understanding – a relationship. It already feels more natural to be mouth to mouth.

But David is not in the moment this time. He is overcome by a growing mixture of dread and panic, each one vying for control of his fevered imagination. Because he has just realised the full import of this trip away.

Sex. The invitation is an invitation to sex. He has imagined sex so often – yearned for it, obsessed over the possibility of it, and now that it looms towards him he feels like he is being pushed onto a stage without his lines. Or his clothes.

In his dreams and fantasies it has been something that just happened; something that he took part in without thought. In these sexual fever dreams he is in control, knows exactly what he is doing – without knowing what exactly it was he actually did. He was the director. He called the shots.

The problem is that, in the cold light of day, that all seems like just a silly game.

Chapter 22

Nobody's Perfect

It's the third anniversary of the death of David's father and it's already become a tradition that David and his mother mark this occasion by having his father's favourite meal – takeaway pizza (always pepperoni) – and watching his favourite movie – *Some Like It Hot* – on DVD.

No matter how he and his mother might be getting on, no matter how uncommunicative David has become, they reluctantly put that aside to take part in this annual ritual.

David feels ambivalent about it, but it feels like an act of betrayal to his father and too deliberately hurtful to his mother not to take part. Besides, how could he ever explain that, for him, that day is replayed endlessly – that he needs no reminder.

'To Dad,' says David, raising his bottle of beer.

'To Dad,' she says, lifting hers.

They clink bottles and drink while they're waiting for the pizza to arrive. There is a minute or two when neither of them knows quite what to say or do next. They are intimidated by the gravity of the moment and by the effort they both know they are making to find this common ground.

David's mother breaks the spell.

'Look at you,' she says. 'I feel like I'm sitting here with a grown man. When did you stop being my little boy?'

David shrugs.

'I don't feel much like a grown man,' he says.

She smiles, watery-eyed.

'Everybody feels like that when they're sixteen. That feeling of floundering about for a few years.'

'Is that what you did?' he says. 'Flounder about?'

She nods and takes a sip of beer.

'Yeah. I did my fair share. I was shy – really, painfully shy. So for me it was mainly about not making an ass of myself. Not that I always succeeded.'

David raises his eyebrows. He tries to imagine his mother as a teenager – making an ass of herself – but it is too hard. She seems so un-teenagery – like she has never been sixteen in her whole life, and yet he knows she must have been and he feels bad that he can't see it in her. He wishes he could.

'I never really enjoyed school that much,' she continues. 'I wasn't clever like you and your dad. Exams weren't easy for me.'

David stiffens, thinking that this is a dig about his lack of concern over his upcoming exam results, but he can see in her face that it isn't. That's just how she feels.

'But you're really clever,' he says.

She waves this away.

'I am a lot cleverer now,' she says. 'I love to learn now that it's not a competition. That's how I used to feel at school. Even with your dad sometimes. He always knew more than

165

me about everything. I always felt like I was struggling to catch up with him.'

'Me too,' says David. 'Sometimes I used to hear him sigh with frustration when I said something stupid.'

He wishes he hadn't summoned that memory up, and his mother sees this in his face and leans towards him.

'Your dad would be really proud of you, you know.'

'I don't know about that.'

She frowns and puts out a hand to touch his.

'Why would you say that? Of course he would.'

David shrugs.

'What is there to be proud of?'

She squeezes his hand.

'Don't talk like that,' she says. 'I don't want to hear you talking like that. He'd be very proud of you. He would.'

David nods, but he isn't convinced. If it is to mean anything – being proud – then it has to be deserved, surely. What has David done to make anyone – including himself – proud? Really?

Even in his alter ego he is useless. He is a superhero who cannot do the one thing he is put on this planet to do. The doorbell goes and his mother gets up to answer it, relieved at the distraction.

'Pizza time!'

But it isn't the pizza.

'Sorry,' says Marie, walking into the lounge followed by Mark. 'Sorry, David.'

'It's fine,' says his mother, following them in. 'Honestly.'

'No,' says Mark. 'We're intruding. We were on our way

166

out and we just wanted to, you know, say hi. And . . . well, you know what I mean.'

Marie hugs David's mother and David stands up, not sure what to do. Marie lets go of his mother and puts her arms around David. Her face is moist with tears. He isn't sure whether they are hers or his mother's.

Mark hugs David's mother and then grips David in a man-hug, slapping his shoulder. David is mightily relieved when he finally lets go.

'We'll leave you two alone,' says Marie. 'We just wanted to . . . you know.'

David's mother nods.

'Where are you off to?' she asks, smiling again now.

'Actually we're off to two different places,' says Marie with a nervous chuckle. 'I'm off to a friend's fortieth and Mark is playing squash with someone from work.'

'You still play?' says David's mother.

Mark nods. David has a clear image of his father and Mark leaving to play squash together, rackets in hand. His father turns his head towards David and disappears.

'Sometimes,' says Mark with a sad smile. 'I'm very rusty now of course.'

The doorbell rings again.

'Ah,' says David's mother. 'That'll be the pizza!'

'Come on,' says Marie, tapping Mark's arm. 'Let them get back to their movie.'

'Absolutely,' he says as David's mother comes back in holding two pizza boxes. 'Night, you two!'

'Bye,' says David's mother.

'Bye,' says David.

His mother sees them to the door and then comes back rolling her eyes.

'Oh my God,' she says. 'I thought they were actually going to ask to stay!'

'Me too!' says David.

She takes the plates out of the oven where they've been warming and puts the pizzas on them.

'I mean I'm very fond of them both, in their way, don't get me wrong,' says his mother, 'but today is . . . Well, it's just about me, you . . .'

'And Dad,' says David.

She nods.

'Yes. Come on – get the movie started.'

They watch the film, side by side on the sofa. David looks directly at the TV, never veering to right or left as he leans forward to grab his beer. Because all the time he keeps from looking to his left he can pretend his dad is sitting next to him on the sofa, just like he always used to.

It's good to laugh and David wonders at how weird it is that he is happier in that moment than at any time he can remember, even though they are doing this in memory of his father's death.

Mostly though he just enjoys the movie, which is one of his favourites too and has been since he first saw it years ago when someone bought it for his dad for Christmas. And the ending has to be one of the very best.

Disguised by being dressed in drag, Jack Lemmon comes up with all kinds of reasons why he can't run away with Joe

E. Brown, who won't listen to any of them. Finally he takes off his wig and confesses.

'I'm a man,' says Jack Lemmon.

'Well – nobody's perfect,' says Joe E. Brown.

There is a big moon rising, part-way between half and full – a gibbous moon, bone white and pin sharp. David can't resist having a look through the scope and pans across the chimney-tops until he reaches its luminous surface, pockmarked and fractured.

David stands up and looks at the view with his naked eye. The moon is bright enough to cast shadows and these moon shadows criss-cross the gardens below. It looks fake. Like a day-for-night shot in an old movie.

He has decided that owing to the special nature of the day he should refrain from any of his spying – it would seem disrespectful somehow – but he discovers, not for the first time, that he has little or no will power in this regard. He is hooked on the scope – he is an addict.

Even after he begins to pan across the backs of the houses, loitering at each window in turn, he pretends to himself that he still won't look at the Millers' window – he won't look for Holly. He doesn't need to look for Holly. Why would he? He has Ellen. Lovely Ellen. And yet, a few minutes later, and that's where he is feverishly focusing.

A filthy thrill fingernails its way up his back when he sees the curtains open and the back of Holly's head above the armchair by the window. Her hair shines under the reading lamp above her head.

She is on her own tonight. Or is she? No – he sees some movement behind her as her boyfriend walks into the room. She stands up and they talk and then he moves closer and grabs her – quite roughly, David notes, pulling at her clothes. David's throat dries up and he can hear his breath booming in his ears.

Just when David thinks he is going to drag her to the floor there and then – they pull apart and he strides over to the window.

'No!' hisses David.

Don't close the curtains!

He wants to see. He wants to watch. Just as the boyfriend is pulling the curtains closed, he looks out almost as though a sixth sense is telling him someone is watching. His face is pressed to the window, peering out.

It's Mark Miller.

Chapter 23

Black People Aren't Allowed to Fly

David hovers in the air outside the curtained window. The curtains are red and the light behind makes them glow. The silhouetted figures of Mark and Holly shed their clothes in time to a slow beat and then embrace and set off on an erotic dance, limbs coiling, hips thrusting – like some adults-only shadow-puppet show.

'It's Joe!'

David wakes. What? What's that?

'It's Joe!' shouts his mother again.

'On the phone?' shouts David dozily.

There's no reply. He gets up and starts towards the door, but he can already hear Joe's feet on the stairs. David dashes towards the window and moves the scope. Joe knocks and opens the door, putting his grinning head round.

'Here's Johnny!'

'What?' says David.

'You know – *The Shining*.'

'Never seen it,' says David.

'You've never seen the clip where Jack Nicholson axes the door open and pushes his –'

'I haven't seen it,' says David. 'What do you want anyway?'

'Oh, that's friendly. Thanks.'

'Sorry,' says David. 'There's a bit of a . . .'

He doesn't know why he starts the sentence and doesn't know how to end it.

'A bit of a what?'

'I can't talk about it.'

Joe shrugs.

'Listen, I just wanted to say thanks for stepping in. At the party. I meant to come round earlier but I've been away at my gran's.'

'No – I should be thanking you. For sticking up for me in the first place.'

Joe smiles.

'How's the nose?' says David.

'Fine. But . . .'

'What?'

'Doesn't matter.'

'What?'

'Why get so angry on my behalf and let him talk to you like that? You need to stand up for yourself.'

'I thought I needed to be more friendly.'

'You know what I mean.'

David shrugs. Why was he never what people wanted him to be? Why do people think they know you – or know what's best for you? Joe slumps down in the chair next to David's desk and picks up a comic.

'Still into this stuff then?' he says.

'Yeah.'

Joe curls his lip.

'You know, I don't really get comics.'

David shrugs. He is not a comic nerd. He doesn't care if no one likes them but him. But Joe wants to explain anyway.

'Maybe it's because there aren't any black superheroes, you know what I mean?' he says after a moment of thinking about it. 'Specially in those ones you read – the ones from way back.'

'Yeah, but there are though.'

David drags a box out from under the bed, opens it and takes a comic out.

'See – Luke Cage: Power Man.'

'Power Man?' says Joe. 'No offence, but he's not exactly famous, is he? I've never heard of him. What the hell is he wearing?'

'I think he looks kind of cool.'

'Cool?' says Joe. 'You're kidding. For the seventies maybe. And what superpowers does he have anyway?'

'Er . . . he's really strong.'

'But he can't fly or any of that really good stuff?'

'Well, no.'

'You see!'

'There's Blade – from *Tomb of Dracula*.'

'Like the movies – the vampire hunter?'

'Yeah.'

'OK – he is kind of cool.'

'And what about the Black Panther?'

David leans over and picks up a comic he's been reading and hands it to Joe. The cover shows the Black Panther being grabbed by men in gold metallic suits who are pulling him through a rock face. It says: 'Through walls of stone they stalk! Beware . . . the agents of Kiber.'

Joe studies it for a while.

'And the Black Panther is black? He doesn't just wear a black suit? It's kind of hard to tell.'

'No – he's black. He's African. He's from a made-up African country called Wakanda.'

'Wakanda?'

'Yeah. He's probably the first black superhero. He joined the Avengers and –'

'So can he fly?'

'Well . . . no. He has super-strength, super-speed, agility – that kind of thing.'

'Well, there you go. We aren't allowed to fly. Black people aren't allowed to fly. What's that about?'

David says he's sure there must be black superheroes who fly, he just can't bring any to mind right at that moment. He picks up a box and starts to look through it.

'I don't care!' shouts Joe, louder than either of them is expecting.

'Sorry,' says David, frowning.

'I don't give a monkey's about Black Panther or whoever. They're made up. Who cares?'

Joe leans back, clearly feeling bad about the hurt look he sees on David's face. He softens his voice.

'It just gets a bit boring, you know?' he says. 'Movie after movie, book after book – and barely a black guy in it. You'll never get what that's like.'

David doesn't know what to say when Joe says things like

this. It's true – how can he know what that's like? But what was he supposed to do about it?

'Every now and then we're supposed to feel grateful that some white guy's put a black character in his story – like he's done us a big favour, you know?'

David nods and takes the Black Panther comic from Joe, laying it down on the top of the box he'd pulled out. Joe will periodically say these things – remind them both that there is this irreconcilable difference between them, and David knows it's true but wishes it wasn't.

'You know I'm not into this stuff.'

'I know,' says David with a shrug.

'I think you should get out more, to be honest.'

'Yeah – that went well last time.'

'It's not helping, sitting around in here reading comics.'

'Not helping what?' says David.

He knows what.

'I just think you should be out in the real world, you know?'

'Then I wouldn't be so weird? Is that what you mean?'

'Don't be like that. Don't make me feel bad for saying you should have some fun.'

'Yeah – sorry. I know. Actually, I need a favour from you on that score,' says David.

'Yeah?' asks Joe.

David takes a deep breath and hopes the pause might signify the gravitas of what is to follow.

'Ellen has invited me go away with her. To a cottage. Overnight. With some friends.'

Joe stares at him. He tries – unsuccessfully – to disguise his amazement.

'And . . . ? How am I supposed to help with that?'

'Because . . . Mum's never going to agree. So I need you to say I'm with you.'

Joe shakes his head, jaw firmly set.

'No.'

'Wait,' says David. 'Let me just –'

'I'm not doing it,' says Joe. 'I'm not going to lie for you. Not to your mum. Certainly not about this.'

'I'd do it for you.'

'Would you?' he says, with a sceptical raise of an eyebrow. 'I'm not sure. In any case, you know I'd never ask.'

'Why? Because you're such a goody-goody?'

David knows his tone is too sneering, but it's too late. Joe smiles wryly, gets up and walks over to the door.

'I'm going to head off.'

'What? Come on. You're not even going to think about it?'

'What the hell are you doing, David?' says Joe, looking at the floor. 'You don't even like these people, remember?'

'Yeah – and you were always on my back, saying I should give them a chance. So I did.'

'Well, I was wrong and you were right, OK?'

'About Matt – even Ben,' says David. 'But not Ellen. You can't lump her in with them.'

'You did.'

'Yeah, but –'

'She was going out with Matt until a few weeks ago. For

a long time. Do you think they're really that different? You saw what he was like at the party. Plus he's going to kill you when he finds out. You know the kinds of people he hangs out with. Is it worth it?'

'Look – if you don't want to do it, then fine,' says David, turning away. 'I just thought I'd ask.'

'OK then,' says Joe with a smile. 'I'll see you around.'

David nods and Joe leaves.

'The Falcon!' shouts David. 'He's black and he flies.'

But he can already hear the front door slamming.

Chapter 24

There's Always Room for More

David lets go his hold on the wall of the church tower and floats free, a gust of wind buffeting him and making him drift to the south.

He swoops down over the graveyard, so low his body almost brushes the lichen-dappled headstones. The grass flattens at his passing. Dead flowers shake in their plastic vases.

Up now. Up and over the boundary hedge, blood-dropped by berries, bristling with thorns. Up and up and over the stand of ash and oak, rook infested, a cacophony of flapping black.

The river below, picking up light and sending it shimmering down its arcing length, and the road alongside dull and unconscious of the drama in which it now plays its part.

David peers into the wind. There. The car is only now climbing up the side of the embankment. It has not yet even entered the water. If he can only –

But Lightforce is on him before he even realises, blinding light made solid, smashing into him, knocking him off course and driving him down towards the ground, picking up speed all the time until they hit the road, tearing up the tarmac and sending fragments spraying into the air.

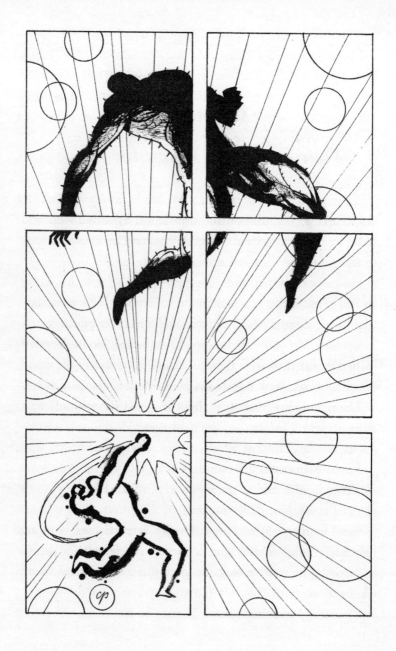

David struggles to push Lightforce away, but it's no good. He is being driven further and further down until he can see nothing at all and he wonders, even in his panic, how deep they might go. Maybe they'll just keep going and going until they end up at the Earth's molten core.

David makes one last effort to struggle free and –

'So?' says Holly, clattering into the room with the hoover. 'How was the party?'

David is wrenched back to his room in an instant and sits up, blinking, Lightforce still burned into his mind's eye.

'How did you get on at the party with Helen?' says Holly, pulling out the lead and reaching down for the plug socket.

'Ellen,' corrects David. 'It was OK.'

'Just OK?' says Holly with a half-smile.

Ordinarily it's a rule of David's to give no more information than is strictly speaking necessary. But he finds to his surprise that he wants to tell Holly. He wants to talk to her. He wants to talk to her about Mark, but knows he needs to take care and pick the right time. This will serve as a distraction.

'It was good – me and her. The party was pretty crap though. I almost got beaten up.'

'What?' says Holly. 'Over Helen? I mean Ellen.'

'No,' says David. 'Well, sort of. She invited me. Some people didn't want me there. Her ex in particular. Him and his mate jumped me. They smacked my friend Joe in the nose when he tried to help. Joe's black and, well, things were said.'

'Bastards,' mutters Holly.

David nods.

'Yeah. But I knew that already. I shouldn't have gone.'

'What happened?'

David gives Holly a quick run-through of the main facts of the evening.

'Does it worry you that this is who your girlfriend was going out with before you?'

Yes. Of course. Of course it does.

'No – you can't judge someone by their friends, can you?'

Holly frowns.

'I'm not so sure. I think maybe you can. A bit.'

He sees Joe in his mind's eye and feels a pang of guilt. But it isn't fair. Ellen can't be blamed for Matt.

'OK – well, not by boyfriends,' he says. 'Boyfriends are different. People go out with each other for all kinds of reasons.'

'So you're saying he's so good-looking she ignored the racism and general assholery?'

David smiles.

'No. Maybe. He's not that good-looking.'

'Ah – not to you maybe,' she says. 'Men never get what women find attractive. They have this idea about what is and isn't good-looking, and if a man is attractive to women and doesn't fit, they behave like he's cheating or the women are stupid.'

David shrugs.

'What about women?' he says. 'Don't they think the same way when men fancy women?'

She shakes her head.

'Men are led by their dicks and nothing more.'

182

'You sound like Marie,' says David.

'What?'

'Er . . .'

'Why would you say that?'

'Because she's always saying stuff like that. My mum's always telling her to shush.'

His own mentioning of Marie trips him up and he can't think of what to say next. Holly peers at him. David shifts uneasily.

'What is it?' she asks.

'I don't know what you mean.'

'You've got something on your mind, I can tell.'

David sighs. He has to tell her, and there is no safe way to phrase it.

'I saw you with Mark.'

Holly flinches like she's been burnt.

'What?' she says, colour rising to her face. 'Mark who?'

'Don't. I saw you,' says David. 'So . . .'

Holly stares at him. David can see the effort on her face; the effort to come up with any plausible explanation for whatever David witnessed. And then the anger as she knows she can't.

'That bloody telescope. You've been spying on me again?!'

'Yes.'

'You promised you'd stop.'

'No, I didn't.'

'Fuck!' she says, followed by a low growl.

She closes her eyes and clenches her fists and mumbles words to herself that David can't catch.

183

'That's why you were so panicked when I saw you the first time, isn't it?' he says. 'Not because you had just any boyfriend?'

Holly puts her face in her hands.

'Why?' says David.

She slowly lowers her hands, opens her eyes and stares at him.

'Why what?' she says mechanically.

'Why are you having an affair with Mark?'

'An affair?' she says with a bitter chuckle. 'My God.'

'What?' says David, confused. 'Isn't that what it's called?'

She sighs.

'In a Jane Austen novel maybe.'

'So why?'

'Why an affair? Why a married man? Why Mark?'

'Yes,' says David. 'Any of those. All of them.'

'None of your fucking business actually,' says Holly. 'What happened to it being none of your business what people did? What happened to you being cool with it?'

'That was before the "it" was Mark! It does make a bit of difference.'

'What – are you shocked?'

'No,' says David. 'Yes. Of course I am. A bit. I know him. I know Marie. I know their kids.'

She puts her hands to her face again.

'You and that fucking scope,' she says bitterly. 'Happy now? If you spy on people you'll get secrets.'

'You're the one with the secrets,' he says. 'You can't blame me for that.'

'Yes, I can!' she shouts. 'You have no business knowing. It has nothing to do with you.'

David says nothing. He would leave if he could, but it's his room – that would just seem weird. What seems like a lot of time passes before Holly speaks again.

'You think you're like some kind of god up here, spying on people, don't you?'

Sometimes. Kind of.

'No,' says David.

'We're like your little playthings, aren't we? Going on about our lives while you watch.'

'It's not like that!'

Although it is a bit like that.

'I thought you'd lose interest now you had something a bit more exciting in your life. I thought you'd put all that behind you and get on with life.'

'So did I,' says David.

She lets out an exasperated groan.

'So?' she says. 'Are you going to tell?'

'No. Of course not.'

To David's surprise, Holly begins to cry. For a few moments it is as though he is watching something on TV and his main reaction is one of fascination as her body heaves and rocks with her efforts to stifle her sobs.

Then, tentatively, fearfully, as though stroking a sleeping leopard, he reaches across and puts his arms around her and she lets herself be pulled towards him.

David holds her close, her face hidden behind her hair, pressed against his chest, and he realises that he has never

185

held anyone before – that he has always, always, been the one to be held.

The whole wide world comes to a halt and hangs in freeze-frame, in a frozen orbit around that moment. David feels the thud of a heartbeat and can't quite tell whose it is – and he does not care.

The Hulk himself could not have pulled David's arms from around her and yet, when she slowly pulls away at long last, his arms become self-conscious, clumsy things once more and he draws them in like the recoiling tentacles of a shy anemone.

Holly's face is pale and pained and David is lost for words. He had felt fine when he was holding her – more than fine – more than himself – but now he realises uncomfortably that he too is close to tears.

'I don't know what the fuck I'm doing any more,' says Holly.

David stares at her.

'I've never known what the fuck I was doing,' says David.

She smiles as though he is trying to be sweet when it is just the plain truth, and he frowns. He doesn't want her thinking he is just saying some crap to make her feel better. He hates people doing that.

'You think that everything is shit already,' she says. 'But that's one thing I've learned – there's always room for more shit. There's always room for more.'

She takes a deep breath, hunching her shoulders up to her ears and making her hair spill over them. She lets out a long sigh of world-weariness that seems to go on and on, and when it's finally over, she sits miraculously transformed.

Holly has now become restored to the Holly of half an hour before and there is almost no visible sign of the frail and vulnerable Holly whose warmth is still clinging to him. David can see it – just – in the redness around the eyes, a more hesitant set to the jaw – but he wonders how many others would – or ever had.

Or ever will.

Chapter 25

The Stillness of a Quiet City

David's exam results come through. They are fine. They are more than fine. His mother is delighted, although she is clearly surprised at how well he's done. So is David for that matter.

He texts Joe to check on his and gets a terse response giving him the grades and little else. David eases himself back into the sofa. He is tense but is trying to exude relaxed nonchalance – something that does not come easily to him at the best of times.

This display is for the benefit of his mother, who luckily is too busy to notice. Each time she walks by, David sets himself to speak, but he does this so languidly that she is gone before the words even form in his mouth. This charade might have gone on indefinitely had his mother not spoken first.

'Are you all right?' she asks. 'You look like you need to go to the toilet and keep changing your mind.'

'What?' says David. 'No. What?'

His mother shakes her head and begins to walk away.

'Oh – yeah,' says David. 'I meant to ask you something.'

'Yes?'

'Joe's asked me to go to this festival with him,' says David. 'It sounds a bit rubbish, but he's got no one to go with.'

His heart is racing now. He has lied before but this is a big lie.

'A music festival?'

'Music . . . all kinds of stuff. It's called the Lapwing Festival. I can show you the website if you want.'

'I've heard of that,' says his mother brightly. 'It always looks exciting. Not rubbish at all. I'd have loved to have gone to something like that at your age. But wouldn't you need to stay over? It's miles away.'

'That's what I mean,' says David. 'It's a bit of a drag, but Joe's really keen. It doesn't matter. I can tell him no.'

'I haven't said anything yet,' says his mother with a smile. 'You're old enough and Joe's certainly sensible enough for the two of you.'

'Cheers.'

'You know what I mean.'

He doesn't really but it's not the time to argue.

'So it's OK then?'

'I don't see why not,' says his mother. 'How will you get there?'

'Train.'

'And what about a tent?'

'Joe's got all that stuff apparently,' says David, amazed now at how smoothly the lies are coming. 'His family are into all that kind of thing.'

'Really? I can't see Jasmine in a tent.'

David just shrugs and his mother smiles.

'It's good that you two are still such mates after all these years. I like Joe.'

'I know you do, Mum.'

And that, to David's amazement, is that. He sits back feeling a little dizzy. He feels like a great bubble of nervous excitement has been building up in him ever since Ellen first mentioned the possibility of going away.

Part of him had maybe hoped that his mother would not countenance his going away for the weekend so that he wouldn't have to give it any more thought and would not have to worry about that first night alone with Ellen.

But it was on. It was happening. It was an actual thing and he was going to have to deal with it. All those fantasies he's filled his nights with, and here was real life outdoing it. He really ought to feel more keen.

David goes up to his room, still a little dazed and feeling hungry and nauseous at the same time. By the time he reaches the top of the stairs all he can do is collapse face down on his bed.

After a moment, he turns over and stares at the ceiling. It slopes away from him, rising up to meet the other sloping ceiling in a sharp crease like a folded piece of white paper.

It is one of those strangely quiet spells – when all the clamour of the city has somehow come to a halt in synchronised silence. There is nothing quite so still as the stillness of a quiet city.

He picks up a Conan comic – *Conan the Barbarian* #24. The artwork is by Barry Windsor-Smith, who did all the early Conan comics. His style is so different to most comic-book artists, like Jack Kirby, with a much softer look to everything – more like illustrations from an old book. He inked his own stuff too, whereas normally the artist just did the pencil drawing.

This one was 'THE SONG OF RED SONJA' and has a story where Conan and Red Sonja meet for the first time and raid a jewel room in a high tower. On the way they go for a swim in the palace pool and Red Sonja takes off her chain-mail shirt to stop herself sinking. Conan stands staring open-mouthed, just as David imagines he would himself in similar circumstances.

That's the fun of Conan. He's powerful and skilled as a fighter, but he's also a bit dim. He has the body of a man but the mind of a teenage boy. Marie would say that was true of all men.

Conan falls for Red Sonja but she – of course – gets the better of him and rides off into the night, leaving him to punch the wall in frustration.

A crack of thunder shakes the room and makes David start and sit up. There is a pause of about thirty seconds and rain starts to hammer down on the roof above his head.

It is so incredibly loud, it makes him get up and go to the window to gaze out in wonder at the hailstones battering the slates below his window and causing a kind of mist between him and the rest of the houses in the street.

He raises the blinds and opens the window, stretching out his arm and letting the stones hit his open hand. They sting his flesh – his palm and wrist and lower arm. It's a strange sensation – painful and exhilarating at the same time.

191

The hailstones continue to fall, easing for a moment and then finding new power as lightning flashes and another crack of thunder shakes the air, sounding even louder and even more close, like giant hands clapping overhead.

A small pile of pill-sized stones gather in his hand and he cups it to try to keep them from bouncing off. They begin to melt almost immediately they touch his skin and he brings his hand in to study them more closely before they disappear.

They are tiny, irregular balls of ice, each a clouded grey-white. He tips them out of the window as water drips though his fingers. Surprised to realise how cold his hand has already become, he puts it to his mouth and blows warming breaths on it.

Then, as suddenly as the hailstorm came, it ends. The roofs of the sheds and garden offices and the lawns they stood on were for a while littered with the debris of the storm, but in minutes there is no sign as it melts away and everything is as it was.

Chapter 26

Sex and Death and Comics

David had thought that all his desire to talk to Holly came from him – and initially this had undoubtedly been true – but he can tell now that Holly has found an oasis in that room too.

David has barged his way, unwanted, unwelcome, into her secret life with Mark, but now that he has it means that, here at least, Holly does not have to pretend. There is a kind of peace.

David knows all about that – the white noise that hisses away continually in his ears, that makes it so hard to be alone, to be quiet. How he needs the distraction of the comics to escape, if only for a while.

David likes it. He likes it a lot that she seems so content to be in his company now. So content that he worries that he might ruin everything with the request he now hears himself making.

'Am I hearing right? You're saying you want me to coach you?' says Holly. 'You want me to be your sex coach?'

'Well . . . yeah . . . I suppose – in a way,' says David.

Holly raises her eyebrows and then laughs.

'Oh my . . .'

She shakes her head and chuckles to herself.

'I don't think so, David, sorry. It would be weird.'

'Would it?'

'Yes!'

'Why?'

'It just would!'

David slumps back against the wall. He had rehearsed this moment many times and it wasn't like he hasn't imagined Holly refusing – it's just that that doesn't seem to have prepared him for the disappointment.

'Are you going to sulk now?' she asks.

'I just don't see what the big deal is,' he says.

He does. He does see what the big deal is.

'It's not like I'm asking you to have sex – just talk about it.'

Holly laughs.

'Oh – that's OK then. You know there are chat lines for that kind of thing?'

David frowns.

'I don't just want to talk about sex,' says David. 'Not like that. Not the way you mean. I want to know about it. I want you to give me some tips. Like with the kissing.'

'But kissing is one thing, David,' she says. 'This is something else. Seriously. What the hell would your mother say if she found out?'

'Why would she ever find out?'

Holly sighs.

'I'm not going to do it, David, so can we just drop it?'

'Maybe I'll ask Mark then,' he says.

The humour drains instantly from Holly's face. David wishes he could unsay it, but he can't. It's there in the room, hovering, glowing between them.

'Oh – I see,' she says. 'It's like that.'

Her voice is cold and hard. David puts his hand up as though she has pulled a gun on him.

'Sorry – that was out of order.'

'Yeah – it was.'

She mutters these words in a low, barely audible hiss, like an angry cat, and then scowls and looks away towards the window.

David has a very strong sense that whatever he might say will be the wrong thing and says nothing. He picks up a comic and flicks through the pages.

'What's the sudden panic about sex anyway?' she says without turning round.

David puts the comic down.

'Ellen has invited me away. You know – overnight,' says David.

'OK,' she says, sitting at his desk. 'What does your mother have to say about this?'

'She doesn't know. She thinks I'm going to a festival with Joe.'

Holly screws up her face. She looks tired – tired of talking to him.

'I'm not sure I should be hearing this.'

'Come on,' says David. 'I need to tell someone, and you're the only person I can trust.'

She shakes her head.

'Jesus – I hope that's not true. Why are you so intimidated by this girl anyway?'

'I told you – she's more, you know, experienced than me.'

'She wants to have sex?' says Holly. 'And you don't?'

'No – I do. I really, really do. I just don't know how to, you know . . .'

Holly stares at him in disbelief.

'You don't know how? Do they not teach you anything at school? And don't teenage boys watch porn 24/7?'

'Look, it's not that I don't know where things go,' says David defensively. 'I know what goes where. Mostly. It's just that I don't have any, you know, technique.'

'Technique?'

'Yeah.'

Holly shakes her head and, finally, smiles.

'You're a strange one, David,' she says with a sigh.

'Why?' he asks. 'I mean, why especially?'

'First you want help kissing and now this. Most boys just get on with it, you know. Most men too.'

'And that's a good thing?'

'Well, since you ask – maybe not. But good or not, that's what normally happens. I don't think too many men would have the balls to ask, to be honest. It's part of the whole macho thing, to act like you know it all.'

'You think it takes balls?'

'Yes!' she says. 'Of course. It always takes balls to admit you don't know something. Most men don't care whether they know or not.'

'I just don't want to look an idiot.'

'You won't look an idiot.'

'How do you know?'

'I guarantee she won't be as experienced as you think,' says Holly. 'Even if she has – you know – done it – more than you, that doesn't mean she's been doing it with anyone who is any good at it.'

'If she's done it at all she's done it more than me,' says David. 'It feels like everyone's done it except me.'

'Well, that can't be true.'

Holly is softening. The cool edge has gone from her voice.

'I'm still a bit confused as to what you want from me,' she says. 'I don't exactly have any experience with girls either.'

'No – but you are one,' says David.

'True,' says Holly, nodding. 'That is true.'

'So you must know some stuff. I know everyone is different and all that, but not everything is different. You know?'

Holly folds her arms and studies him for a while.

'OK,' says Holly, looking him up and down. 'Seriously. Well, my first tip is cleanliness.'

'Cleanliness?' mutters David. 'You sound like my mother.'

Holly shrugs.

'If you are planning to put something into someone else, you want whatever it is to be clean.'

David blushes.

'I'm sorry – but it's true. Some women may get a kick out of being mauled by someone with filthy nails and a stinky body, but best to assume not.'

David casts a quick look down at his nails and hides them under his legs.

197

'What else?' he says.

'OK. Appearance,' says Holly.

David groans.

'I'm not talking about whether you think you look handsome or not – she's already asked you to go away with her so she must see something the rest of us don't.'

David smiles. Banter. That's nice. Banter is good.

'So what do you mean?'

'OK – now don't get all moody,' says Holly, 'but what is going on with your hair, David?'

'What?' he says, instinctively raising a hand to his head. 'I like my hair.'

'Really?'

'Yes,' says David, frowning. 'So does Ellen.'

'She's said that, has she?'

'Not in so many words, no.'

'What words has she actually used?'

'I don't know,' says David. 'You can just tell.'

'OK . . .' says Holly. 'But if you're going to have hair that long, you need to wash it, David.'

'Seriously – you are sounding exactly like my mother.'

'Can I remind you that she is also female,' says Holly. 'So maybe she knows what she's talking about too.'

David waves this unwelcome intrusion from his mother away.

'Look,' says Holly, 'it's you who wants the advice. I don't care if I give it or not, so –'

'No,' says David. 'Sorry. You're right, you're right. Clean body, clean hair. Then what?'

Holly leans forward, her face now a mask of calm.

'The most important thing to remember about sex,' she says, 'is that you can have sex with anyone, anyone at all, but the only time it will be something memorable is when you have it with someone you really, truly love.'

David lets the words sink in. He nods.

'OK.'

Holly's face cracks into a grin and then she puts her head back, laughing.

'Ha!' she says. 'Nooooo. That's bollocks.'

David blushes. Holly laughs even louder. David peers at her, frowning. But it's good-natured laughter, if a little wry. It's certainly not the spiteful laughter David had feared it to be. She seems to be laughing at herself more than him in any case. But he's never imagined her laughing out loud that heartily, shoulders shaking. It takes him a little while to adjust.

'Oh,' he says, simply because he's realised he has to say something.

Holly stops laughing and puts her hand on his knee.

'There's all kinds of sex, David,' she says. 'Sometimes it's just fun and nothing else, you know. An entertainment. Like watching a movie or eating nice food.'

He nods without really understanding. He looks at her hand on his knee. Her hand. On his knee.

'Look,' she says, 'I'm not saying that having sex with someone you love isn't special. It is. But sometimes it's the sex that makes the relationship special – not the other way round.'

She giggles to herself.

'Sex can just be fun,' she says. 'It doesn't have to be a big deal. As long as both people understand that.'

'Is that how it's been for you?' says David. 'Just fun?'

Holly's smile disappears.

'No – not really,' she says. 'I've never really managed to pull that off to be honest. No matter how much I tell myself it doesn't have to mean something, it always does. I'm a romantic. It's a curse.'

A romantic? David hadn't thought of her as a romantic. Is she lying? Is she joking? Is Mark a romantic? She studies her hands for a while and then looks up at David with a smile.

'But it's different for men,' she says. 'Men don't get bogged down in all that stuff. Men are more realistic. It must be great.'

David doesn't recognise this image of himself. He certainly doesn't feel realistic. Is this because he isn't a man? Maybe sex will make him more realistic. Maybe sex is going to be the introductory welcome pack from his adult self to his child self and everything will make sense after that.

'But, David,' she says, 'if you're not ready, then wait. Go at your own speed.'

'That's easy for you to say,' says David. 'I don't have a speed. Or if I do, I don't know what it is. I think about sex all the time. All the time. Well, sex and death and comics.'

'Sex and death and comics?' says Holly.

David smiles.

'Yes. It's true. But mostly sex. I think I should actually do it instead of thinking about it. That's got to be healthier. Hasn't it?'

'I don't know about that,' says Holly with a chuckle.

'More normal then.'

'Normal?'

'Yeah.'

'And is that what you want to be: normal?'

'I don't know,' says David. 'I just know I don't want to be like this forever. You know what I mean?'

Holly nods.

'Yes. As a matter of fact I do.'

Chapter 27

Superhero Porn

David is sitting at his desk looking at the website for the Lapwing Festival. He scrolls through lists of bands and performers, settling on a few to concentrate on, and then looks them up on YouTube to watch them in action.

He finds a few that he quite likes and downloads some of their songs to listen to – all in the service of answering the questions his mother will inevitably ask on his return from the weekend with Ellen.

There are, happily, a couple of acts he already knows and likes. But he leaves nothing to chance. He looks up all the information about buying tickets, the campsite, the travel – trying to anticipate any line of enquiry she might make. Mostly he just tries to immerse himself in everything the website tells him so that he can actually imagine himself there. By the time he's finished he actually wishes he is going – it would certainly be simpler. And it does sound good. Maybe next year.

He's still doing this when there is a knock at the door and Joe's head appears.

'Your mum let me in,' he says, walking in, moving a comic and sitting on the end of the bed. 'What's happening?'

David closed his laptop as soon as Joe walked in.

'Not a lot. You know, just watching crap on YouTube. How about you?'

'Nothing much. Mum was pleased with the exam results, which means things are bit more relaxed.'

David nods.

'Yeah – mine too.'

'It's good to have it all over and done with to be hon— Wait – have you done something to your hair?'

'What? No.'

He blushes.

'It looks different. Kind of fluffy.'

David puts his hand defensively up to his hair and pushes it back from his face.

'I washed it, that's all. What's with the sudden interest in my hair?'

Joe grins.

'OK . . .'

David smiles sheepishly and Joe picks up the Hulk comic he's moved aside, looking at the cover, which shows a bald man swinging a ball and chain and hitting the Hulk in the head. David smiles. It's typical Joe. He's trying to make peace.

'That's got to smart,' says Joe. 'Who's the bald dude?'

'He's called the Absorbing Man.'

'What? Like a sponge?' says Joe with a chuckle.

David frowns. He doesn't care if Joe isn't into the comics, but he has a low tolerance of him mocking them.

'He can become whatever he touches – metal, rock, whatever he wants.'

'What happens when it rains?' says Joe. 'Does he just turn to water and go down the nearest drain?'

'He can control it,' says David. 'There's no point in having a superpower if you can't control it.'

He flinches a little as he realises what he's said. If only.

'What about the Hulk?'

David nods and has to admit this doesn't apply to the Hulk, whose whole story revolves around poor old Bruce Banner not being able to stop himself becoming the Hulk or controlling the green monster once he's changed. David's always liked the Hulk though.

'Why the ball and chain?' says Joe. 'Why has the Absorbing Man got a ball and chain?'

'He was a convict. It's a long story.'

'Why are they standing on a missile?'

'Read it if you want,' says David. 'Then you'll find out.'

Joe lays the comic down.

'Nah – not really interested enough.'

David shakes his head. Joe ignores him. He wants to talk about something else.

'What happened about the weekend with Ellen in the end?' he says.

'Still haven't really decided,' says David. 'I shouldn't have asked you.'

'No. You shouldn't. You're still going though?'

David shrugs.

'Yeah – I think I am. If I can.'

'Wow.'

'I know.'

'Are you nervous?'

'Why would I be nervous?'

Joe grins.

'Er . . . Because I'm pretty sure you've never had sex with anyone but yourself and you're the nervous type.'

'What? I'm not the nervous type. Bollocks. Besides, who have you ever had sex with?'

'Yeah – but I'm not going off on a dirty weekend, am I, so that doesn't really matter, does it? We're not talking about me, are we?'

'We're not talking about me either!'

'Imagine if Absorbing Man had sex!' says Joe. 'What happens then?'

'He can control it,' says David. 'So he wouldn't turn into a – whatever it is you're imagining.'

'Ewww,' says Joe. 'I wasn't. But I am now. Thanks.'

'Luckily I'm not Absorbing Man so it's not a problem I have to think about.'

'Does the Hulk have sex?'

'No one has sex in comics,' says David. 'Well, not these comics anyway. They're from the seventies. Things were different then.'

'People still had sex though, right?'

David sighs. Joe grins.

'Superheroes must have sex,' says Joe. 'The ones who fancy each other. It stands to reason.'

It's not like David hasn't thought about this himself.

'I suppose. Mr Fantastic and the Invisible Girl in the Fantastic Four are married, so . . .'

Joe laughs.

'Mr Fantastic? I bet he gave himself that name.'

'Reed Richards then. That's his real name.'

'How does he know he's having sex with her though – if she's invisible?'

'She's not invisible all the time, you chump.'

'I know. It was a joke. What other superhero couples are there?'

David puts his hand to his chin and muses.

'Well . . . There's Cyclops and Jean Grey in the X-Men. Batman and Catwoman have a thing going on. Superman and Wonder Woman. There are a few.'

'Wow – Superman and Wonder Woman. That must be something to see. Superhero porn would be pretty amazing, wouldn't it?'

David shakes his head, smiling. All this talk of porn is just that – talk. He doubts Joe has ever watched that much of it.

Joe picks up an oversized squidgy tennis ball from by his feet and hold it up in front of his face.

'Alas, poor Yorick! I knew him, Horatio.'

David smiles.

'You never get bored with doing that, do you?'

'We'll never have to think about Hamlet again. Weird, huh?'

'I didn't mind it.'

To be or not to be, that is the question.

'I know – you weirdo. It's because you're as bonkers as he is.'

'How's Fuzz by the way?' says David. 'You never did tell me how you got on at the vet's.'

Joe's eyes glisten. He huffs out a big breath.

'She got put down.'

'What?' says David. 'No!'

Joe nods. David is surprised at how upset he is, but Fuzz has always been there. She felt like his cat. He was never allowed to have one because his mother is allergic. Although he has always suspected she just says that because she just doesn't like cats.

'She was really old.'

'I'm really sorry. Poor Fuzz.'

'I know. Still. The vet says it's kinder.'

'I suppose.'

'She'd have been in real pain and, well, it's better this way.'

David nods. There is a window of opportunity for a man-hug, but neither of them seizes the moment and they sit there in silence for a while thinking of Fuzz the cat who used to be young and silly, just like a kitten. Time is a bastard.

'So this is it then,' says Joe after a long moment, his voice quieter, huskier. 'The big one. Sex.'

David nods. Joe shakes his head.

'What?' says David.

'How can it be possible that you are going to be first out of the two of us? I mean, look at you, then look at me.'

David grins.

'And yet . . .'

Chapter 28

Low Expectations

David clings to the window of the church tower, listening. He hears the sound of distant traffic and then, above the mournful caw of rooks, the cries for help.

He pushes himself off, throwing his arms out in front, the dull light shimmering on the spikes of his costume. He swoops to the north and banks to the west, skimming the uppermost twigs and leaves of the trees that edge the river.

He sees the arc of the tyre tracks and the car sinking in the water just as Lightforce hits him from below, hurling him up and up, higher and higher.

He turns his head away from the blazing glare and looks down at the receding fields below as they hurtle on upwards. The river is just a curved wire, then the finest of hairs and then nothing at all.

Soon they'll leave the Earth's atmosphere. David wonders if he will be able to breathe – will that be one of his superpowers? Or will he just die there gasping, left to float out into the blackness and silence of space? Is this how he dies? A failed superhero no one even knew existed?

PING.

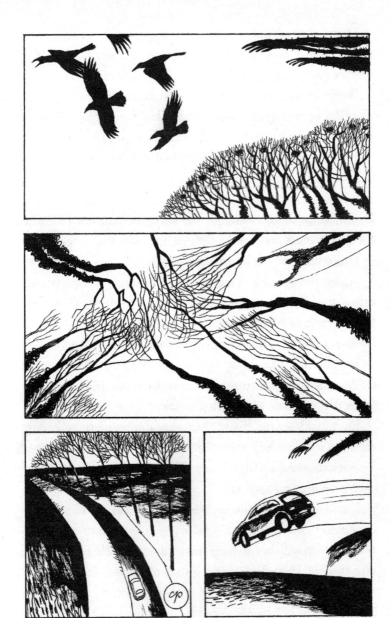

David sits up and reaches for his phone. It's a text from Ellen: 'See u at the weekend!! Heart. Heart. Smiley face. Smiley Face. Heart.'

David groans and lies back down. He feels a little woozy, like part of him is still being pushed out into space. The air feels heavy, like there's going to be another storm.

He gets up and wanders over to open the window. He is still standing there when Holly walks in.

'Hi,' she says. 'How are things?'

'I'm going next weekend!' he says, slapping his palms to his head. 'Next weekend!'

Holly lets out a long breath.

'Calm down – for goodness sake. You're getting yourself into a state. If it's causing you this much grief then don't go. You're making it matter too much.'

David walks back and slumps down on his bed. Holly sits at his desk.

'Making it matter too much?' says David. 'It's huge!'

'Is it now?' she says with a smirk.

David isn't in the mood. Banter is not going to relax him today; it's only going to make him feel worse.

'Seriously,' he groans, 'I just don't want to be useless.'

'You won't be useless.'

David closes his eyes and shakes his head.

'Please!'

'What do you want from me?' she says. 'I'm not talking you through the whole thing. You can't rehearse sex, David.'

'Why? Why not?'

She waves her hands around.

'I don't know – you just can't!'

David scowls, unconvinced.

'It's like I was saying about kissing,' she says. 'You have to be in the moment. You can't treat it like an exam.'

'What do you even mean?' says David. 'It is an exam! It's just an exam that apparently I'm not allowed to revise for.'

Holly chuckles.

'But it's the same for everyone, David. We all had to go through this. And people have been fumbling their way through since time began.'

'But it's not fair. If Ellen was doing it for the first time too then it would be OK – we could fumble away and it would be whatever – but it's not her first time and I don't want her to think it's mine.'

'But it is,' says Holly.

David groans. Why won't she listen? Why is she making this so hard?

'In any case,' says Holly, a bit bored now with the whole conversation, 'Ellen will have low expectations.'

'How do you work that out?'

Holly smiles a crooked smile.

'Believe me – if she's ever had sex, she'll have low expectations.'

'Is this supposed to be helping?' says David. 'Because it really isn't.'

Holly reaches over and touches his arm.

'You need to calm down. Keep it simple. People are into all kinds of weird stuff, but best not to assume any of that –

whatever you may have seen online. Let her take the lead. Let her show you what she likes.'

David nods and sees that this might make sense.

'But supposing she wants me to take the lead?'

'Well, then you're fucked, my friend.'

David growls in exasperation. Holly shakes her head and then makes a calming gesture with the palms of her hands.

'All right, all right,' she says. 'Give me strength. What do you want to know?'

David stares at her.

'I don't even know what to ask,' he says quietly. 'I just don't even know where to start. I imagine myself in bed with her and I just don't know what to do. I don't know what to do.'

Holly looks at him with a face David wishes wasn't quite so filled with pity.

'OK – I'm assuming you know you need to buy condoms.'

'Yes. I've done that.'

'Good. Then you'll get into bed and you'll be naked or you'll get naked – depending on how bashful you both are. And then it goes where it goes. You may hold each other. You may explore each other. Hands. We're back to hands. Clean. Nails cut.'

'Don't start all that again!' says David. 'What do I do with them?'

'Let them go for a wander,' she says. 'Trace the outline of her body. Enjoy the feel of her skin.'

'What about – you know – erogenous zones?'

'Oh my,' says Holly. 'Someone's been doing some research.'

'Very funny.'

She shakes her head.

'You've seen that *Friends* episode, right?' she says with a grin. 'The one where Monica and the girls teach Chandler about erogenous zones?'

He has seen that. He'd watched it with his mother. It had been embarrassing. He'd laughed without knowing entirely why and felt like she was looking at him the entire time although he didn't want to check.

'Yeah – but they don't even show us what they're talking about!'

'Anything can be an erogenous zone,' she says.

David knocks a couple of comics across the room.

'OK,' says Holly. 'A couple of things. Nipples don't unscrew.'

'What?'

'Nipples? You know? You said you wanted practical advice. I don't know what it is, but men seem to want to twist and turn and tweak them like they're a fisherman trying to find *The Shipping Forecast* on the radio. I've even had them flicked. My advice is flick your own nipple a few times and see if you find it sexy.'

'OK . . .'

'The important thing is to remember that it's not the same as when you're, how shall I put it, on your own.'

David stares at her.

'Don't look at me like that,' she says. 'You're a teenager. You're at it all the time at your age.'

David opens his mouth to contest this, but what would be the point?

'What I mean is,' continues Holly with a sigh, 'when you

213

do it yourself – then it's kind of about friction. You know what I mean.'

David nods, tentatively.

'But if you want to have the same effect on someone else, it will have to be about intensity.'

'Intensity? What's that supposed to mean?'

Holly sighs.

'It means you're not trying to polish a shoe or start a fire. Well – I suppose you are trying to start a fire . . . in a way.'

Holly grins. David stares at her, baffled.

'Look, it means you have to start slowly and get more and more powerful. Start too quickly, too powerfully, and you'll just exhaust yourself and irritate her. It's like music – building up to a crescendo. Do you play the piano?'

'No.'

'Shame.'

'What about . . . ? What about . . . ? You know . . .'

Holly raises an eyebrow.

'You may have to give me a clue.'

'How will I be intense in, you know, the right place?'

'I'm imagining your research has involved pictures?' says Holly.

David bites on his bottom lip.

'So you know where things are – roughly?'

'Roughly.'

'OK then,' she says. 'So just take it slowly and see how it goes. You're worrying too much and that's never a good thing. Maybe – if you are so stressed out about it – you're not ready. Maybe you should just say you're ill or something.'

This has already occurred to David and been rejected. He can't stand the idea of not being there; of being given this chance and not taking it – of not knowing.

'I have to go. I just have to.'

'Then go – and let things happen they way they want to. You'll be fine.'

David lies back on the pillow and Holly switches on the hoover and begins to clean. David closes his eyes and tries to accept that Holly must be right. He has to believe she knows more about this than he does. If she says it will be fine then it probably will.

When she finishes, she crouches down and pats him on the leg.

'Best of luck, David,' she says. 'You can tell me all about it the next time I see you.'

He has an overwhelming urge to grab her and hold her but he nods and she leaves, clunking and clattering down the stairs.

David trains the scope on the scaffolding across the other side of the gardens. It is deserted. The roofers seem to have finished their work. The new dormer window waits to be painted.

David zooms in on the scaffolding planks and ladders, edging his way along almost as though he is walking on them himself.

The sensation is so real in fact that he is forced to step back from the eyepiece, his legs suddenly weak with dizziness. An unwelcome memory creeps forward in the gloom at the back of his mind and he shakes his head to send it scuttling back where it came from.

215

Chapter 29

Keep Your Hair On

The train journey is a short one but seems to have lasted for hours. David had wondered if it would feel awkward being with these people – people he has avoided for so many years – and now he has his answer. It is indeed awkward – painfully so.

He and Ellen sit opposite each other across a small table, next to the window. Tilly sits next to Ellen, Finn next to David. Dylan and Kate sits across the aisle. An older couple sits next to them, the woman frowning every few minutes at Dylan's constant swearing as she tries to read her Kindle.

Ellen's efforts to include him in every conversation have only made his exclusion feel all the more deliberate, when in reality it is simply because there is no overlap in the Venn diagram of his life and theirs – everything and everyone they talk about is alien – or anathema – to David and he would have been as happy gazing out of the window if Ellen had not felt the need to explain every reference to him.

Joe was right. What the hell is he doing with these people? Sex. It is really just about sex. Because in the end he knows that he has only agreed because he fears that such a chance to be with a girl like Ellen may never come again, and the idea that his place on the train – in the house – in her bed – would be taken by someone else is unbearable.

It is made all the stranger because he used to be one of these people. There is another life, another David, where he carried on hanging out with them all and maybe ended up at this very same spot, only by right instead of by some weird random turn of fate.

He looks in their general direction and smiles and nods occasionally just to look as though he is paying attention, but their conversation is just a kind of background radio hum. No one but Ellen seems in the slightest bit bothered by his lack of input.

'What did you think of him?' says Ellen, giving him a nudge.

'About who?'

'Have you really not been listening at all?'

'No, not really,' he says.

Tilly laughs. David smiles and sees that Dylan and Kate are engaged in their own private conversation, snippets of which float across above the noise of the train.

'We were just talking about Mr Denton in history,' she says. 'We were saying how creepy he is.'

'Is he?'

David quite liked Mr Denton. Ellen smiles.

'Don't you think he's got that serial-killer look about him?'

'Not really, no.'

Tilly laughs.

'You're so sweet,' says Ellen. 'He's so sweet.'

David soon allows himself to drift back out of the conversation. He looks at his own face reflected in the carriage window, superimposed in ghostly fashion over the passing countryside of wide flat fields and distant farmhouses. Huge wind turbines tower above, their white blades turning lazily against the pale blue sky.

After they've stopped at several little stations, David sees the others getting restless and realises they are approaching their stop. Sure enough Ellen nudges him and says, 'We're here,' as they slow down.

They grab bags and jump off. Looking back at the train, David sees the couple who had been subjected to Dylan for the entire journey talking and shaking their heads.

'We won't all fit in the same cab,' says Ellen as they all exit the little station, grabbing David by the arm. 'We'll follow you.'

'You sure?' says Kate.

'It's not far,' says Finn. 'You've got the address, haven't you?'

'Yeah. No problem. We'll see you later.'

The first taxi drives off and Ellen snuggles into David and pulls him close. David tenses at her touch.

'What's the matter?'

'Nothing.'

She shakes his arm.

'What's the matter?'

'They don't like me.'

He knows he should not voice this. What's the point? But he cannot stop himself. Ellen laughs.

'Sure they do.'

'They don't,' says David firmly. 'They don't want me here. I shouldn't have come.'

Ellen lets him go and takes a couple of steps backwards.

'Maybe if you made more of an effort.'

You see? he tells himself. Idiot. Now he has to defend his idiocy.

'What?' says David. 'Why have I got to make an effort?'

'Because they're my friends, David,' says Ellen.

David shrugs. Ellen frowns.

'I thought you wanted to come.'

'I did,' says David. 'I do.'

'Well, you don't look like it.'

'I just wish it was us – just us.'

Ellen smiles. OK. Good.

'It will be. Later.'

Ellen slips her arms round his waist.

'Where to?' says the driver of the taxi through a half-open window. Ellen laughs.

'Look at us – heading off for a dirty weekend!'

She hugs him again.

'Hello?' says the taxi driver in a heavy accent. 'You want cab or not?'

'All right, all right,' says Ellen. 'Keep your hair on.'

The taxi driver gets out of the car and opens the boot. He is short, dark-skinned. Ellen bursts out laughing when she sees he is bald. She gets in the back of the car while David hands their bags to the driver and gets in the back with Ellen, who is still giggling.

'Keep your hair on,' she whispers.

David smiles at the frowning driver as he opens the door.

'Where to?' the man says as he gets in.

Ellen gives the taxi driver the address and the detailed explanation she had been given to go with it and they pull away from the station out towards the main road.

It is a small town and it isn't long before they have reached the outskirts. Ellen looks out of the window on her side and without turning round slides her hand onto David's crotch and squeezes, making him whimper slightly and shift in his seat. Ellen giggles and squeezes again. The driver frowns in his rear-view mirror. There are prayer beads hanging from it.

'Should be ashamed,' he says.

'What?' says Ellen with a snort.

'You are young woman,' he says. 'Educated young woman. Not whore.'

'Hey,' says David. 'You can't say that.'

'Yeah!' shouts Ellen. 'You're not in Iran here, mate.'

'Ellen!' says David, pulling her away.

'I am from Turkey,' says the taxi driver. 'Lived here now for twenty years. Longer than you've been alive, miss.'

'Who cares?' says Ellen. 'Iran, Turkey. You're in Britain now. If you don't like how we live then –'

'Ellen,' says David. 'Jesus.'

'What?' she says.

The cab driver turns his music up a little and they drive on in silence, Ellen scowling out of the window. David is aware of the cab driver trying to make eye contact with him in the mirror but he avoids his gaze.

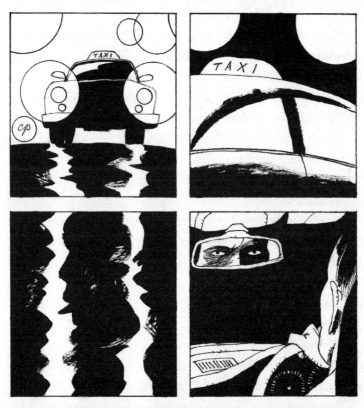

'Here!' says Ellen. 'Just here.'

The taxi stops and Ellen springs out, standing on the road-side staring darkly into the distance. David goes to the boot to collect their bags and pays the driver, refusing the change.

'I should report you!' she yells as the cab pulls away.

David picks up their bags.

'Don't you ever try and tell me what to do either,' says Ellen, turning on him.

'I wasn't,' says David. 'You just sounded a bit . . .'

'What?' she says.

'Racist,' says David.

'What?' says Ellen. 'Rubbish!'

David shrugs.

'I'm not racist.'

'OK,' says David.

'I'm not.'

'You said.'

'Oh, fuck you,' says Ellen, snatching her bag from him and striding off up the drive.

David seriously considers turning round there and then and heading back off in the direction of the station. Instead of which he sighs and follows Ellen up the drive.

Chapter 30

Like a Jelly Tower Block

The driveway is long, gravelled and shaded by a group of tall trees that partially block the view of the house, which David now sees is Georgian – a style he knows well because it had been his father's stated aim to one day live in a Georgian rectory very like this. He takes a deep breath and rings the doorbell. Tilly opens the door.

'Wow,' says David, walking in. 'This place is amazing.'

Tilly smiles – the first genuine smile she's given David all day.

'I like it,' she says. 'My parents have had it ever since I was a little kid. They rent it out mostly, but sometimes they let me or my sister use it for the odd weekend. We don't normally get the summer, but they had a cancellation.'

David looks round as they enter the hall, a big wooden staircase right in front of them.

'My dad was an architect,' says David. 'He loved Georgian houses. He kind of passed it on.'

Tilly nods. They hear Ellen's voice upstairs.

'Ellen . . .' begins Tilly quietly. 'She can be a bit . . . you know.'

David smiles.

'There was a bit of a thing with the cab driver . . .'

Ellen appears on the stairs.

'There you are,' she says as though nothing had happened. 'I thought you'd run off.'

'No. Not yet.'

'Well, don't just stand there,' she says. 'Bring your bag up.'

Tilly smiles and David picks up his bag and follows after Ellen.

'This is our room,' she says, opening the door.

It is a bigger room – far bigger – than the bedroom he has in his own house – the ceilings are high and there is a huge sash window looking out onto the drive and to the lane beyond.

'It's great, isn't it?'

'I know,' says Ellen. 'It's bloody lovely. I'd like to live here. If it wasn't in such a dump, that is.'

David bristles a little at the familiarity Ellen seems to have with this room. How often had she been here with Matt? With how many others? He looks at the bed. He has to put his bag down. It suddenly seems to weigh a ton.

'I'm sorry about before – about the cab,' he says.

Although he isn't really. Ellen was out of order. But people expected you to say sorry, even though you weren't. It was a way of drawing a line under it and moving on.

'I'm not racist.'

'I know,' says David. 'Of course you're not.'

For some reason, even as he says this, he sees Matt about to call Joe a black something or other. But Ellen isn't Matt.

'He called me a whore,' says Ellen. 'I'm not having that.'

David resists the impulse to correct her or defend the taxi driver. He had been rude, whatever he'd actually said. It was a misunderstanding mostly. Let it go.

Ellen lunges at him, grabbing hold of him and squeezing him against her body. She grins lasciviously and raises an eyebrow.

'Mmmmm,' she says. 'Shall we just stay up here?'

'Erm . . . I . . . They might think it's a bit weird.'

Ellen laughs.

'You are such a hoot,' she says.

Is he? Is he a hoot? He's never thought of himself as a hoot. He is pretty sure he is the opposite of a hoot. Whatever that is. What the hell is he doing here?

They kiss and then go downstairs to join the others, who are all gathered in the kitchen, doing a passable job of pretending they haven't been talking about them.

'Pasta OK with everyone?' says Tilly.

'Absolutely,' says Ellen. 'I'm bloody starving. Tilly's a great cook, David.'

'Tilly is not a great cook,' says Tilly. 'She's just better than Ellen – who refuses to cook at all.'

'That's not true!' says Ellen in mock outrage. 'No, wait – it kind of is.'

She laughs.

'Thought we'd have a tomatoey-saucy kind of thing.'

'Kate's a veggie,' says Ellen. 'That's why she's so skinny and sickly-looking.'

Kate – who is an Amazon, tall, lithe and toned – smiles wearily at what is clearly a very old joke.

'Shall we get some booze in?' says Dylan.

'Sounds good to me,' says Finn.

Dylan and Finn head off. They don't ask David if he wants to come and he doesn't offer to go.

Ellen is right about Tilly's cooking. The food is great, and somehow the eating of it makes David feel included in a way he hadn't before. He starts to forget that he doesn't belong here and he feels the others forget too. Or at least give the appearance of forgetting. And that is good enough for starters.

David is quiet as they eat but that does not hamper the conversation, which becomes louder and louder with each drink. Every now and again, Ellen touches his arm, his leg, his hand – turns and kisses his face. These little oases nurture him through the desert of the evening and conjure up mirages of the soon-to-be-naked Ellen – the Ellen whom he would soon embrace.

David drinks more than he had wanted to, for fear of looking uncool. He wants to have his wits about him but they are becoming fogged. This may be an everyday experience for the others, but it is momentous for David. He needs to concentrate on looking like it isn't momentous.

Tilly offers to make tea for everyone. No sooner have they all collapsed onto sofas and armchairs though, than Finn nods his head towards the door and he and Dylan get up and head off.

Ellen turns to David and says they are going for a smoke and does he want to come. He shakes his head, she kisses him and follows Finn and Dylan outside. Tilly brings a mug of tea over and puts it on the table in front of David.

'I'm going to kill Dylan,' says Kate, staring off at the door.

'You don't smoke then, David?' says Tilly sitting down.

'I didn't even know that Ellen did,' he says.

'Only dope,' says Tilly.

David nods, trying to look as though he knew they'd been talking about dope from the start, but can't stop himself glancing over at the door.

While he thought they were smoking cigarettes he hadn't minded opting out, but now he worries that he looks a prude or that he is taking sides with Kate in an argument he hadn't even known was taking place.

He has a sudden urge to get up and go outside to join them but it is smothered completely by his fear of looking like an idiot and that fear itself is smothered entirely by a bigger panic about drugs in general.

He has never smoked anything in his life. He has never had the remotest desire to. And yet he still feels lame sitting inside with these two girls he barely knows, resenting the fact he has clearly gone up in their estimation as they shake their heads disparagingly at the shouts and laughter coming from outside.

David forgets his tea and lets it go cold, but drinks it anyway, not knowing what else to do. When Kate and Tilly say they are bored with waiting for the others to come back in, David meekly follows them upstairs.

He brushes his teeth – then brushes them again – then gets undressed. He does this very speedily so as not to be caught in some embarrassing halfway stage. Holly had already warned him about this.

'Always take your socks off first,' he hears her saying. 'Never last.'

Did he leave something on though? Should he leave his pants on? Would nakedness be making too many assumptions? He decides in the end to take them off. There is nothing coy about Ellen. This is why they are here, isn't it?

David jumps swiftly into bed, suddenly catching a glimpse of his pale flesh in the mirror and feeling horribly exposed and ridiculous. Two new spots on his neck. He pulls the duvet up to his chin and watches the door.

And watches . . .

He is almost asleep by the time the door opens and Ellen's flushed face appears.

'Sorry!' she says in a loud stage whisper, stumbling into the room. 'Lost track of time. Hope you didn't start without me!'

She comes over to the bed and gives David a long, lingering kiss that smells like the smoke from a pile of damp leaves: musty and fungal and not at all pleasant.

Ellen has none of David's foibles about undressing. She simply takes her clothes off seemingly without a care in the world or a thought to David's presence in the room. She stands with her back to him in only a pair of knickers, throws on an oversized black T-shirt and heads for the bathroom.

When she returns she has the knickers in her hand and throws them nonchalantly onto the chair with the rest of her clothes. She stands for a moment, a little unsteadily, hands on hips. The T-shirt, which reaches the top of her thighs, has a picture of the Silver Surfer on the front, arms stretched out across her breasts.

228

'Hey,' says David. 'I didn't know you liked comics.'

'I don't,' she says, looking down. 'This is Matt's.'

Of course it is. It's huge on her and why, oh why, did David have to ask and bring Matt into this scene. Idiot. Idiot. Idiot.

'Did you bring . . . you know – protection?'

She says the word 'protection' in a strange warbly voice with wide eyes. David laughs.

'I did. They are . . . Fuck – where did I put them?'

'Them?' says Ellen, wiggling her eyebrows. 'Getting ahead of ourselves, aren't we?'

'No . . . No . . .' says David. 'I just, you know . . .'

'I'm messing with you,' says Ellen, grabbing hold of her T-shirt with both hands and pulling it off. David can't help but stare as her breasts fall back and tremble to a standstill. She gets onto the bed and under the duvet, and settles back onto the pillow, arms above her head.

David begins to explore her body with his hands. He wonders if his breathing sounds as loud to her as it does in his own ears, where it roars like waves on a shingle beach. He tries to remember what Holly told him, but he is utterly lost to the moment and to the wonder at the end of his fingertips. Ellen's own breathing sounds heavy now and her voice is dreamy as she urges him on.

'Here!' he yells as he remembers he put them in a drawer of the bedside table. 'They're here. Look.'

He waves the packet of condoms triumphantly.

'Very good,' says Ellen. 'Well done.'

David opens one of the wrappers and takes the condom

229

out. He had taken the precaution of practising this at home when he was sure his mother was out, and was very pleased he had because he found it far more difficult than the instructions suggested. He puts it on with a practised ease and turns to face Ellen, trying to mask his feelings of triumph.

She is lying on her back, with her head not quite on the pillow. He moves towards her, deliberating where first to rest his hands and gingerly opts for her thigh. She does not move. Leaning further towards her he realises she is fast asleep and beginning to gently snore.

David remains frozen in this attitude for a good thirty seconds before slowly pulling away to sit upright, his back turned to her once more.

He stares mournfully into his lap and watches the condom and its contents collapse in slow motion, like a jelly tower block on demolition day.

Chapter 31

The Sea, Of Course

When David awakes there is a magical re-erection of the tower, but Ellen is lying in precisely the same position as the last time he looked.

Attempts to rouse her – beginning with whispers and ending with increasingly violent flicks of her arm – only bring an angry grunt and Ellen turns away from him onto her front, almost falling out of bed in the process.

Ellen has thrown off the duvet and David sits looking at her long legs, slightly parted. Tentatively he reaches forward to touch her thigh, but Ellen moves again and he loses his nerve. He gets up after a few muttered curses, throws the duvet over her, gets dressed and goes downstairs.

Tilly is at the stove.

'David,' she says. 'Morning. Eggs? Bacon?'

'Er . . . morning. No, not for me, thanks.'

'Sleep well?'

'OK.'

'Do you want some cereal or something? Toast?'

'I'm OK, thanks.'

Dylan walks into the room. Ignoring David, he leans on the counter looking at the bacon Tilly is cooking.

'Morning.'

'Eggs and bacon?'

'I might just have some toast,' says Dylan. 'I don't feel that great.'

'You shouldn't bloody smoke so much then,' says Tilly.

'Yeah, well, fuck off.'

Tilly hands David a mug of tea.

'Quite the little housewife, aren't we?' says Dylan.

Tilly ignores him.

'How'd you get on with Ellen last night?' says Dylan. 'It was a bit quiet.'

'Dylan! Don't be such an arsehole.'

'What?' he says. 'You know what she's like. It's normally World War III in there. It was a bit quiet, that's all I'm saying.'

'Well, if you were busy listening to David, I'm guessing your night wasn't great.'

'Neither of us could be bothered, to be honest.'

Tilly laughs. David laughs too in the hope that this will hint at a spurious man-of-the-worldliness and end all talk of him and Ellen, but Dylan doesn't like David laughing, he can tell.

'So,' says Dylan, a new ragged edge to his voice, 'are you and Ellen an item now? Have you sealed the deal?'

David shrugs.

'Don't you know?'

'He's always like this in the morning,' says Tilly. 'Ignore him.'

'Fuck off,' says Dylan.

'See?'

Dylan glares at her but Tilly either does not notice or does not care.

'I hope someone's going to eat this,' she says, turning the bacon over.

'Always weird though,' says Dylan. 'The first time with someone new?'

'Give it a rest, Dylan,' says Tilly.

'What is this? Are you his protector all of a sudden? He's a big boy – aren't you, David? He knows I'm only messing with him.'

David takes a sip of tea.

'Rude not to answer,' says Dylan.

'It was great, OK?' says David. 'She's still asleep, so . . .'

Tilly laughs. Finn walks in, looking at David as if he's forgotten he was staying there.

'Morning. Have I missed anything?'

'Nothing at all,' says Tilly.

He grabs Tilly round the waist and kisses the back of her neck.

'Mmmmm – bacon,' he says. 'Hope I'm not too late.'

'This is yours if you want it,' she says. 'No one but you and me seems up for it this morning.'

'Really? Dylan?'

Dylan shakes his head. He's still looking at David, but David ignores him. If he could press a button that would transport him back to his own room he'd press it right now.

Kate then steps in to say that she and Ellen are going for

a walk to get some fresh air. Ellen walks forward and leans over to kiss David on the lips.

'We won't be long,' she says before walking away.

The door slams, and after a pause Dylan chuckles to himself.

'What's so funny?' says Finn, sitting down to eat.

Dylan nods at David.

'Ellen and Kate have gone for a walk.'

Finn slaps his hand down on the table, making Dylan wince and David jump.

'Man – your ears are going to be burning.'

David smiles and shrugs. Dylan chuckles some more.

'Don't let them get to you, David,' says Tilly, sitting down with them, cradling a mug of tea.

'He knows we're only yanking his chain,' says Finn.

'Yeah,' says David, not sure of anything except a vague desire to call it quits and just go home before Ellen comes back.

'So what's happening today?' says Dylan.

'The sea, of course!' says Tilly. 'We can't stay here and not go down to the sea.'

Dylan yawns, nodding.

'When?'

'As soon as Ellen and Kate get back. Which hopefully won't be too long.'

They weren't gone that long but it felt like an age to David, who resorted to looking through the library of books round the walls rather than talk to Dylan or Finn, asking Tilly if it was OK to take them down and then sitting in an armchair flicking through a succession of photography books.

Eventually Kate and Ellen reappear and Ellen beckons him from the doorway and, holding his hand, leads him upstairs to their room.

'Sorry, David,' she says, closing the door.

'What for?' he says.

'For drinking too much – and smoking – and falling asleep on you. I'll make it up to you.'

David shrugs.

'We OK?'

'Yeah,' he says.

'You're pissed off with me,' says Ellen.

'I'm not pissed off with you.'

'Jesus. You are. You're mad at me because we didn't have sex,' she says.

'So?' says David. 'What's wrong with that? I was looking forward to it. Is that a crime?'

This isn't close to being the whole story of course. He has been dreading it as much as looking forward to it. It was more a sense of overwhelming anticipation.

She smiles and grabs him, pulling him close.

'There's still tonight.'

'I know,' he says, frowning.

'You're not going to sulk, are you, David?' she says. 'Because that would be really annoying.'

'Sorry,' he says. 'No. It's not that. Dylan has been winding me up.'

'Don't mind him,' she says. 'Come on – let's go down to the sea. The sea always makes everything seem better.'

And Ellen's right. It does. David has always loved the

sea – the sound of waves rolling in, the smell, the wide flat horizon. They walk along the drift of pebbles near the water's edge and then go for coffee at a cafe looking out onto the promenade, seagulls braying from the masts of the fishing boats hauled up on the shore.

He is surprised at how many people are about. The house had seemed so claustrophobic that David had forgotten they are in a pretty English seaside town in summer – although in true English seaside form, the sky is thick with cloud and it threatens to rain.

The walk, the sea, the caffeine – it seems to lift everyone's mood and David is amazed to find himself chatting to Dylan about comics on the way back. For the first time since they set off for this place, he begins to feel at ease. But they are just walking through the door of the house on their return when Ellen grabs his arm as the others go inside and steers him upstairs to their room.

'Why would you tell Dylan we'd had sex?'

David opens his mouth, but no appropriate words make themselves available.

'That's pretty weird, David,' says Ellen, her frown deepening.

'I don't know,' says David. 'I told you. Dylan was on my case and I just said it to shut him up.'

'To shut him up?'

'Yes.'

She shook her head.

'You made some comment about me being still asleep,' she says. 'Like you'd worn me out.'

236

David sighed.

'Look – Dylan was being really annoying. I just wanted him to stop. You'd passed out right in the middle of . . . and then you leave the house as soon as you get up and –'

'So you *were* pissed off with me?'

'No! Yes. A bit.'

David can't make sense of what he is supposed to feel now. He can hardly say he had been relieved, can he? Even though part of him had. He had felt annoyed too – annoyed that he had been put through so much stress for nothing. Annoyed with Dylan, annoyed with Ellen. Annoyed with himself. What is he supposed to say?

The healing magic of the walk down to the sea has been immediately reversed and Ellen turns on her heels without another word and walks out, heading downstairs. David looks out of the window at the trees outside. A flock of tiny birds takes flight. Goldfinches, he guesses. He sighs and follows Ellen downstairs. Again he has an overwhelming desire to be back in his own bedroom.

He feels right back where he was on the train. They have now coalesced once more into a group apart from him and he walks over to the sofa and slumps down while the others sit round the table talking. Ellen's phone rings.

'Speaking. Oh yeah, right. I should bloody well think so too. OK. OK. All I want is for him to understand he's out of order. You can't have someone like that driving cabs, you know. It's not right. OK. OK.'

She hangs up and puts her phone on the table.

'What's going on?' says Kate.

237

'It's that bloody cab driver. I complained and they've just got back to me.'

'Good for you.'

'The guy says he's getting him in today and he's going to sort him out. Says he'll fire him if he can't get a straight answer out of him.'

David gets up.

'Wait,' he says. 'They might fire him?'

'If he doesn't have an explanation, yeah. So?'

'What did you tell them?'

'I told them the truth!' says Ellen. 'That he called me a whore.'

'Actually he specifically said you weren't a whore. He said you were an educated young woman.'

They all look at Ellen.

'I can't believe you're taking his side, David,' she says. 'He was really nasty. If I'd been on my own I'd have been really scared.'

'No, you wouldn't,' he says.

'I think you'd better go,' says Ellen.

'What?' says David.

'I said I think you'd better fucking go!' she yells. 'I don't want you here and neither does anyone else.'

David laughs but no one joins him.

'Sorry, David,' says Tilly. 'Maybe it's for the best.'

'Don't apologise to him! Weirdo. And don't tell people we've screwed when we haven't. Because that's never going to happen, OK?'

David takes a deep breath and goes upstairs to fetch his

238

bag. When he gets back downstairs, Ellen and Kate have disappeared.

'Bye then,' he says.

He stares at Tilly, unable to say anything else for fear that he might simply burst into uncontrollable sobs. He feels it welling up inside him but manages to keep it strapped down, despite Dylan's chuckling, until he has walked to the bottom of the drive and is sure he is out of sight.

David hurries down the road in the direction of the centre of the village. He skids to a halt, takes a deep breath and grabs a nearby car, lifting it over his head and hurling it down the road.

Furious as he is, he realises immediately what he has done and takes off, catching the car in mid-air, dragging it to a halt and then flying back to replace it where it was. He does it all so super-quickly that no one sees a thing.

He carries on, head bowed, and sits down in a bus shelter where he bursts into tears and violent blubbering and bawling in a way he has not done since he heard of his father's death.

That night he had cried so much he was sure that he would never cry again, and now here he was, sobbing his heart out over nothing more than looking like a fool. And this realisation simply makes him feel all the more wretched because he feels it cheapens the grief he felt then.

'Are you all right, son?'

David looks up, his eyes tear-blurred and stinging. An old man is standing beside him, leaning on a cane.

'Yes,' gasps David. 'I'm . . . I'm . . .'

But he begins to cry again, leaning over and sobbing and

sobbing, and the man moves closer and places a hand on David's shoulder.

'There, there, lad,' says the man. 'I've lived a long time. Things are seldom as bad as they seem.'

The words are meant kindly and David has to stop himself from hugging the old man, but instead he struggles to control himself and sniffs his tears to their conclusion.

He nods and looks up at the man, whose watery eyes look as though they might overflow with tears themselves.

'I'm all right,' says David. 'I'm all right now.'

'If you're sure,' says the old man, patting his shoulder. 'I'm in no hurry.'

'I'm fine, honestly.'

'Well, if you're sure.'

'Thank you,' says David. 'Thank you.'

The old man smiles and nods and walks away. David lets him go before getting to his feet, pulling out his phone and calling a cab.

Chapter 32

Perfectly Up

The door bangs open as Holly drags the vacuum cleaner into David's room.

'Oh dear,' she says, looking at his dazed expression. 'You look knackered. The weekend went well then?'

'It was . . . OK,' he says, sitting up and pushing the hair out of his eyes.

'Sooo,' she says, sitting down at his desk with a grin, 'tell me everything. I want to know every sordid detail.'

David shrugs.

'Not much to tell really,' he says.

'That doesn't sound good.'

He doesn't want to talk about it. It already feels like it happened ages ago to someone else. Her grin disappears. She puts her hand on his shoulder.

'Hey – there'll be another time. It's no big deal, let me tell y—'

'Don't,' he says, pulling away. 'Don't talk to me like I'm a kid.'

'I wasn't,' she says. 'Although you clearly are.'

David looks away towards the window. After a moment,

Holly gets up and, plugging in the hoover, begins to clean the room.

David puts his headphones on and listens to music, closing his eyes and returning to the other Holly in the garden, in her bikini – until the one in his room taps him on the foot.

'Stopped sulking now?' says Holly, when she eventually switches the hoover off. David removes his headphones.

'What?'

'I said, have you stopped sulking?'

'I wasn't sulking,' mumbles David.

What is it with girls and sulking? Did they all get together and agree to accuse boys of sulking just to wind them up? His mum does it too. It is so annoying.

'OK then.'

'Why are you being so miserable?' he asks.

'Me?' she says. 'You've been in a grump since I came in the room.'

'No, I haven't.'

Holly sits back down at his desk and slaps her hands down on her thighs.

'Let's start again,' she says. 'How did it go with . . . what's-her-name – Ellen?'

There's a pause. Should he tell her what happened? All of it? The truth? No.

'OK.'

'Just OK?'

'Yeah,' says David. 'I don't know what you want me to say.'

'I don't know,' says Holly. 'You were just so hyper before that I thought you be a bit more . . . I don't know . . . up.'

'Up?'

'Yeah.'

'I'm up,' he says. 'I'm perfectly up.'

Holly smiles. David doesn't. Some of the bitterness and hurt of that morning creeps back into his mind and he feels his heart clench at the memory. There is no way he is going to discuss it.

'Look,' he continues, 'we did it and that's that. There's nothing really to tell.'

'You don't sound very happy about it, that's all.'

David shrugs. Something about her tone, about her lovely face, makes him want to tell her even while he knows he can't. It feels like a defeat and it feels defeatist to tell her – to admit to the failure.

'I don't like to brag,' he says.

'You have something to brag about?'

Now he smiles. They can just joke about it and move on. No one ever has to talk about it again.

'Not brag,' says David. 'But she seemed happy enough. It was good actually. It was really good.'

'So are you and Ellen an item now?' she asks.

'Yeah,' says David, surprising himself at where this lie is wandering off to. 'Definitely.'

'Well, that's great,' says Holly. 'Isn't it?'

'Of course.'

Of course it is. Why wouldn't it be?

'So why the long face before?'

That is a very good question.

'Well,' he says, 'I don't know. I suppose it still feels weird for me.'

'To have a girlfriend?'

David nods. His attempts to cut this enquiry short seems to have inadvertently extended it. But he can't stop now.

'I've never really had one before,' he says. 'I mean – I've never had one at all actually.'

Holly shrugs. He notices again how beautiful she is.

'Well, it's the same for everyone. Everyone just learns as they go along.'

This is crazy. Why are they talking about Ellen? He doesn't want to talk about Ellen.

'But I was hoping –'

'What?'

'You know – that you might give me some advice.'

Holly laughs, dry and humourless.

'Seriously? You've come to the wrong place for that kind of advice, believe me. Kissing maybe, but relationships – no.'

She gets up and starts to leave.

'What about the sex stuff then?' he says. 'You can't have told me everyth—'

'For God's sake, David,' she snaps, spinning round and scowling at him. 'Is that all you see when you look at me? Or Ellen for that matter?'

David stares at her. A speeded-up slide show of Holly in her bikini and Ellen in her Silver Surfer T-shirt flashes by.

'No! Of course not.'

She sighs, calming herself down.

'All right,' she says. 'Sorry.'

David nods, happy to see an end to another flare-up of Holly's wild temper.

'OK then, if that's true – ask me something else. Anything. Ask me something that isn't for you or your . . .'

She points at his crotch. David thinks. Then thinks a little more. There must be something . . .

It occurs to him to ask her why she was crying that day when she was sitting on the sunlounger, but he doesn't want to draw her attention back to the fact of his spying on her.

'Why did you drop out of university?' he says after a while.

Holly peers at him.

'Where did that come from?'

'I don't know,' says David. 'I just wondered.'

Holly is still staring suspiciously at him. He worries that she is about to lose her temper again.

'Look,' he says, 'this was your stupid idea. Ask you something that isn't about sex, you said. So I did.'

She nods.

'Yeah – sorry. OK, OK.'

'So, why did you?' says David, now, seeing Holly's reaction to the question, genuinely interested in the answer.

'I was stressed out,' she says. 'I just couldn't go on. I got myself into trouble. With a boy, of course.'

'Trouble, how?' says David.

'Isn't that a new question?'

'I don't know,' he says. 'I thought it was still the same question.'

Holly pauses for a moment and looks as though she might

storm out. But for whatever reason she decides to stay. And it was a decision – David can see it taking place. She is deciding that, despite clearly not wanting to, she is going to tell a piece of her story. He can feel the gravity of it.

'There was a boy,' she begins, with a sigh. 'I was working in a coffee bar, to earn some extra money. He came in one day. Then he came back and came back and we got to talking and he left the biggest tips and then he finally picked up the nerve and he asked me out.'

She breaks off here, looking off into nowhere in particular.

'We became inseparable,' she continues. 'I spent more and more of my time at his place, less and less time with my friends. I changed bit by bit, without really noticing it until a friend pointed it out and I told her to get the fuck out of my life. She was a good friend. Maybe my best. But I was lost to her. Lost to all my friends.

'But I didn't care because I had Duncan. I didn't need them. I only needed Duncan. What did I care what they thought about me – about him – about our life?

'I suppose if you like who you are it must be a trauma to move on – to change – to evolve. But you see, I never did really like myself, so I was happy to embrace this new life. If Duncan wanted me to be different, then that was fine. That showed me that he was in it for the long haul, you know?'

David nods. He doesn't have to pretend to understand. He feels as if he really does know how that would be.

'But he wasn't?' says David. 'In it for the long haul?'

Holly smiles and tears appear as though by magic in her eyes, little stars twinkling at the pupils' edge.

246

'No,' she says. 'I was such an idiot. I never saw it coming at all. Not at all. Pathetic.'

She shakes her head and sighs. David waits for more but only silence follows.

'What happened?' he says eventually.

'He started getting cross with me – over little things. Stuff that used to make him laugh now exasperated him. I became an irritant. I felt like I was in a trap. Whatever I said or did, he took exception to it. And never worse than when I tried to make up for whatever it was I'd done. That just annoyed him all the more. I became weak and servile and it disgusted him. It disgusted me. I would have done anything to keep him. Anything. But he didn't want me.'

'He went off with someone else?'

'I found out he was seeing someone. I confronted him about it and he lied of course. He even tried to make it up to me. He said we'd make a new start. Jesus – I don't know whether he believed that or not, even when he was saying it. But it was bollocks of course.'

'Who was she?'

Holly twisted her face into a grimace.

'No one I knew. She wasn't even from the uni. She worked in an office across town. But the thing . . . the thing that really did me in was . . . was that she looked like me.'

'Looked like you?'

'Yeah,' says Holly. 'And not like the limp and bland fucker he made me, but how I was before. He'd turned me into something he didn't like and then gone after what I used to be. I mean – how sick is that? And yet . . .'

Again she comes to a halt, biting on her lips as though punishing them for what they had allowed to escape.

'And yet?'

'And yet it was me they said was screwed up,' says Holly. 'Me! He was allowed to mess with my mind but I wasn't allowed to show it!'

She throws her head back until the top of it rests against the wall.

'I just lost it, you know? I absolutely lost it. I lost me. Do you know what I mean?'

David nods. He did. He does. Holly doesn't speak for a while and then quietly when she does.

'So here I am,' she says. 'Back with my parents. A poor little damaged bird back in the nest.'

'I'm sorry,' says David.

'That you asked?'

'No – that you're a damaged bird.'

Tears sprang to her eyes again.

'You won't make me blub,' she says. 'So don't think you will.'

But her voice is faltering. She smiles a crooked smile.

'You're a nice kid,' she says. 'Deep down. Ellen's a lucky girl. I hope she knows.'

Chapter 33

The Truth Game

Holly almost drops her drink when she walks out of the back door and sees David standing there on the lawn beside her sunlounger. She looks around, confused.

'How the hell did you get into the garden?' she says.

David smiles and puts his hand through his hair.

'That's what I wanted to talk to you about,' he says.

'Seriously,' she says, looking past him, 'did you climb over the fence? From where? What the –'

'Shh,' he says, patting the air with his palms and urging her to calm down, 'and I'll tell you.'

'You'd better,' she says, scowling. 'Because spying on me is one thing; actually creeping up on me is another.'

She sits down on the sunlounger. David can see how self-conscious she is in her bikini with him actually there nearby, hugging herself, covering herself.

'Well?' she says. 'This better be good.'

'First off, you've got to promise me that you won't tell anyone about what I'm going to tell you.'

She shakes her head.

'David,' she says with a sigh, 'just get on with it.'

'No,' he says, his voice now deadly serious. 'I'm not joking around. It's really important. No one can know.'

'No one can know what, you weirdo?' says Holly. 'You're in my garden. Why have I got to promise anything?'

'Promise,' he says.

'God – all right, all right. Tell me what the hell you're doing in my garden, or I ring your mother right now.'

David takes a breath, staring at his own feet for a moment, hesitating at the thought of such a momentous step. Can she be trusted? Can she? But he's determined to go through with it and so he looks up at Holly and nods.

As she looks on witheringly, David crouches down as if he is about to tie his shoelace and then springs up, leaving the ground, shooting into the air. Holly is so taken aback that she cries out and tumbles sideways on the lounger.

David soars higher and higher until Holly can only see him as a speck against a distant cloud and then, with lightning speed, he hurtles back down, scattering leaves as he lands back on the grass two feet from where Holly sits, mouth agape.

'You . . . You can . . .'

He nods.

'Fly,' he says. 'Yes. Yes, I can. And quite a bit more besides.'

Holly pushes herself back into a seated position and puts her hand to her forehead, rubbing the furrows of her frown as though she is massaging her poor, befuddled brain.

'What?' she says. 'You're telling me you're like, what – like Superman?'

'We share some powers,' he says. 'Although Superman was never a favourite of mine. I was more of a –'

'Wait. You're a superhero?' says Holly, peering at him. 'Is that what you're saying. You?'

'I'm going to try not to be offended by that tone,' says David with a grin. 'But, yes – I'm a superhero. If that's what you want to call it. I have superpowers. Not sure if I qualify as a hero exactly.'

Holly puts her drink down and gets to her feet.

'This is crazy!' she says. 'There's no such things as super-heroes.'

'And yet . . .' says David, grabbing hold of the metal pole the washing line hangs from and bending it with gentle pressure from one hand – and then back to straight again.

'No!' shrieks Holly. 'It's not possible.'

'I know it seems that way,' says David. 'And I know I seem pretty unlikely as a superhero, but it's the truth, I swear it.'

'And no one knows?' says Holly.

David shakes his head.

'A superhero identity pretty much always has to be a secret,' he says. 'Otherwise it gets complicated.'

Holly nods, dazed.

'I can see that it might. But then, why tell me?'

David steps forward and reaches out to take her hand in his. She looks nervous – as though he might crush it.

'Because I trust you,' says David. 'Because I want you to know the truth about me. Because I –'

The door bangs open as Holly bursts in with the hoover.

'Don't you ever knock?' says David.

'Sorry – did I interrupt something?' she says with a smirk.

251

'What? No! I just think you should knock when you come into –'

'Yeah, yeah,' she says. 'Boring. What's happening, handsome?'

'H-handsome?'

Holly laughs.

'You are looking kinda handsome today as it happens. It must be the light. Or maybe I forgot to put my lenses in.'

'Very funny.'

'So what's new?'

'Nothing much. Er . . . saw Ellen yesterday.'

He impresses himself with how nonchalant he sounds.

'Yeah? How's that going?'

'Good,' says David. 'It's going good.'

'Uh-huh? So are you two serious?'

There is an odd tone to Holly's voice. David can't quite make out what it signifies, but it's there, bubbling under the surface.

'Well, you know, I wouldn't say –'

'I need to get on, David.'

She turns away from him and starts cleaning.

'Wait – can't we talk?'

'Talk?' she says with a sigh. 'Talk?'

David frowns, confused at the exasperated way she says the word.

'OK. You want to talk? Well, I've got a game we should play.'

'A game? What kind of a game?'

'A truth game.'

'A what?'

Holly bends over and, picking up his oversized tennis ball, sits down at his desk.

'Whoever holds the ball has to tell the truth.'

'Huh?' says David.

'Whoever is holding the ball has to answer the other person's questions truthfully,' she repeats. 'And the other person can ask whatever they like.'

'What?' says David. 'Why?'

'You said you wanted to talk.'

'Yeah – but that's not the same as playing some weird truth game.'

'But that's the point,' she says.

'What is?'

'Talking for us isn't a truth game, is it?'

David scowls. What is this?

'Why?'

'Because we're both liars, David,' says Holly. 'Don't you see? Wouldn't it be interesting to tell the truth. Just for once. Just us. Liar to liar.'

David mumbles something inaudible.

'What? Are you really going to protest that you are in fact a person who tells the truth? We both know that isn't the case.'

David knows it would be useless to protest. She passes the ball to him.

'Why do I have to start?'

'Why not? Did you have sex with Ellen?'

What is this? he thinks. Can girls just read my mind? Resistance is clearly futile.

'No,' says David after a long pause.

'And I'm guessing you aren't still seeing her.'

He shakes his head.

'You see?' she says. 'That wasn't so bad, was it?'

And it isn't so bad. David has to admit that, oddly, he does feel a little better not having to persist with that particular lie. It would have just got more and more complicated, and life seems complicated enough.

'My turn,' says David.

He throws the ball to Holly and she catches it in one hand.

'Well?' she says.

'Do you love Mark?'

Holly stares at him.

'No,' she says.

He waits for more, but there isn't going to be any – that is all too clear from Holly's face. She drops the ball on the floor and smiles.

'Enough questions for today, I think.'

Chapter 34

A Big Deal About Everything

David slumps back onto the sofa as though he's been shot. No. No. No.

'Do I have to?'

'Yes,' says his mother. 'Come on, David – after dinner you can do whatever you like, but you're going to eat with us like a normal human being.'

'What's that supposed to mean?' he says.

'What? It's normal to talk to people,' she says. 'It's normal to socialise with friends.'

'But they're not my friends.'

'Not like Joe, you mean?' she says.

'Why are you bringing Joe into this?'

'No reason,' she says, with a weird smile.

Why is she mentioning Joe?

'Anyway, you've known them all your life. And you like Mark.'

'Not especially,' says David.

She stares at him, but there's nothing he can say.

'Since when?'

David doesn't respond.

'David?'

'Forget it.'

She opens her mouth to say something, but thinks better of it, alternately straightening her fingers and clenching them into fists.

'Look, I don't know what's the matter. All I'm asking you to do is eat some nice food and be pleasant for an hour or so. I'm a terrible mother. Report me.'

David groans like an injured bear, squeezing his eyes tight shut and grimacing. She snaps.

'For God's sake, David, you go from zombie to drama queen in an instant. Stop making such a big deal out of everything.'

This is a favourite phrase of hers and it never fails to rile him. He doesn't make a big deal out of everything. He doesn't make a big deal out of most things in fact. That's kind of his style – not making a big deal out of things. He makes a small deal out of big deals if anything.

But sometimes things are, incontrovertibly, a massive great huge deal and they have to be acknowledged as such. Or else how would you ever know what is and what isn't. A big deal, that is.

Maybe when you get to a certain age some things stop being such a big deal. But when you're sixteen – well, there's really no limit to how big a deal something can be. It could be so big it could block out the sun. Maybe forever.

But David knows from bitter experience that there's no point in sharing these thoughts. Things are only ever as important as the person listening decides them to be. They demand you have the same sense of scale as them.

David's mother is already busying herself around the kitchen, talking to herself and opening cupboards and drawers like she's doing an inventory of everything they possess. David leaves her to it. What can he say?

'Hey!' she calls as he reaches the bottom of the stairs. 'I could do with some help later. I realise you have a lot on.'

'OK,' he says over his shoulder.

David's bedroom has felt like a sanctuary ever since his father died. It seems to have a sense of being a joint space – part David's and part his father's. This is of course both sweet and sour. He is painfully reminded of his father's absence and also comforted by the memory of the office it had once been – an office that David had only ever been allowed to peek into. Don't disturb your father. Don't disturb your father.

It doesn't feel quite like a sanctuary now though, and it's David's fault. It is tainted. David has sullied it, cheapened it, with his spying, with his febrile, sweaty thoughts, with his naked, squirming imaginings.

David lies on his bed and clamps his eyes tight shut. Everything is so big, so deep, all of a sudden. How is he just supposed to sit there and chat with Mark as though nothing has happened? How is that even possible?

He has promised Holly not to say anything – but he had hoped that this might simply involve avoiding Mark altogether.

He doesn't have the luxury of being able to tell Mark what a hypocrite he knows he is. How he would love to puncture that cosy little bubble. The look on their faces –

257

But no – he has Holly's trust and that is important to him. He wants to be worthy of it. He has an opportunity to demonstrate that he isn't a little kid – that he can show some maturity when he needs to. This is grown-up stuff by any reckoning and he is going to deal with it like a man.

All David's resolve to pull himself together and behave sensibly dissolves, however, as soon as Mark walks through the door with Marie, a bottle of wine in his hand and a toothy grin on his face. Only then does David realise quite how much he despises him.

'Hey, David,' says Mark.

'Hey.'

Mark laughs, slapping him on the arm. It is all David can do to stop himself lashing out and punching Mark in the face.

'You're clearly delighted to see us,' says Mark, misreading his rage for sullenness. 'Are we forcing ourselves on you, young man?'

'Don't start being annoying, David,' says his mother.

He ignores her and stares at Mark, who frowns back, his smile faltering. David registers the slight shift. He is making Mark a little uncomfortable. It feels good. That in itself isn't wrong, surely? Why should he give him an easy ride? He doesn't see why he is under any obligation to be pleasant to him.

Mark hands the wine to David's mother and Marie takes her jacket off and starts talking to her as she cooks – something she has told Marie time and time again she doesn't like.

'Please sit,' she says.

Marie doesn't take the hint and carries on a one-way conversation, following David's mother about as she tends to her pans. Mark sits down and David joins him.

'So,' says Mark. 'What's happening with you, David?'

'Nothing much,' he replies.

'Not still stuck in that room, I hope,' he says with a wink.

'Actually,' says David, 'I went to the Lapwing Festival with a friend.'

David's mother drops a pan noisily into the sink, making them all turn to face her. She smiles back – the same odd smile she'd used on David earlier.

'Sorry,' she says. 'Why don't you tell us all about the festival, David?'

'I've always wanted to go to that,' says Mark. 'Marie says I'm too old.'

'You *are* too old,' calls Marie. 'Isn't he, David?'

David barely even registers that Marie has spoken and makes no reply. He is still looking at his mother out of the corner of his eye as she prepares the food. She is behaving strangely. Why?

'Pah!' says Mark. 'I bet there were loads of people my age, weren't there?'

'Some,' says David.

'You see!' shouts Mark.

'David's just humouring you.'

Mark smiles and takes the glass of wine Marie hands him, sipping appreciatively.

'That's nice. That's very nice.'

David studies Mark's face. He looks different somehow. Smaller. Weaker. He realises he has never really looked at Mark before – not properly. What on earth does Holly see in him?

'What about girls?'

'What?' says David.

'Stop it, Mark,' says Marie. 'Don't embarrass him.'

'I'm not embarrassing you, am I?'

David shakes his head. He doesn't give a toss.

'You see!'

Marie and David's mother start bringing the food over.

'This looks delicious, Donna,' says Mark.

'It really does,' says Marie, sitting down.

'Sorry,' whispers Mark to David.

He winks at him.

'I've got a girlfriend actually. She's called Ellen,' says David.

'What?' says his mother, joining them. 'No, you haven't.'

'Yes, I have,' he says, still looking at Mark. 'She invited me to that party the other night. She went to the festival with me and Joe.'

'Oh,' says his mother. 'Really? You didn't say. But then there's so much you don't say.'

There is an awkward pause during which they all look at David, knives and forks poised. But David says nothing else.

'Please,' says his mother with a sigh, 'start. Don't let it go cold.'

'I didn't know she was going,' says David. 'That's why –'

'Sorry,' says Mark, looking at David's mother. 'I didn't mean to say anything to –'

'Don't be silly,' she says, smiling. 'You know how kids are – full of secrets. I'm the last person to know anything.'

'Pretty, is she?' asks Mark.

Marie slaps him and frowns.

'Yeah,' says David. 'She is. I mean, not as pretty as Holly.'

'David! What an odd thing to say,' says his mother.

Marie chuckles. David sees Mark bristle at the mention of Holly's name. He peers at David, searching his face.

'Thank goodness your girlfriend wasn't around to hear that,' says his mother.

David can tell by her voice she thinks he's making it up. Which in a way he is. But still, he finds it annoying.

'She is very pretty though, it's true,' says Marie. 'Holly, I mean.'

'Don't encourage him,' says David's mother. 'I had no idea he'd even noticed Holly.'

'Come on, Donna,' says Marie. 'He's a teenage boy. Have you seen the way she lies out there in her bikini? Shouldn't be allowed. Mind you, if I had a figure like that I'd do the same.'

'What do you think, Mark?' says David.

'He knows better than to say,' says Marie.

Marie laughs. Mark doesn't say a word. He's been staring at David with a fixed expression on his face ever since David mentioned Holly's name. David does his best to avoid direct eye contact with him, but Mark's gaze bores into him regardless.

'So tell us about this girl of yours,' says Marie.

'Ellen,' says David.

'Ellen. Someone from school, is it?'

David nods. His mother studies him as he speaks, making him falter slightly.

'Yeah . . . I've known her for a while, but we've only just started going out.'

'This is all news to me,' says his mother, frowning and putting her cutlery down. 'You've never mentioned an Ellen.'

Why would he? What does that prove?

'You're always saying I never see people.'

'I'm not complaining,' she says. 'It's lovely if you have a girlfriend. But that's the point. You never go out. How on earth have you managed to see each other? I just don't get the need for the secrecy, that's all. Why would you not tell me. Is it serious?'

'Mum,' he says, rolling his eyes. 'This is why I never said anything.'

'Sorry,' she says. 'But it's OK to ask, surely? I'd like to meet her sometime.'

'All right,' says David. 'Yeah.'

'OK then,' she says. 'More chicken, Mark?'

Mark is still staring at David, oblivious to the conversation around him.

'Mark?'

'Sorry – what?'

'You all right, darling?' says Marie. 'Not thinking about Holly sunbathing, I hope.'

'What? Me? No. Of course not,' he says. 'I'm fine.'

He takes a swig of wine and turns to face her with a tight smile. Then he says he would love some more chicken and the conversation moves on and away from David and Ellen and Holly.

David is soon forgotten and sits apart studying the other three – but Mark in particular. He is playing his part in the conversation, but whereas he might normally be expected to dominate it, he is, that evening, a far more reserved presence, content, for once, to let Marie do most of the talking.

David enjoys the feeling of power – enjoys seeing Mark rattled. He clearly did not like David mentioning Holly, but what could he do? David smiles and finishes his wine while the pudding plates are being cleared away.

'Do you mind if I leave the table?' he says.

'No – that's all right,' says his mother. 'You get off.'

'G'night, David,' says Marie. 'Sleep tight.'

'Goodnight,' he says, looking straight at Mark, who looks straight back at him, saying nothing.

David climbs the stairs with a satisfied spring in his step. There has been a shift in power towards him and he likes it. He likes it a lot.

Chapter 35

Man to Man

The next day comes round bright and sunny and filled with the babble of birdsong. David gets up and prises open a couple of slats in his Venetian blinds and squints out into the blazing morning daylight, still smiling to himself at Mark's discomfort the previous evening. Jerk.

The scaffolders are back. They are dismantling the scaffolding with breathtaking ease, dropping twenty-foot-long poles to each other as the edifice speedily reduces in height.

The workmen whistle and call to each other, laughing and singing while they work, with that careless, inconsiderate air that builders always have, owning whatever space they're in without regard for the people around them.

Boards and poles clatter down to be carried to a waiting truck while the clamps that held them in place are in turn hurled down and taken away. David watches the whole process, fascinated. Soon the whole building is clear and it's as though they have never been – apart from the presence of the new window and the neat new slates.

He gets dressed and trots downstairs. There is a note on the table from his mother saying she is out for the day, which

triggers some vague memory that she was talking at dinner about having to go to London.

There is a twenty-pound note next to the message, which tells him to go and buy a small list of supplies as well as whatever he fancies for lunch. David pockets the money and goes to the sink, fills a glass with water and drinks, almost dropping it on the floor as he turns to see Mark standing in the kitchen.

'What the f—'

'Language!' says Mark with a smile.

His presence is so incongruous, David wonders for a moment if he is dreaming.

'How did you get in?' says David looking round the room. 'What are –'

'Calm down. We have a spare key. For emergencies.'

'So my mum's out?'

'Yeah. Or I wouldn't have needed the key.'

'W-what's the emergency?' says David. 'Why not ring the doorbell?'

Mark sighs. For once he doesn't look completely in control. His voice has an edge to it. He's holding himself back.

'The emergency? The emergency is that you appear to want to wreck my marriage.'

'Me?' says David. 'How am I supposed to be doing that?'

Mark takes a step closer. The smile has disappeared.

'I love my wife. Can you understand that?'

'Not really,' says David.

'Don't think you can judge me,' says Mark.

David says nothing.

'Look, I've spoken to Holly,' says Mark, his voice calmer again. 'I figured she must have said something to you.'

'About what?'

Mark bows his head and waits a few moments before resuming.

'Don't make this more difficult than it is, David,' he says. 'OK? I know you know. If you wanted it to be a secret, you should have watched what you were saying.

'Like I said – I'd assumed Holly had let something slip when she was here cleaning. But then she told me you'd found out . . . via your little spying game.'

These words hit David in the stomach like a punch. Holly told on him.

'I don't think that's what your dad had in mind when he bought you that scope, is it?'

'Don't talk about my dad,' says David. 'Don't –'

Mark holds a hand up.

'OK. Low blow. I'm sorry. But you'll understand that I'm under a great deal of stress.'

'It's not my fault that you –'

'Look, I'm not here to fight with you, David. It's really none of your business at the end of the day, now, is it? But you promised Holly you would keep your mouth shut, so just keep your promise. OK?'

David scowls at him but eventually nods.

'And don't start talking about Holly around my wife. Or I'm afraid we will fall out.'

David stares at him. Is that a threat? It feels like a threat. He is filled with rage all of a sudden – for Mark, for Holly.

He would like to just walk up to Mark and grab him by the throat and crush him, smash him to atoms. But he knows he can't. He mustn't.

'Do you think I don't know what's going on here?'

David doesn't answer. He doesn't want to talk to him any more.

'With you spying on Holly? Zooming in on her lovely flesh with your little telescope? And it is lovely, let me tell you. You're jealous, right? Of me – who gets to touch that body rather than just look at it? Fair play to you. I get that.

'But this isn't a fantasy, David. This isn't a game or one of your comics. She won't have told you why she had to leave college but –'

'She has. She told me everything.'

'Really?' says Mark sceptically.

David says nothing.

'Then you know? OK. I hadn't realised you two were so close.'

'We talk,' says David.

Mark nods. He puts his hands together, palm to palm, like he's praying.

'You feel angry with me. OK. That's OK. I'm cheating on my wife – your mother's friend – and I'm screwing a girl you'd like to screw yourself. OK. I get it.'

David wants to hit him. Hard. Over and over again – pulverise him. He wishes Mark knew what he was capable of – what restraint he is showing.

'But you can't punish me without punishing her – or Marie or the kids. That's just . . . well, that's just the way it is.'

'That suits you, doesn't it? And anyway, why should I care?'
Mark smiles.

'But you do though, don't you? Not about me, clearly – maybe not even about my family. But about Holly.'

'No.'

Mark smiles.

'Listen, David,' says Mark. 'I've said all I have to say. You'll do whatever you have to do in the end, but Holly won't thank you for causing trouble.'

He steps closer to David. His face softens and he looks almost tearful. He's desperate; David can see it in his eyes.

'I like you, David. I've done more than my fair share for you and your mother. I know you're pissed off with me now – but I was there when everything went to pieces.'

David hates him all the more for mentioning this – because it's true. He was.

'Come on,' says Mark, growing quiet now. 'Please. I'm asking you, man to man, to give me – and my family – a break. They didn't do anything. This is my mess. They did nothing and it would be them who'd suffer the most. Things have got a bit crazy but I'll sort them out, I promise.'

David shrugs.

'OK,' he says.

Mark smiles.

'Thanks, David – I owe you one.'

David sits on the sofa when Mark leaves, staring at the blank black screen of the television and simmering with cold fury over Holly telling Mark about the scope.

He knows Mark is hardly in a position to say anything about it to David's mother, and he realises that it is not the indiscretion but the mere fact that Holly would confide in him at all.

It had not really occurred to David that they might talk – any more than it had clearly occurred to Mark that Holly might talk to David.

David saw them in his mind's eye simply having sex – and even that was problematic enough, in that while he liked imagining the sex, he did not want Mark there in his thoughts, naked, and naked with Holly.

At no point has he seen them chatting to each other. It makes it seem more of a relationship and harder to dismiss in the way he had up until that moment. It makes them seem close when David had tricked himself into believing that Holly saved that closeness for him.

And this simply makes David all the more furious, because he realises how ridiculous and childish it would sound if he tried to explain that to anyone. Not that he had anyone other than Holly he could explain it to.

Ironically.

Chapter 36

End-of-a-Film Finality

The text from Joe is short even for him and terse even by text standards. He replies telling him to meet him by the tennis courts. He has a desperate urge to confide in Joe.

'You told your mother we went to that festival together,' says Joe.

David can feel the anger glowing, cold and hot at the same time. He nods, wary of saying anything that might tip him over the edge.

'I specifically said no.'

David nods.

'Look, I know,' he says quietly. 'It's just that –'

'I don't want to hear it, OK?'

David has never heard this particular tone to Joe's voice. It's not harsh or even especially aggressive. It's distant. Final.

'I know, I know,' says David. 'But just let me –'

'Lie? Bullshit? I don't think so.'

'I'm not going to lie. Come on.'

'Well, that would be a first anyway.'

'What's that supposed to –'

Joe snarls at him.

'I stuck up for you, man. From the start. Through all the lies and weirdness and shit. You know – after your dad died and you started making stuff up. I defended you. It wasn't always easy. I never asked for thanks. I just want to have some respect, you know?'

'Respect? What are you on about? I respect you. Why wouldn't I? How do you even know anyway?'

Joe takes a step forward. David takes another step back.

'Because,' he says between gritted teeth, 'your mother bumped into me yesterday and asked me about it! That's how.'

David groans.

'Fuck,' says David. 'What did you say?'

'I didn't have the faintest idea what she was talking about, did I? You didn't even bother to tell me about the shitty lie you involved me in.'

'But you didn't say that? You didn't say you didn't know what she was taking about?'

Joe shakes his head, a wry smile on his face. David puffs out a breath.

'Thank Christ for that.'

Joe's smile disappears.

'I tried to cobble something together but it was too late. She knew I was lying.'

'Knew . . . or just suspected?'

'Knew.'

'Shit!' says David. 'That's why she's been acting weird. Damn it. You're sure she –'

'Of course she knew. She's not an idiot. I know you think we're all stupid . . .'

272

David's not listening. He paces round and round trying to assimilate the new information and predict the fallout. No matter how he turns it over in his mind, the outcome is never good.

'I should've told you that I'd used you as cover,' says David after a moment. 'I should have told you I was going to stick with the festival plan. Then you'd have been prepared.'

Joe lurches at him but stops short of actually grabbing him. He has told himself over and over that he will stay in control. But it's proving harder than he thought.

'Then I'd have been prepared? Then I'd have been *prepared*? You selfish shit!'

'All right. Sorry. For fuck's sake.'

'You don't get it, do you?' says Joe. 'You asked me, and I told you no! I told you no and you just went right on and did it anyway.'

'And I've said I'm sorry,' says David.

'You've said it, but you don't feel it, do you?' says Joe. 'You knew I liked your mum.'

'What?' says David. 'What has that got to do with anything? And why "liked"? She isn't going to blame you. Besides – I'll tell her I dropped you in it. It'll be f—'

'You made me lie to her!' shouts Joe. 'You made me look like I'm the kind of person who doesn't give a fuck, and I do give a fuck. I'm not a liar. Not everyone is, David.'

David takes a deep breath and sighs.

'Look, I'm sorry,' he says, 'but I think you're going a bit over the top. It's me that's going to get grief for this, not you. I just –'

'Shut up, David,' says Joe.

'Look, what is this?' says David. 'I think I'd rather you just thumped me.'

'Don't worry,' says Joe. 'It could still happen.'

David can see by Joe's odd demeanour that this isn't an idle threat. He can't get in a fight with Joe. It's too dangerous. David tries to concentrate – to sharpen his mind. He needs to stay in control. For Joe's sake.

'I am sorry,' he says. 'Honestly. Whether you believe me or not.'

'I believe you,' says Joe, his eyes half closed and looking away as if looking at David is painful to him. 'I believe you're sorry – sorry about pissing me off – sorry about lying to your mum. But I also think you're mainly just sorry you were caught and you'd do the same thing tomorrow. Like that!'

Joe turns to face him with this last line and snaps his fingers in David's face. David opens his mouth to respond but his brain hasn't supplied him with the words he means to deliver.

'If the same thing happened,' says Joe, 'if you thought you needed to lie more than you thought you needed to keep me as a mate, you'd do the same, you know you would.'

'No, I don't,' says David. 'Neither do you.'

Would he? Is Joe right?

'We've been mates for ages,' says Joe, a weak smile flickering for a moment. 'Since we were little.'

David can see now that Joe isn't so much angry as upset and he doesn't want David to see how upset he is. That's why he's refusing to catch his eye.

'But I don't want a mate who's gonna lie to me – or make me a liar for him. I'm sorry.'

David stands there, baffled as to what he is supposed to say other than repeat – again – that he is sorry.

'What? Are you splitting up with me?' he says, with a smirk.

'See you,' says Joe.

And then he walks away with such an end-of-a-film finality to it that David has to suck back on the sob that threatens to burst out of him.

Chapter 37

Like It's Unravelling

David wonders if his mother is ever going to mention the fact that she has caught him in this lie. He toys with the idea of confessing but wonders if that will only make it worse. He has missed the opportunity to own up and he knows it. You can't really confess to something someone already knows. Instead it is two whole, tense days before she finally looks him in the face – and with the expression he knows means trouble.

'I spoke to Joe,' she says.

They are having breakfast. Has she been preparing for this all night? She looks tired.

'I know.'

'Well?'

Her voice is constricted – angry and sad. He puts his spoon down and looks her in the eyes.

'I'm sorry.'

She slams her mug down on the table, tea splashing over the side. David jumps. Flashes of temper from his mother are rare, and all the more startling because of it.

'You're sorry? You're sorry?'

'Yes.'

'Where the hell were you? Were you at that festival with this girlfriend of yours? Sneaking around behind my back – so you could screw some girl from school?'

'I didn't go to the festival.'

'What?'

'I didn't go to the festival.'

'You told me about the bands you watched. You went into such detail.'

'I know,' he says, suddenly filled with the shame of it all. 'I wanted you to believe me. I'm sorry.'

'Then where did you go? That was so important to lie about? Clearly somewhere I wouldn't have given you permission for. Let's hear it. The truth, please.'

David has been given ample time to prepare for this inevitable question, but all the lies he has come up with seem to sound ridiculous. As annoying as it is, the truth, on this occasion, seems the best option.

'I went to a house on the coast. With friends.'

'Friends?'

David is stung by how implausible she assumes this to be.

'Yes – friends. Kind of.'

'What the hell is that supposed to mean?'

'I don't know. They aren't my friends now.'

'Why all the secrecy?' says his mother. 'Why lie?'

'Because I didn't think you'd let me go.'

'Is it drugs?'

'Is what drugs?'

She slaps her hands down on the table.

'Is that why you're like this?'

'Like what?'

'Is it drugs?' she shouts. 'Are you on drugs? Tell me!'

'I'm not on drugs!' yells David.

They are both wide-eyed now. David can see his mother's hand trembling. He feels nauseous. Everything feels like it's unravelling.

'Then what?' says his mother after a long pause.

David closes his eyes tightly shut and leans back.

'It was Ellen,' he says to the ceiling. 'The girl I told you about. I wanted to be with Ellen. She invited me.'

'Oh – she exists then? You're sure?'

He lowers his head and opens his eyes.

'Yes – of course she exists.'

'There's no of course about it. You seem to have become a very efficient liar. I know nothing about her. You suddenly announce it at dinner.'

'I thought I'd told you about her,' says David.

'No, you don't. Do you think I'd forget you telling me about a girl? Do you seriously imagine I don't spend my whole time worrying about you – wanting you to have friends and be happy. If you'd told me you had a girlfriend, I'd remember, OK?'

'All right then,' he says. 'What do you want to know? Her name's Ellen Emerson. From school. We met at the shops a while back and we got talking. It was her who invited me to that party.'

His mother looks at him for a while, saying nothing for a long moment.

'So it was about . . . sex. The lying?'

278

David's stomach lurches.

'Mum – do we have to talk about this?'

'Yes!' she says. 'You forego the right to be coy when you lie to me.'

David stares into his bowl of cereal.

'Yes – all right. Jesus! I wanted to have sex with her.'

She looks as though she is about to burst into tears but she doesn't.

'You tried to get your best friend – your only friend – to cover for you; to lie for you. Good for Joe for refusing to have anything to do with it.'

'Is that what he said?'

'He didn't need to.'

'Because Joe's perfect, I know.'

'Oh, stop being so childish! Something could have happened and I wouldn't have known where you were.'

'But nothing did happen,' says David. 'Nothing.'

David's mother holds her head in her hands. She says nothing for a long time and David wonders whether he is meant to leave and leave her to it, but he can't make himself get up from the chair.

'What's going on, David?' she says eventually, so quietly he only picks it up with his super-hearing.

'What?'

'To you. To us,' she says, taking her hands away and staring at him pleadingly. 'To me . . . and you.'

David can't look at her. He doesn't know what to say.

'We were so close before your dad died,' she continues. 'You don't seem to even remember . . .'

David's eyes start to sting.

'It feels like when he died that died too,' she continues. 'The fun we used to have together. I tell myself that it's just because you're growing up and so you don't need your mum like you used to, but it's more than that. You've shut me out. You've used his death to shut me out.'

'I haven't.'

Has he?

'Well, it feels that way,' she says.

'I'm sorry, Mum – honestly.'

She throws her head back so she is looking up at the ceiling and David can only see the underside of her chin. It feels a very long time before she looks at him again.

'I don't know what to say, David,' she says. 'Whatever I say to you seems to have the opposite effect. I'm lucky if I get so much as a grunt in reply. You seem to talk to Holly more than you talk to me.'

'I don't think that's true.'

It is. He talks more to her than to anyone. More than Joe even. That has never seemed strange until now.

'I hear you talking up there,' she says.

'You do?' he says, startled.

'I can't hear what you're saying obviously,' she says. 'Which judging by your expression is clearly a good thing.'

'No – it's just – you know . . .'

'No, I don't know,' she says. 'I don't know anything. There could be something going on between you and Holly, for all I know.'

'Mum – there's nothing going on –'

'I know, I know!' she says, frowning. 'That's ridiculous, obviously. All I mean is that I don't know anything about what's going on in your head any more. You're a mystery.'

She shakes her head, lost in her own thoughts. He is filled with a sudden desire to tell her about his superhero alter-ego, but though he opens his mouth he cannot form the words.

'Sorry,' says David eventually.

'I've got to get on,' she says, scraping back her chair and leaving the kitchen without another word.

Chapter 38

Everyone Wants to Believe They're Special

The room is airless, but David refuses to get up and open a window. It feels right. It is appropriate to his state of mind – his brain feels as if it is being crushed in a vice.

He lies on his back and gazes at the imperfections in the ceiling – imperfections that become more and more exaggerated as he studies them, until he feels as though he is hovering over a vast ice field, chilled despite the warmth of the room.

He has been idly flicking through the Red Sonja Conan comic, looking at the bizarre range of jobs advertised therein:

BOYS, 12 OR OVER, SELL GRIT FOR CASH PROFITS AND PRIZES

THE KEY TO YOUR FUTURE: BE A LOCKSMITH

TRAIN AT HOME FOR A BIG INCOME CAREER IN
ACCOUNTING

HOW TO WRITE, SELL AND PUBLISH YOUR OWN SONGS

SELL ENGRAVED METAL SOCIAL SECURITY PLATES

David doesn't even know what social security plates are or why anyone might want them engraved. He is waiting for

Holly to arrive, lying in a state of near self-hypnosis, until he hears her footsteps on the stairs, the clunk and slither of the hoover against the wall. But when she finally enters his room he does not acknowledge her at all.

Holly does not respond to this lack of response. She knows what it's about, and if David wants to signal his annoyance without discussing it, then that suits her just fine.

But David can't keep it up.

'You told Mark I spied on you!'

Holly rolls her eyes and turns to him, hands on hips.

'Look – what was I supposed to do? It's your own fault. He told me what you were like when they were round here. What the hell was that about?'

David scowls.

'He was getting on my nerves.'

'He was getting on your nerves?'

'Yes.'

Holly shakes her head.

'You're messing with people's lives,' she says.

'No! *You're* messing with people's lives. It's not my fault if you're screwing Mark.'

She glares angrily at him.

'Keep your voice down!'

David slumps down, muttering to himself. After a moment, Holly comes and sits on the bed beside him.

'Look, I'm sorry I told Mark about you spying on me. It seemed the best thing to say.'

'For you, maybe.'

She nods.

'For me, yes.'

David wants to stay mad at her, but he knows in the same situation he'd have done the same.

'He thought I'd told you,' says Holly. 'He was really angry. I couldn't have him thinking I'd just been randomly blabbing. Sorry.'

David lies back down on his bed. Holly stands up and goes to the window, silhouetted against the slats.

'Look,' says Holly, 'he can't exactly tell anyone about it, can he? So one more person knows about your little secret. Now we're in the same boat.'

It doesn't feel like that to David. He wants to say that he doesn't think that spying on people doing something is the same as actually doing the thing that the people are doing, but he thinks better of it.

'Come on,' she says, bending over and grabbing the ball. 'Ask me something. Anything.'

David shakes his head. He isn't in the mood. He was sick of the whole sorry mess – a mess that just seems to get more and more tangled and complicated at every turn.

'All right then . . .'

She throws the ball at him and he only just manages to stop it hitting his face. She laughs at his look of surprise, and after a moment he joins her, holding the ball with both hands.

'So . . .' she says, looking around the room for some focus for a question.

She glances towards the drawing of Lightforce.

'Tell me a secret,' she says. 'Something no one knows.'

'That's not a question,' he says.

'All right then,' she says. 'What is your biggest secret?'

'It won't be a secret if I tell you.'

'Well, maybe that'll be a good thing,' she says.

'How do you work that out?' he says. 'I don't see you telling everyone about you and Mark.'

'Yes – but you know about it,' she say. 'So it's not a total secret.'

'And that feels better, does it?'

She smiles.

'No. But I thought maybe, as you know such a big secret of mine, there might be something you could tell me. If you tell me a secret, I'll tell you one. How would that be?'

David frowns dubiously.

'You already know that I spy on you.'

'True,' she says. 'But speaking as a person with secrets, I think you have other secrets. I can see it in your face. I can see the effort of keeping them all hidden.'

She reaches out and lays her hand on his face. He closes his eyes. He is so very tired. The weight of it all. It's exhausting. Enough. Enough. Give in.

'I think – I thought – I had superpowers,' says David.

As soon as he has said the words he wants to reel them back in – to unsay them.

'Really?' says Holly.

After a moment David nods. He feels like he's falling out of the sky, plummeting to earth.

'Go on,' she says. 'Tell me about this dream of yours.'

'It isn't a dream. I mean, I'm not asleep. It feels real. It

285

feels more real than what everyone else is trying to tell me is real.'

He shrugs. There seems no way to explain it that won't make him seem ridiculous. He has never wanted to talk about it because on some level he knew to do so would destroy his powers. The truth is kryptonite.

'Go on,' says Holly.

David feels as if the words are slipping back into the darkness and he has to wrench them free before they disappear. Why isn't she laughing?

'Oh!' she says, pointing to the drawings on the wall. 'You're Lightforce!'

David shakes his head.

'The other one.'

Holly frowns and nods as though that makes sudden sense to her.

'And you, what, rescue people from burning buildings – save the world . . . that kind of thing?'

'No – I only have one thing to do. One thing. And I can't even do that.'

'What is it? What do you have to do?'

David takes a deep breath. Why is this so hard to say?

'I have to save my dad.'

Finally. He gasps with the effort. It's like having a massive splinter wrenched from his flesh.

'Oh, David,' says Holly.

She leans forward and puts her hand on his shoulder. David fights to hold back tears. Now nothing in the world can stop him from continuing.

'Every time it's the same,' he says. 'I see the car going into the water or I see the car sinking and I fly there and I use my super-strength to pull it out. Or that's how it was for a while. I'd rescue him. I'd stop him from dying.'

'And then what happened? What changed?'

'Right at the point where I'd be about to save him, something always stopped me.'

'You changed your mind?'

David winces as the very thought of Lightforce hits him with a blinding burst as though his enemy is there with him at the river's edge.

'No – there was something else there. Someone else – with superpowers. Someone stronger than me.'

'A supervillain?'

'I guess.'

Holly peers at him, cocking her head to one side.

'What did it look like, this supervillain?'

David feels his muscles clench. The light bursts again behind his eyes, like a migraine.

'I can't see. It's just like a human-shaped blinding light. Too bright to look at. It's too powerful for me. More powerful than anything.'

Holly sits back, pondering all this.

'Wait! You mean him,' she says, pointing to his drawing on the wall. 'It's Lightforce!'

David nods.

'So Lightforce stops you from saving your dad.'

David nods again, pushing his fingers through his long hair.

'But why?' she asks.

David has asked himself this many times of course.

'I don't know.'

Holly sits back, staring at him.

'I know, I know,' he says. 'Feel free to laugh.'

'I'm not going to laugh.'

'Why not?' says David. 'It's pretty hilarious.'

'No, it's not,' says Holly.

David chokes back a sob and can't speak for a while.

'So now you know,' he says at last. 'I'm even crazier than you thought.'

'Not crazy.'

'No?'

'Everyone wants to believe they're special,' says Holly.

'Even if they're not,' says David.

'Hey,' says Holly. 'That's not what I meant.'

'Please,' he says. 'I'm not special. And you don't have to try and pretend I am. I'm not a kid.'

'You are a kid,' says Holly. 'No shame in that. So am I most days. Everyone thinks there's this big moment where you suddenly become an adult, but there isn't. It's a process.'

'I love you,' says David.

'No, you don't,' says Holly, kindly but with a sigh.

'I do,' says David. 'Don't tell me what I feel. Why does everyone think they know better than me how I feel?'

Holly takes a deep breath and exhales slowly.

'OK. If you do love me, it's because I'm the only girl you've taken the time to get to know,' she says. 'A girl you've talked to, properly. A girl you've been brave enough to be weak in front of.'

'You don't know that.'

'Don't I?'

'I don't care!' shouts David.

'It's powerful stuff,' she says, 'getting inside someone's head. Much more powerful than getting inside their pants, believe me. But you have to get inside someone's heart for love.'

'And I haven't got inside yours, is that it?'

Holly smiles a gentle smile and David feels it like a hot needle in his heart.

'I'm very fond of you, David,' she says, 'but I don't love you. I'm sorry. Not in that way.'

'Because . . . you love Mark?' says David.

'Mark? I've already told you – I'm not in love with Mark.'

'What then? Is he in love with you?'

'No – he's in love with Marie.'

David frowns, confused.

'How? I don't get it.'

Holly smiles.

'He's a little bit obsessed with me,' she says. 'But it's not love. He still loves Marie. He just can't stop himself.'

'Why would you –'

'Why would I allow myself to be the object of an obsession?' she says with a sad smile.

David tries to make sense of what she is saying. Is she talking about him? Is she saying he is obsessed with her too? Maybe he is. Holly looks away and shakes her head.

'Anyway, a deal's a deal,' she says. 'I promised you a secret, didn't I?'

Chapter 39

Like an Animal

Holly seems to lose her nerve and covers her face with both hands.

'It doesn't matter,' says David. 'You don't have to tell me anything you don't want to.'

'No – I do. I do want to.'

David looks at her. It doesn't look much like she wants to. It looks like it is causing her the same pain it caused David to reveal his secret.

'You know that I dropped out of university, but you don't know why,' says Holly.

'You told me. You had a breakdown,' says David. 'You were stressed out about that boyfriend – Duncan – who went off with someone else.'

She licks her lips and holds out her hands. David throws her the ball. He wants to know now.

'Did something else happen with Duncan?'

She nods. She trembles a little, as though about to break down and cry, but regains control, looking him straight in the eye.

'Truth is, I didn't exactly tell you the whole story.'

291

'Oh?'

Holly hugs the ball to her stomach and rocks back and forth.

'I became obsessed with Duncan,' she says. 'Really, really crazy obsessed. I mean, I'd loved him when we were together. But when we were apart it was like he took over my whole fucking world. Or the world inside my head anyway. Have you ever had that?'

David nods. Yeah. Just a bit, he thinks.

'I'd lost all my friends when I was with him, so I had no social life – no shoulder to cry on when we split – no distraction. I just thought about him. All the time.

'I followed him around uni like I was a spy or a detective or something.'

Holly smiles, but it is a cold, hard smile.

'At first it was just embarrassing,' she continues. 'Not for me, I hasten to add. I was already beyond that. No – to everyone around me. To Duncan it was only mildly annoying for a while.

'But I persisted and persisted. It started to get to him, and to his girlfriend. I started to freak them out. Everywhere they went, I seemed to be there watching, and even if I wasn't, they probably thought I was.

'I didn't really do anything else for months. I couldn't relax. I couldn't work. I couldn't do anything else other than obsess over where Duncan was and what he was doing.

'Then it all came to a head . . .'

Holly breaks off and every muscle in her face seems to flex and tremble.

'What happened?' asks David quietly.

Holly smiles, her eyes swimming in tears. She takes a deep breath before continuing, and when she lets it out, it's with a shudder in her shoulders and a tremble in her lips.

'I got more and more obsessed,' she says. 'My tutor got to hear about it too. He called me in and warned me that what I was doing was going beyond what could be thought of as normal and if it did not stop there would be consequences.

'I promised him – of course – that I would stop and that there was nothing to worry about, but I had no intention of stopping. I couldn't if I tried. It was all that got me up in the morning. I had ceased to care about my course or why I was at university.

'The only real reason I was there now was so that I could keep an eye on Duncan. But of course it could never carry on like that.

'I was going to get kicked out eventually and I knew it. Perhaps that's what spurred me on to the final confrontation I had with him.'

'Final confrontation?'

'I followed him and his girlfriend to a restaurant. They were actually having a meal on the anniversary of the day I first met Duncan. Of course he was oblivious to that. That's what made it all the more upsetting.

'So instead of just following them, I walked over to their table and yelled at them in front of everyone. The girlfriend called me a bitch so I threw a glass of wine in her face.

'A couple of waiters came over and tried to shepherd me out . . .'

She tries to form the next words but she can't. She puts her hand over her mouth as though to gag herself. She closes her eyes tightly, but can't stop the images forming in her head.

'Holly?' says David. 'It doesn't matter. You don't have to tell me.'

'I do,' she says, with a gasp and a sob. 'I do have to tell you. I want to.'

She sighs and tries to calm herself.

'When the waiter grabbed me to push me out, I flailed my arm in the air as I turned to shout at them one last time and my . . . my hand – it caught a light fitting above my head and it smashed.

'It was such a weird, freak accident. I mean, what are the chances? I looked at my hand and there was blood pouring out and then I heard a scream.

'I thought it was her – the girlfriend, screaming at me smashing the light or the blood or whatever but . . .'

She stares ahead, swallowing the words before they can come.

'What?'

'It was Duncan. He was screaming. Like an animal. The glass had gone in his eye, you see.'

Holly breaks down into sobs and can't continue. David tries to put his arm round her but she shrugs him off.

'Was he OK?'

She shakes her head.

'He lost the eye.'

'Fuck.'

She lowers her head and sobs.

'Look, it wasn't your fault,' says David. 'It was an accident. A weird, freaky accident, like you said.'

'It was my fault though,' says Holly. 'If I hadn't been crazy jealous, if he'd never met me . . .'

She wipes the tears from her eyes with her fingertips and David watches, his own eyes welling with tears now. The pain he carries with him always seems to join with hers. He can no longer fully distinguish between the two.

'I told Mark,' says Holly. 'I knew Marie and Mark before I left for university. I'd done some babysitting for them in the past and when I came back I was looking for work again – for distraction.'

'I don't know why I told him. It just all came out one day. But that's the strange thing about Mark – he can be such a lovely guy. I didn't think he'd let me look after the kids once I told him, but he was kind. He seemed to understand that I was only that way with Duncan. I wasn't a danger to anyone else. Except maybe myself.

'I knew he was a lawyer, but I never really thought about that. But he offered to help and I was grateful. He wrote to the university for me and helped me word a letter to Duncan. I don't know what I'd have done without him. Duncan's parents were threatening to take me to court.

'One night I was babysitting for them and Mark came back early, on his own. He'd been drinking – I could smell it on his breath – but he wasn't drunk.'

'I should have stopped him,' she says. 'I did try. I didn't try very hard though. Like I say, I was grateful for his help.'

David stares at her.

'You mean . . . ? You mean he raped you?'

She shakes her head.

'No – he didn't rape me, David,' says Holly, tears brimming in her eyes again. 'He would have stopped, if I'd wanted him to. He didn't force me. He's not like that.'

'But you didn't want to?'

'I don't know. I felt indebted, I suppose, and –'

'You felt you owed him?'

She shakes her head again. A tear rolls down her cheek.

'I don't know. He'd been good to me.'

'Yeah – but that doesn't mean –'

'All right, maybe in some way I thought it was all part of my punishment. That probably sounds crazy.'

'No,' says David. 'Not crazy. But not fair. Why should you be punished?'

'Why should Duncan be blind in one eye?'

David scratches his head.

'But it wasn't your fault. And it has nothing to do with Mark. He took advantage of –'

'Look – I had been deserted by Duncan and he'd driven me crazy and here was this man who seemed willing to risk his marriage to be with me.

'I never thought it would get to this stage. Neither of us did, I'm sure. It's a mess, I know that.'

'Then why not just stop seeing him? What about Marie – or the kids?'

Holly frowns.

297

'I don't want to talk about it any more,' she says, wiping her eyes.

'I just meant that –'

'Seriously, David,' she says. 'I know you mean well, but you're out of your depth. Honestly. Leave it alone.'

Chapter 40

What If Everything Is Significant?

David has previously taken refuge and comfort in the idea that nothing outside of fiction has to mean anything. In a comic every detail is there for a reason – but in real life everything is random.

Isn't it?

Now he isn't sure. What if everything is significant? What if everything does mean something? What if all the things that happen to him are only random because he has not seen the pattern?

What use was there in Holly telling him her story if David can do nothing to help her. What was the point? Whatever she said, or even thinks she meant, surely on some level she wants David to save her?

Is this what his superhero fixation is all about? Was it always about this? Maybe he has always been trying to save the wrong person. Maybe it isn't about being a superhero in his fantasies, it's about being a hero in his real life.

Why have they chosen each other to be honest with? Surely the truth is more naked than any bare flesh could ever be? He knows how he feels about Holly, but could she – can she – feel the same about him? Surely it's not impossible.

He sees her face so vividly. Whenever his mind is at rest, that's where it goes. She is his mental screensaver. She is his Lois Lane – she is every superhero's girlfriend rolled into one. Mark is his nemesis – his arch-enemy, his Lightforce.

But the danger she is in is not the obvious danger of comics. She isn't tied up on a railway line or trapped in a burning building or at the mercy of some giant robot or something. This is complicated. It's real. But it's just as urgent.

And didn't these messy real-life perils need superheroes too – maybe they needed them even more. Holly is in trouble and she needs his help.

David resolves in that instant to act. To do something. It is so much easier to do nothing – he knows that more than anyone. But if he doesn't act, then who will. Only Mark knows the whole truth of what happened to Holly at university, and now only David knows the whole truth about Mark.

Holly has to be rescued, and who else is going to do it? If she didn't see David as someone she might love, then this was the way to show her!

David rings the doorbell and steps back, looking up and down the street. It's dusk and the street lights are just beginning to come on. After a moment, the door opens and Holly is staring at him in confusion through the crack.

'David?' she says. 'What are you doing here? Mark and Marie are out.'

He says nothing, but shoves past her into the hallway.

'Mark!'

'Mark's not here, David,' Holly hisses. 'Keep your voice down. You'll wake the girls.'

'Mark! Mark!' yells David.

'David! Stop.'

Mark appears over Holly's shoulder

'Oh – Mark,' says David. 'Sorry – Holly said you weren't here.'

The sarcasm doesn't have any noticeable effect on Mark. He just stands looking at David with a kind of weariness on his face.

'What do you want?'

'I want you to leave Holly alone,' he says.

Mark laughs. It's a genuine laugh. He is clearly amused. But then he is also clearly drunk.

'What exactly has it got to do with you?'

'Holly's my friend,' says David.

'David!' says Holly. 'You need to go.'

David stares at her, pained by her lack of support. But he needs to be strong. She needs his help even if she doesn't know it.

'Friend?' says Mark, walking unsteadily forward. 'Interesting. I wouldn't have thought of spying on someone when they're semi-naked and wanking about it as friendship these days. But maybe I'm out of touch.'

'Mark!' hisses Holly, and then, turning to David, says, 'Please go.'

Go? He can't go.

'You see?' says Mark. 'Holly wants you to leave. She doesn't

301

require your help, apparently. So – off you trot, there's a good boy.'

David doesn't move. He needs to be strong.

'Please,' says Holly.

'No,' says David, turning on Mark and raising his voice. 'I want you to leave her alone!'

'Don't upset yourself,' says Mark. 'We know you're a bit fragile, the Deacons. Don't want you going loopy like your dad, eh?'

'Stop it, Mark!'

'I told you before,' says David, spitting the words through gritted teeth, 'don't talk about my dad.'

'Oh, I think we should,' says Mark. 'I really do. I was at the hospital with your mum. We both know he didn't swerve to avoid anything that night. There were no tyre marks on that road. Did you not think that was a bit odd? Why did he not try and brake if he saw something in the road?'

'What?' says Holly. 'Mark, don't.'

'No – it's time the truth was out there,' says Mark. 'David's been humoured far too long. He's not a kid, is he?'

'What are you on about?' says David.

'Your father killed himself. That's the truth. He drove that car into the water and drowned himself. He probably –'

Mark never finishes his words though because David throws himself forward like a wild animal. But Mark is ready for him, blocking his arms and pushing him back against the wall, his forearm against his throat. David tries to break free. It should be easy. It isn't.

'Mark!' calls Holly. 'Stop it! Leave him alone.'

'This is all your fault,' he hisses at Holly.

'Leave him alone or so help me I'll call Marie!' she says.

'No, you won't,' he says.

Holly takes out her phone and starts to dial. David tries to summon his super-strength one last time but it won't come. Mark pushes him aside to grab the phone and David is hurled into the banister, banging his head as he falls to the floor.

There is a stunned silence. David just sits there slumped against the side of the stairs, rubbing his head. Mark looks at him, then at Holly and then puts his head in his hands. His shoulders begin to rock. David is shocked to see he's crying. Then there are footsteps above them.

'Daddy?' says a voice at the top of the stairs.

'Everything's all right, Morag!' says Mark, getting to his feet and wiping his eyes. 'Daddy's here. I'll come and say goodnight in a minute. David is just leaving, aren't you, David?'

He nods and Morag smiles and waves and runs off back to her room. Mark teeters a few steps and slumps down at the bottom of the stairs.

'David – you need to go home,' says Holly.

David straightens out his clothes, turns and heads for the door. He hasn't reached the gate when Holly calls after him and he turns to see her, smudged by his tears, standing in the doorway.

'David . . . About your dad . . .'

He shakes his head and goes to turn away.

'How can you be with him?'

'I'm sorry, David. But it's got nothing to do with you!' she says.

'It has! I came to help you!' he says, turning back round. 'I came to –'

'Oh my God!' she says, putting her hands to her head. 'You came to save me, didn't you? Like you really were a sodding superhero.'

She shakes her head.

'Jesus, David,' she says. 'You need to grow up and you need to get some help.'

'What about you?'

'I'm fine!'

'Are you? Because you don't look it!'

'Well, it's none of your fucking business one way or the other, is it?'

'So you're just going to carry on like this, letting him –'

'Go home, David,' she says, already walking away. 'Just go home.'

Chapter 41

Drifting Among the Rubble

David lies on his back, floating in some distant part of the universe. He appears to be in a vast asteroid belt. Rock fragments – some as small as a tooth, some as large as a very big house – surround him on all sides, hanging suspended in the same horizontal plane, stretching off as far as he can see.

It's as though he is floating in the aftermath of a great explosion, adrift in the dispersed rubble. His suit is torn to shreds and he is bruised and cut, the blood oozing out of him in droplets to join the other particles in suspension.

There is no sound. No sound at all. Not even the sound of his own breathing or the blood pumping near his ears. It feels like some massive part of him has been damaged and he will simply float here, wrecked, for all eternity.

'David,' says a distant voice, so faint that he thinks he is remembering it rather than hearing it.

'David,' it says again.

'David!'

He opens his eyes and there is Holly standing at the foot of his bed, hands on hips.

'What?' he says, and he says it without rancour or sarcasm or anything at all that might be seen as interest in what response the question might elicit.

'You had no business coming round like that the other night,' she says.

Is this how it's going to be? he thinks. Is she going to tell him again how little he matters? Can't she see that he knows that?

'Why would you do that?' she asks. 'Don't just lie there like that. Speak to me!'

'Why?' says David. 'What would be the point? I get it. I had no business trying to help.'

'Help?' she says, frowning. 'Is that what you thought you were doing?'

In spite of himself, David sits up.

'Look – you wouldn't be with him if it wasn't for what happened to Duncan. He's using you. You shouldn't let him.'

'And what about you?' she says.

'What?'

'You don't have any problem when it comes to using me, as some kind of sex coach.'

'That's hardly the same.'

Holly moves a couple of steps closer and drops her voice.

'Don't start acting all heroic. You spied on me and then you used what you knew to get me to do what you wanted. You pretty much blackmailed me. You knew I had no choice.'

Holly looks away. David sinks back down onto the bed.

'OK, OK,' he says. 'Whatever. You're right. It's none of my business.'

Holly's voice softens.

'That was a horrible thing he said about your dad.'

David turns away from her and looks towards the window. A flock of birds flies by, just visible through the gaps in the blinds.

'Take no notice of him,' she continues. 'He was just trying to hurt you.'

'No,' says David. 'It's true.'

'What?'

David rolls back and holds out his arms, wiggling his fingers. Holly finds the ball and tosses it to him. He holds it to his face.

'It's all true,' he says, fighting back tears. 'I heard Mark and my mother talking that night. I've always known it. I just never wanted to think it.

'He'd been depressed for ages. Thinking back now, I can see it, but I was just a kid, wasn't I?

'Mark's right. There were no skid marks because he didn't even try to stop. He drove straight up the embankment and into the water and by the time a passing driver had run up there it was too late.

'They told me it was an accident – that he'd swerved to avoid a deer and I decided to pretend that I didn't know the truth. But soon, the more I told people that that was what happened, the more it became easier to believe it was actually true.

'Then I started to have the visions – I don't know what

else to call them – about being a superhero and trying to save him. They seemed so real – more real than the rest of my shitty life if I'm being honest.'

'But you couldn't save him,' says Holly. 'You knew you couldn't save him so you made up a supervillain to thwart yourself.'

David nods.

'Yeah,' he says. 'Lightforce wasn't really a supervillain. It was just the truth. So bright I couldn't look at it . . .'

'I'm so sorry,' says Holly.

'Don't be,' says David. 'Like you say – it's my own fault for coming round. None of my business.'

'Come on,' she says. 'Don't be like that.'

David lies on his back. Holly sits down on the end of the bed.

'You're still a kid,' she says. 'You've carried that round with you all this time? Why didn't you tell anyone?'

David shrugs.

'What good would it have done? Who would it have helped?'

'You,' says Holly.

David knows she's right. All those sessions with Dr Jameson without ever once talking about the stuff that was really gnawing away at him. They only ever talked about the symptoms – the lying, the introversion.

'But I told you – I obviously wanted to believe that version. I must have done.'

'But you didn't. You didn't. Don't you see?'

He tosses the ball onto the floor, lets it roll silently away and closes his eyes. Holly says something else but he is already back in the silence of the asteroid belt, drifting among the rubble.

'David!'

'What?'

'You need to talk about this,' she says. 'You need to speak to your mum. If you don't, I will.'

'What? After all the secrets I've kept for you?'

'This is for your own good,' she says. 'Did you even tell your shrink?'

He shakes his head.

'We need to sort you out,' she says.

'Why me?' he says. 'Or why just me? How am I worse than you? Jesus – look at us. We're both as pathetic as each other!'

'Talk to your mum,' she says. 'Please.'

David nods. She's right. Why not? Things are so smashed now, he might as well. There's nothing to lose, is there? He's lost everything that he thought he had – every solid thing in his shaky life.

'What about you?' says David.

'What about me?'

'Please . . .' says David.

Holly sighs.

'Look, for what it's worth, you're right, OK? I finished with Mark that night, after you left. I realised that it was only ever going to end badly if we carried on. I always knew that, of course. But seeing Morag come out onto the landing – I just couldn't carry on. It's finished, OK? It's over.

'So in a way you did save me after all.'

She says this kindly, but somehow all it does is remind David, sickeningly, of how preposterous the episode must have seemed – of how childish he had been even as he thought he was being grown-up – finally acting like a man. He feels tears welling and looks away.

'Stop being so hard on yourself, David,' she says.

'That's rich, coming from you,' he replies to the wall.

She reaches out and turns his face around, resting her forehead against his and looking into his eyes.

'Talk to your mum,' she whispers.

He takes a deep breath.

'It's so hard.'

'I know.'

She leans in and hugs him, her face pressed against his. And for a moment – just for a moment – everything seems so much simpler.

David picks up his phone and heads out of the house. Without thinking, he starts to head for Joe's place and then remembers that this route is not open to him – or not today.

He wanders with studied randomness, turning this way and that, trying to deliberately go down streets he would not have chosen, simply as a way of distracting his thoughts, which are scurrying and clambering over each other like ants on a log.

He walks along with head bowed, studying the knots of his shoelaces, muttering to himself, going over old conversations, imagining others.

'Well, well, well,' says a voice he recognises but can't immediately place.

He looks up to see Matt and two other boys he doesn't know.

'David,' he says. 'Don't run off.'

David has already turned and is on the kerb waiting for a car to pass before crossing. Matt grabs him by the shoulders and pretends to push him in front of the car before pulling him back. David yanks himself free.

'I'm not in the fucking mood, OK?'

'Oooooh . . .' says Matt, wide-eyed in mock fear, turning to his two friends. 'David's not in the mood.'

David ignores him and turns back to the road. Again Matt pulls him back. David shoves him away.

'I said I'm not in the mood. Now leave me alone.'

Matt moves to block his way.

'And supposing I d—'

Before he can finish David punches him in the face, knocking him to the ground. He leaps on him and punches him again and again until he is being pulled off by one of the friends.

David turns on the boy who pulled him off, wild-eyed, but the boy backs off, as does the other one. David looks down at Matt, who is groaning on the ground, and then at his own fists; skinned knuckles throbbing. He turns and walks away.

Chapter 42

Too Many Secrets

David flies out over the fields, dark now below him – darker than they have ever seemed before. The flying feels an effort now, rather than natural, and he has to concentrate, fearing he will fall out of the sky if he doesn't.

He flies over the trees, thick with rooks, and the birds sit on their branches and observe him passing by, like mourners solemnly watching a hearse.

David is acutely aware of the air passing over his suited body. It feels thick – as though it has congealed around him and he is being carried on a fast-moving current rather than consciously moving himself forward. For the first time he feels the cold.

There below him is the car as always. He flies above it, wobbling awkwardly, keeping pace with it as it moves along the road, watches as it lurches to the left and drives up and over the embankment and into the water.

David dives down as the car begins to sink, plummeting rather than struggling through the air. But instead of grabbing the car and trying to wrest it from the water, he comes to a halt hovering in front of it, staring through the windscreen.

There is his father looking out. The windows are open and the water floods in, but David does nothing. His father looks straight at him, his face calm, relaxed. As the water rises to his chin he smiles.

David does not move. He stays there, hovering, as the water fills the car entirely and the whole thing sinks. Lightforce does not come. He doesn't need to come. The car disappears with one last gurgle.

The rippling water smoothes itself until soon there is no sign that there has ever been a car or the life it contained. Birds twitter in the trees, the leaves rustle in the breeze.

David closes his eyes and when he opens them he is back in his room and he knows his days as a superhero are over.

He has been sitting at the table for three quarters of an hour waiting for his mother to come home. He has slipped into a kind of trance, the almost inaudible whisper of the clock's lisping tick the only sound he registers until he hears the key turning in the lock of the front door.

She comes in and gives him only a passing glance – not even a purposeful one that would signify her annoyance, but a genuine, disinterested passing glance that seems to say, 'Oh – you're still here.'

They have argued so many times and he has upset her so many times, but this feels different. They have become separated. The frayed and tattered bond between them seems broken now, and he feels unmoored. He might just float away – float away and never return.

His mother takes her coat off and hangs it over a chair.

She fills the kettle and stands with her back to him. It's as if she can no longer even bear to look at him.

'Mum?' says David.

There is a barely perceptible ripple in the material across her shoulders. Is his voice now so disagreeable to her?

'Do you want a cup of tea?' she says, without turning round.

'No. Thanks.'

She takes one mug from the cupboard and drops in a tea bag. The kettle begins to hiss.

'Mum?' says David again.

She sighs and turns round. Her face is blank, unreadable.

'What?' she says.

'I want to tell you something.'

She turns back as the kettle comes to the boil in a little burst of steam, pouring in the water and opening the fridge door to look for milk.

'I've had a nice evening, David,' she says in a voice as inscrutable as her face. 'I'm tired, OK. I just want to go to bed and read with a cup of tea. All right?'

'No,' says David. 'It's not all right. I need to tell you now.'

She closes her eyes and lets out a long breath.

'Well, you'd better tell me then,' she says, her voice suddenly brittle with sarcasm. 'It must be very important.'

She slumps down in the seat opposite, both hands cupped around her mug.

'Well?' she says, with pointed disinterest.

It's almost as if their respective roles have become reversed.

She notices his red and skinned knuckles.

'What is all this?' she says, interested all of a sudden. 'And what have you done to your hand?'

'Never mind that,' he says.

She grabs his hand and studies the knuckles. She cannot stop herself from showing concern, however exhausted she might feel with him.

'Have you been in a fight? What the hell –'

'Just listen!' says David. 'Just listen to me – and then you can say whatever you like.'

She opens her mouth to tell him that she's had enough – enough of all his silly nonsense – but she can see it's important. She can see the urgency in his face. He looks older.

'OK. What is it?'

'I know about Dad,' he says finally. 'That it was suicide. I know. I've always known.'

She stares at him, shaken, startled.

'But how?'

'I overheard you and Mark talking that night – the night I came back in the rain. I came down later and you were talking.'

She puts her hand over her mouth, her eyes not meeting his, and he can see that she is replaying that day – seeing him walk in the door.

'Oh, David – why didn't you say?'

'Because it was a secret,' he says. 'Because I knew I wasn't supposed to know. I thought you might be angry.'

'Sweetheart . . .'

She reaches across the table and grabs his hand. He flinches at her touch.

'And I had kind of forgotten I knew. I think I preferred the version you gave me and so I made it true. I saw it in my head so clearly. It was like a memory. It was like I'd actually seen it happen. The accident, I mean. It was like I'd been there myself – a witness. But of course I was a witness to something that never happened.'

'He was ill,' she says. 'He had been ill for a while. In his mind. It was so hard. We kept it from you. I kept it from you. I'm sorry. You seemed too young, but I see now I should have found some way to talk to you about it.'

David stiffens, pulling his hand back.

'But if he'd loved us – really loved us – he wouldn't have been able to do that.'

She shakes her head and reaches out with both hands, leaning across the table towards him.

'No – he was ill, David, and he died of that illness. Just as surely as if he'd died of a heart attack or cancer.'

'But –'

'He loved us, David, but his mind was damaged. Don't be angry with him. That's why I tried to hide it from you. I didn't want you to be angry with him.'

'Are you angry with him?'

After a pause, she nods.

'Sometimes. But I know it's not fair. I'm angry with the illness. I'm angry that he isn't here, well and strong. And I'm angry at myself for being angry.'

'I know,' says David.

She wipes away the tear that is balanced on her lower eyelashes. David looks at her and it feels as if they have both struggled from different directions through the tangled under-growth of a forest and are standing, exhausted from the effort, face to face for the first time, in a clearing.

He gets up and hugs her and she squeezes him with her arms, tightly, like she used to do when he came back from a school trip.

He considers telling her about Holly and Mark but imme-diately decides not to. What would be the point? Why spoil this?

'It's good to hug you again. You never liked being hugged when you were a little boy. It was like you were covered in little prickles.'

'Really?' he says.

'I used to call you my little Cactus Boy. Do you remember?'

And now he does.

Chapter 43

Standing on the Sidelines Moaning

David is even less keen to go to the shops now. The hope of bumping into Ellen has turned into a dread. But he knows it's going to happen sooner or later. Maybe sooner is better. Maybe. So he agrees to go.

But it isn't Ellen he sees, but Tilly. He spots her at the far end of an aisle. She is staring intently at a pack of coffee before putting it back on the shelf and choosing another. She turns her head towards him and he quickly carries on to the next aisle.

He dawdles, pays and leaves and walks out of the shop to find her standing outside.

'Hey,' she says. 'I thought I saw you.'

'Hi,' says David.

They stand there for a moment, neither of them saying anything. Traffic rumbles by, an old woman jostles past.

'Look,' says David, 'if you want to have a go at me about that weekend, I'm not in the mood, OK?'

'What?' says Tilly. 'Why would I do that?'

'It doesn't matter,' says David.

'What happens between you and Ellen is your business,' says Tilly.

'Yeah, well, it didn't feel like that.'

'Look,' she says, frowning, 'it wasn't our fault you messed up, OK? It's pretty uncool to brag about having sex with someone when you have, but –'

'OK,' says David. 'I get it. I screwed up. What do you want me to say?'

'Sorry,' she says. 'I shouldn't have . . . Like I said, it's nothing to do with me.'

'Anyway . . .' says David.

He shrugs and looks at his feet.

'I'm sorry things didn't work out with you and Ellen.'

David raises a sceptical eyebrow.

'Honestly.'

'I don't even know if I care any more,' says David. 'It doesn't seem like the biggest thing right now.'

'Maybe it was for the best then?' says Tilly.

'Yeah. Maybe. My mum says you may as well believe everything is in the end.'

Tilly smiles.

'She sounds wise, your mum.'

'She has her moments. Listen, I've got to –'

'I've broken up with Finn,' says Tilly suddenly.

'Oh?' says David.

'Yeah,' she says, running her fingers through her hair. 'That's probably for the best too.'

David smiles and nods.

'I think it definitely is.'

'Oh? Really?'

'Yeah – really. I don't think he's right for you.'

She raises her eyebrows.

'That's pretty bold, coming from you. What about you and Ellen?'

'Sorry,' says David. 'I didn't mean to . . . I just think . . .'

'What?'

'That he's a bit of a shit, if you want to know, and, well, you're . . . not.'

Tilly laughs. It's a nice laugh.

'I think that may be the sweetest thing anyone's ever said to me.'

David blushes.

'Sorry.'

'Don't be.'

They stand for a few awkward moments before Tilly says she ought to be going and turns to walk away.

'I don't get it,' says David to her back.

'What?' she replies, turning round.

He waves his hands around as though trying to summon the words he wants to say from the air.

'Why do nice girls go for creeps?'

Tilly chuckles.

'Another compliment?' she says. 'It must be my day.'

'Seriously – why?' persists David. 'Why do so many really nice girls hook up with total dickheads?'

Tilly shrugs.

'Life's a bitch, huh?' she says.

David sighs.

'Look, what do you want me to say? And Finn's not a total dickhead. That's not fair. You don't know him.'

David frowns. A van sounds its horn and drowns out David's muttered response. He thinks Tilly is walking off but she is just suggesting that they move back away from the road and stop blocking the pavement.

'Boys like you always complain that girls like me go out with boys like Finn – or Matt or Dylan,' she says when they are standing together beside the post office. 'But the fact is, those are the boys who ask us out while boys like you are standing on the sidelines moaning.'

'Yeah, right,' says David. 'So it was just a matter of me asking?'

Tilly steps forward and jabs a finger towards him.

'Look – if you'd have asked Ellen out after the trip to the Lakes she'd have said yes, but you didn't, did you? You didn't have the nerve or maybe you didn't want to –'

'I wanted to,' says David quietly.

'So you didn't have the nerve. That's not her fault, is it? Don't have a go at her – or me. We work with what we've got.'

She laughs at this thought. David sighs. Has it all really been this simple all along? Just been a matter of who had the nerve. He thinks he prefers the idea that he wasn't attractive enough to it all actually just being down to his cowardice.

'Besides,' says Tilly, 'you didn't even notice me.'

'You?'

'Yeah – me. I always kinda liked you, but you never noticed. Or maybe you did but you weren't interested.'

It's true. He hadn't noticed.

'You liked me?'

'Yeah – a bit. Don't get carried away. Does that seem so bizarre?'

'Honestly? Yes, it does.'

It absolutely does.

'Why?'

'I don't know. I suppose I just never imagined a girl like you would be interested in someone like me.'

'Well, I was,' she says, smiling.

'OK,' says David.

He stares at her, waiting for the punchline or the laugh or whatever it is that's going to signal that she's taking the piss, but it never happens. Tilly sighs out another big breath and shoves her hands deep into her jacket pockets.

'Look – I really had better get going,' she says.

'Yeah,' says David. 'I know. Me too.'

Come on, come on. She's walking away.

'I do too,' he says.

'What?' she says, turning round.

'Like you. I like you too.'

She grimaces.

'I don't want you to think I told you about splitting up with Finn because I wanted you to –'

'Sure,' said David. 'Course. I wasn't, you know . . .'

He nods. She smiles. They stand for a few long seconds before she eventually waves and walks away. And David watches her and watches her until there's nothing left to watch.

325

Chapter 44

The Opposite of a Magnet

It's a while before the door opens and an eternity before Joe seems to know what to say or do as he stands there looking at David on the doorstep.

'Hi,' he says eventually. 'All right?'

David nods.

'I wondered if you were doing anything.'

'Yeah,' says Joe. 'I am actually.'

'Oh?' says David.

'Yeah, so . . .'

'What?'

'What?' says Joe.

'What are you doing – exactly?' says David.

'What's that got to do with you?'

'I'm just curious.'

'Listen – why are you here?'

'Is that David?' says Joe's mother from the kitchen.

'Yes!' shouts Joe with a frown.

'Well, don't keep him standing on the doorstep. Ask him in.'

'He can't!' shouts Joe. 'He's got to –'

'Well, maybe just a few minutes,' says David, barging past him and into the hallway.

'David!' says Dr Jardine. 'We haven't seen you for a while. How are you?'

'I'm good, thanks. You?'

'I'm well, thank you,' she says. 'How did the exam results go?'

'I did OK, thanks.'

'Of course you did. Clever boys, the both of you. I had the feeling you and Joe had fallen out and –'

'Mum!' says Joe. 'Don't be embarrassing!'

Dr Jardine rolls her eyes and walks away tutting to herself.

'See you later, David!' she calls over her shoulder.

'Why are you here?' says Joe.

'Well, that's nice,' says David.

'I think you ought to go.'

'Oh, come on,' says David. 'Stop being such a dick.'

'Me?'

'Look, I'm sorry,' says David. 'Really sorry.'

Joe says nothing.

'You were right and I was wrong. About everything. I wish I could go back in time and do everything differently but I can't. I think I went a bit crazy.'

'A bit?'

David smiles.

'OK – quite a bit. And I know you stuck up for me and I know I never said thanks, so I'm saying thanks now.'

He scratches his forehead, searching for the kinds of words

that might convey the great complexity of the feelings he is experiencing, but all he comes up with is:

'Do you think we could just go back to being mates?'

Joe sighs and looks away. A matter of days ago and this would have been enough for David to give up and go home.

'It would have been easier not to come,' says David.

'No one asked you to.'

'I know you're really hacked off with me, and if I was you I'd feel the same. But then what? If you want to stay mad at me forever I can't stop you, but I just wanted to say that I still want to be mates if you do.'

Joe nods.

'OK.'

'OK, you know what I mean – or OK, you still want to be mates?'

Joe shakes his head.

'You are so annoying, do you know that?'

David smiles. Joe – after a moment – smiles too.

'I've got something for you,' says David, taking off his backpack and unzipping it.

He hands Joe a comic. *Captain America and the Falcon* #171 (guest-starring the Black Panther).

'You see,' says David. 'A black superhero – and he's flying!'

Joe smiles, nods and hands it back. David pushes it back and says it's his to keep.

'I thought these were like precious antiques,' says Joe.

'They are – that's why I'm giving it to you.'

Joe grins and looks at the cover again, which shows Captain

America, the Black Panther and the Falcon all leaping forward together.

'Although technically,' says Joe, pointing to the Falcon, 'he can't really fly, can he? Not like Superman? It's only because of these wing things he has.'

David shakes his head.

'OK – well, if you don't want it . . .'

'I didn't say I didn't want it,' says Joe, clutching it to his chest.

'Anyway – I'll get off,' says David. 'I'll see you around.'

He turns and heads for the door.

'No!' says Joe. 'Since you're here and everything . . .'

'What?'

'I don't know – we could play tennis. My mum'll lend you her racket.'

David nods.

'OK.'

And that is that. Joe fetches the rackets and they set off for the courts, which – and they both privately take it as a sign of some sort – are empty.

They begin playing with the kind of polite restraint that suits this restatement of their vows of friendship, but neither can maintain it, and it soon descends into the usual good-natured arguments over every line call and foot fault.

They play for a long time – longer than normal – and don't stop until a group of adults is standing loitering just outside the court, frowning and looking at their watches. They will remember this game for the rest of their lives. They can't know that yet of course – and yet they do.

'So . . .' says Joe as they sit on the bench afterwards.

David nods.

'Yeah.'

These words of deliberation float away on a river of silent rumination.

'So,' says Joe again, eventually, 'I never did find out. Did you and Ellen – you know?'

David grins.

'It's a long story . . .'

'Go on . . .'

David sighs and then gives him a very edited version of the dreaded weekend away.

'We've split up. Not that we were ever together really.'

Joe shakes his head and smiles wryly.

'I feel for you,' he says finally. 'But you know, it's probably for –'

'For the best – yeah, I know.'

Joe laughs and David joins him after a moment.

'You'll never guess what though,' says David.

'What?'

'I bumped into Tilly and, well, I don't know – there was a bit of a thing there.'

'With Tilly?'

'Yeah.'

'You? Honestly?'

'Yes – honestly.'

Joe stares at him, clutching the sides of his head.

'What the hell is going on?'

'What do you mean?'

'I mean that you appear to have become some kind of a babe magnet when previously you were a . . . I don't know. What's the opposite of a magnet?'

'A magnet,' says David.

'What?'

'The opposite of a magnet,' says David. 'I mean, technically the opposite of a magnet is another magnet only at the other –'

'You see?' says Joe, waving his arms around. 'This is what I mean. You talk like this and still . . . I'm doing something wrong.'

David laughs.

'What can I say?' he says. 'When you've got it, you've got it.'

Ordinarily this is where it would end: in random banter. But David decides that he is, for once, going to tell Joe something of what has really been going on in his life for the last few weeks. If there is to be a re-invention, then why not start here and now?

Chapter 45

No One Is Watching

David sits on the bench in the graveyard. He has divested himself of every secret he has now. All except one. He is not ready to give this one up. Not yet.

He looks up at the church tower, taking in the window and the crenellated top. A casual observer might not notice the scars of relatively new mortar around the small window near the top.

David's eyes were always drawn to that part of the tower, but he had learned to stop his mind being pulled to there too, and usually refused to give room to the memories that it evoked. But not today.

His father had been a devout and outspoken atheist, but he loved old churches and any trip they took would never be complete without him ushering them into some cold, damp medieval pile and pointing out the features to David – some dog-toothed moulding here, a carved corbel there.

He would take David into the choir stalls hunting for misericords and show him the worn engraved skulls on old tombstones set into the chancel floor, the iridescent traces of ancient paintings on wooden screens.

He had stepped in to help when their local church had had problems. The top of the Norman tower had become unsafe and large pieces of masonry had tumbled dangerously into the graveyard. Some people said it had been struck by lightning, but David's father was doubtful and said it was more likely just decay.

His father had offered his services as an architect for nothing and oversaw the work that was paid for by a trust that he himself set up. He had been in the local paper.

When the scaffolding was in place, David's father had asked him if he would like to go up to the top of the tower and see the work. David had looked up nervously from the graveyard and felt he had no choice.

His father had produced an old key from his pocket and grinned and they both went inside the church, down the nave to an ancient wooden door set into the wall to the right of the rood screen.

The arched door was small and opened with a hollow clunk to reveal a narrow spiral stone staircase. His father told him to go first – that way, he said, he would catch David if he fell.

David had never thought he had a fear of heights, but something about the spiral staircase played with his balance and sense of direction, which, added to the feeling of being pursued, albeit by his father, meant that by the time he reached the door at the top and fumbled for the handle, his heart was pounding and he was wheezing asthmatically.

'It's OK,' his father had said. 'It's perfectly safe.'

David pushed open the door, squinting into the relative

brightness of what was in reality a gloomy, cloud-covered day. A brisk wind had made him even more scared and he held tightly to the open door as he edged onto the leaded roof.

His father took him by the shoulders and coaxed him towards the crenellated wall that ran around the tower top. One corner of the roof was cordoned off and David could see where the parts of the wall had fallen away. The tops of scaffolding poles could be seen over the edge.

'Come here, David,' said his father. 'I want to show you something.'

And his father had held out his hand and David had nervously taken it and let his father lead him under the plastic tape to the side of the tower that was being repaired.

'Follow me. Don't be scared. I'll help you over.'

With that his father had stepped onto a box and climbed over the parapet wall onto the scaffolding below, holding out his hands to help David.

'I'm scared.'

'Don't be,' said his father. 'There's nothing to be scared of.'

David had hesitated and then given his father both hands to be helped up and over the wall to stand alongside him. The scaffolding plank beneath their feet shifted slightly and David had anxiously grabbed a nearby pole.

'Look out, not down,' his father had said. 'There's nothing scary about a view.'

David hadn't really been convinced by this thought, and though he tried to look out, the wide, untroubled view only reminded him of how high they were. The wind too. The trees at the graveyard's edge swayed and David imagined – or hoped he was imagining – that the scaffolding swayed with them.

'Look at this,' said his father.

David had looked, grateful for the distraction, and his father was standing next to a window – much larger than it had looked from the ground – and beneath it, below the sill, there was a stone face.

David had edged closer to look at it. It was frozen in an expression of horror. Its eyes bulged and its mouth was wide open as though it had just that second seen something utterly terrifying.

The carving was crude but still sharp, despite being distressed by time and weather, moss growing in the open mouth, pale grey lichen on the staring eyes.

'Amazing,' said David's father. 'So high up on the tower that no one but the men who built it could know how well made it was, and yet still the sculptor did his best – did it as well as if it had been intended for the porch for all to see on their way into church. Touch it.'

David had done as he was asked and reached out and let his fingers trace the features in the cold stone. His father had put his hand on David's back.

'You may be the first person to touch that since it was put there all those centuries ago. Think about it.'

David did. He did think about it. It made him feel even dizzier, like he was falling back through time.

'He knew that God was watching, do you see?' his father

had said. 'He knew that God would know if he skimped in any way.'

'But you don't believe in God,' David had said, confused.

'No,' said his father quietly. 'Sometimes I wish I did. It's hard sometimes, to feel that no one is watching.'

David had looked up into the cold grey sky.

'Do you believe, David?'

He had shaken his head. He saw nothing in those clouds – no hint of something beyond them – and never had.

'Do you see the river there?' his father had said, pointing out at the flatlands in front of them. 'Curving away over there.'

David had followed his gaze and nodded. The water had in that instant caught the light like a sabre.

'Ugly thing, isn't it?' his father had said.

David frowned, not really seeing what his father meant. It hadn't seemed ugly to him at all. It was a river catching the light – splendid in its own way.

'Look at it,' he had continued, as though David's failure to grasp his father's meaning was due to some lack of observation.

'See how it slices through the earth like a great wound, the land on either side now tamed and bullied into service.

'All of that would once have been marshlands, until they drained these fens and put in their pumps to keep the water at bay – channelling it all away into that river.

'You know that if they stopped those pumps these lands would flood within weeks. Imagine that.'

He had tried but could not see why his father found this idea so attractive.

'Don't you see? This landscape is a lie. It wants to be something else.'

He had then scowled and spoken bitterly.

'I sometimes feel that we are all being pulled into that river – to be carried away in its filthy waters. I hate it. I've always hated it.'

David had looked at the river again, but he could not make himself hate it the way his father so clearly did. It was just water.

'Wouldn't it be great to fly?' his father had suddenly said.

David had nodded, nervously looking down at the grave-yard far below.

'Wouldn't it be great just to be able to leap into the air and take off and just fly to wherever you wanted? To sail through the air like a bird? Huh? Like a superhero?'

'Yeah. It would,' David had said.

David's father had leaned on the scaffolding barrier, grinning.

'Maybe we can.'

'Dad?'

'Fly! Maybe we can fly. And all that's stopping us is having the nerve to take that first leap. Maybe all that stops us from flying is that we don't believe we can.'

David had smiled up at him, enjoying this idea. But there had been something about his father's face that worried him. He wasn't looking at David at all. He was looking down, longingly.

'Shall we leap together? Now?'

David had laughed nervously. The flag of St George above their heads clapped as it fluttered in the wind.

'We can't fly, Dad,' he'd said.

His father had looked at him for a long time and there was something about the balance of his body that David felt hinted at a sudden lurch into the void. But it never came.

'I know,' he said eventually. 'I know. Of course. I was just saying. Imagining.'

And then something seemed to change in his whole demeanour – a mask taken off . . . or replaced. He took David by the arm and shepherded him inside and they climbed down.

A week later he was dead.

Chapter 46

To Be

David stands at the water's edge, watching the surface shimmer and quiver as a cool breeze plays across it, masking the blackness beneath.

There is a startling lack of drama, given its place in David's imagination over the past months. It's a scene of almost aggressive dullness. It doggedly refuses to be elegiac. It just is – unaware of its significance in David's life or his father's death.

The passing hum of the morning traffic on the road at the foot of the embankment provides a murmuring chorus offstage. But whatever power David thought this moment might have when he agreed to come here, it refuses to comply.

After a while his mother walks up the embankment and stands beside him, slipping her hand into his and leaning in to rest her head on his shoulder.

'Are you OK?' she asks.

David nods.

'I don't really feel anything,' he says.

She puts her arm around him and squeezes.

'Maybe we shouldn't have come.'

But he is sure they were right to. This story needs an ending. This is as close as it will get.

'He's not there,' says David.

'I'm sorry.'

'No – it's good,' says David, only then realising it for himself. 'It's just the place he died, that's all. It's just a river. I thought I'd still feel like there was something about him here – but I don't. I don't feel him here at all.'

His mother nods.

'Me neither,' she says. 'So, shall we move on?'

'Yeah,' says David.

They walk back to the car, arm in arm. With every metre they drive away from that bend in the river, the better David feels. His lungs seem to grow in volume. He feels healthier. It is as if a damp miasma from those cruel waters had risen up and infected him. Soon he knows he will be free of it entirely.

They drive back towards the centre of town, fields and woods replaced by street lamps and houses, getting more and more tightly packed until they are on the long, busy road on which stands David's sixth-form college.

'I've decided I'm going to do art at uni,' he says. 'Graphics or illustration maybe.'

'Oh?'

'If that's OK?'

'Of course it is. You know it is.'

He nods and looks out of the window. How super-normal everything seems – everyone milling about on their way to work and school. It is a dull scene, but dullness has its own compensations. Dullness can be a comfort – and today, for David, it is.

'This is fine,' says David, as the college building becomes visible in the distance.

His mother puts her indicators on and pulls into a side road, parking the car and turning to face him with a smile.

'Don't want your mum dropping you off at the gates on the first day?'

'No,' says David smiling. 'No – I really don't.'

'You OK?'

He nods.

'Yeah. I think I am.'

'Nervous?'

'A bit. Good nervous though.'

'You'll be fine.'

'Yeah.'

David smiles and grabs his bag from the back seat.

'Have a great day,' says his mother.

David nods and gets out, slamming the door behind him, and walks around the car ready to head back to the main road to cross over to the college.

A tap on her window startles Donna and she turns to see David looking in. She lets the window down.

'David? Have you forgotten something?'

'Yeah,' he says.

Then he leans in and kisses her on the cheek.

'Bye, Mum.'

She drives away. David stands on the edge of the kerb looking at the high college gates on the other side of the road and the gaggle of students milling about in front of them.

A bus pulls up, wheezes its air brakes, blocking his view; a huge advert for some new action movie he hasn't heard of down the side, all frowning faces and flames.

An old woman looks out of one of the windows at him, her face breaking into a smile that David cannot help but mirror. The bus moves off and a hand taps him on the shoulder. David turns. To his amazement it's Holly.

'What are you doing here?' says David.

'Well, that's nice,' she says.

'No – you know what I mean.'

'I thought I'd see you off on your first day,' she says.

David peers at her, confused. Is she mocking him?

'Seriously though,' says David, 'what brings –'

'Friends of yours?' says Holly nodding towards the group across the road.

'Some, I suppose,' says David.

He spots Joe and waves. Holly smiles.

'Is she there? The girl who took you away? Ellen, isn't it?'

David nods. She is there. So is Tilly. Dylan is too. They are looking his way. Holly smiles more broadly.

'Good. Kiss me.'

'What?'

'Kiss me!'

Holly grabs David and pulls him close. When their faces come within a few inches of each other she stops and looks into David's eyes and he into hers and then he pulls her close and their lips lock together. Their bodies too, as his arms wrap around her. He can't make out which tongue is his and which hers as they slide over each other in his mouth.

The kiss lasts seconds. It lasts hours.

Then, just as suddenly, they pull apart and the world floods back in. David gasps for air, like a drowning man coming to the surface.

The sounds of engines and brakes and sirens and talking and shouting and all the music of the world flood back in, more delineated than before, his senses cleaned and polished.

Holly smiles at him and he returns it. It is a smile he has never worn before on a face that he feels he might not recognise were he to look in a mirror.

Holly turns and walks away without saying a word and David swallows a deep breath and watches her go, wondering if she will look back but she never does. Then he turns slowly to see the looks of amazement of the faces of those gathered on the other side of the road

It's like Hamlet says: 'To be or not to be . . .' David knows he has chosen to be. He knows that choosing and doing are two different things and he is not going to fake the newness he wants. No more fakery. To be and not pretend to be, that is the answer.

Then he grins, crouches down and launches himself up into the air, flying higher and higher, bursting through the low clouds until he soars up into the big blue beyond, yelling and whooping with joy.

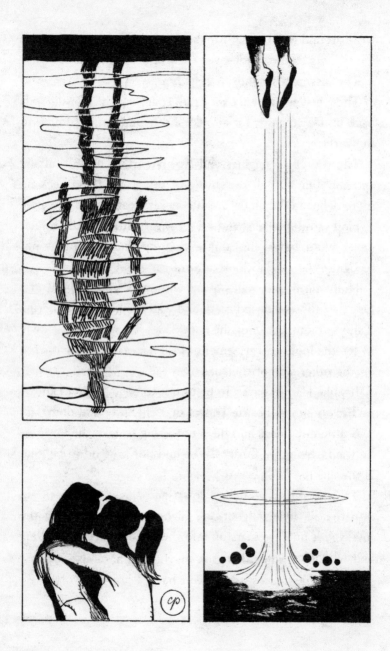

Acknowledgements

I don't normally let anyone read early drafts of my books – anyone besides my wife and my editor, that is – but for some reason it felt right for *Superpowerless*. So thanks to Sam Chamberlain for reassuring me early on, to Rowan Pelling for her encouraging words and to Jon Mayhew for some very sound advice and generous comments.

Thanks to my wife, Sally, and my son, Adam, for reading the first draft – and particularly to my son for declaring it to be the best thing I'd written (he doesn't give praise lightly).

I need also to give a huge thanks to my editors at Hot Key – Georgia Murray, who has been a fantastically friendly and supportive presence from the very start, and to Talya Baker for her sterling work in the last stages.

Thanks also to my agent Philippa Milnes-Smith and her then assistant Elizabeth Briggs for some very well-timed nice comments.

If you are reading this then maybe you have also read the book. Thanks to you too, if you have. I hope it worked for you.

CHRIS PRIESTLEY spent his childhood in Wales and Gibraltar, and his teens in Newcastle-upon-Tyne, before going to art college in Manchester. He moved to London and freelanced as an illustrator and cartoonist for twenty years before getting his first book for children published. He has written lots of books, fiction and non-fiction, has won awards here and abroad and been nominated for many others, including the Carnegie Medal. He now lives in Cambridge and spends a great deal of time looking out of the window . . . Follow Chris at https://chris-priestley.com or on Twitter: @crispriestley

Thank you for choosing a Hot Key book.

If you want to know more about our authors
and what we publish, you can find us online.

You can start at our website

www.hotkeybooks.com

And you can also find us on:

We hope to see you soon!